C.L. Taylor is a *Sunday Times* bestselling author. Her psychological thrillers have sold over a million copies in the UK alone, been translated into over twenty languages, and optioned for television. Her 2019 novel, *Sleep*, was a Richard and Judy pick. C.L. Taylor lives in Bristol with her partner and son.

Also by C. L. Taylor

Young Adult Fiction:
The Treatment

Adult Fiction:
The Accident
The Lie
The Missing
The Escape
The Fear
Sleep
Strangers

THE
ISLAND

C.L. TAYLOR

ONE PLACE. MANY STORIES

HQ
An imprint of HarperCollins*Publishers* Ltd
1 London Bridge Street
London SE1 9GF

www.harpercollins.co.uk

HarperCollins*Publishers*
1st Floor, Watermarque Building, Ringsend Road
Dublin 4, Ireland

This edition 2021

7

First published in Great Britain by
HQ, an imprint of HarperCollins*Publishers* Ltd 2021

ISBN: 978-0-00-824059-2

To my niece Rose Taylor

PROLOGUE

She's dead. She said she'd never leave me but she did. She said she'd never love anyone as much as she loved me. She said I was her everything. She said a lot of things and none of them were true.

She's dead.

And she's a liar.

CHAPTER 1

JESSIE

Life would be so much easier if I were a psychopath. I'd be charming, manipulative and a pathological liar. I also wouldn't be wondering what Danny, Honor, Jeffers, Meg and Milo are talking about on the other side of the pool, their faces cast in shadow, the Thai night sky a black blanket above them. And I definitely wouldn't be convincing myself that they're talking about me. Even if they were, I wouldn't care. But the biggest advantage of being a psychopath, by a mile, would be lack of empathy. Life doesn't hurt as much if you stop caring.

'Who's up for a swim?' Honor, who's been intertwined with Danny on a sun lounger for the last hour, wriggles out of his grasp and stands up. She slips off her flip-flops, strips off her T-shirt and wriggles out of her shorts. It's dark and the surface of the pool is still and calm, striped with the reflected glow of the hotel and dotted with candlelight. Honor dives in, barely making a splash. She pulls her arms through the water, blonde hair streaming behind her.

Seconds later Danny's in too. He tries to grab Honor around the waist but she slips away like a fish and swims almost a whole length underwater.

'Meg?' Honor's voice echoes off the walls of the hotel complex as she breaks through the water, just a few feet away from me. It's after eleven and an older couple to my right, talking quietly on their sun loungers, sigh loudly. 'Milo? Jeffers? You coming in? We could play water polo?' She glances at me and the expression on her face changes: uncertainty replaces excitement. She doesn't know whether to invite me to join them or not. I pull the sleeves of my top down over my hands and shift in my seat. Swimming's one of my favourite things in the world and I'm good at it – I've swum for the county – but I haven't been in the pool since we got here and I'm not about to start now.

'You guys go ahead,' I shout. 'I'll watch.'

As holidays go this is right up there with the time we went to Center Parcs and Danny did a poo in the corner of the ball pit at soft play. OK, so we were all three at the time, but the memory of the warm squelch as I put my hand in it is indelibly burnt into my brain. The walking tour of the Scottish Isles when we were all twelve was pretty grim too. It never stopped raining and I slipped and twisted my ankle when we were still an hour away from the car. Almost every year since we were born there's been an enforced group holiday and now here we are, in Thailand, a disparate group of teenagers forced to socialize with each other because our

4

parents happened to go to the same antenatal group over seventeen years ago. Our friendships have changed over the years. As five- and six-year-olds Honor and I were about as close as two little kids could be. We tried to include Meg in our games but she was more interested in trying to muscle in on the games Milo, her twin brother, was playing with Jeffers and Danny. As pre-teens Meg gravitated back to me and Honor and there was a distinct girls versus boys dynamic. That all changed when hormones kicked in and Honor and Danny got together and me and Milo... well, I'm not sure how to describe that. We danced around each other, I guess. Sometimes I fancied him and he didn't fancy me. Sometimes it was the other way round. It's not that we've got a 'thing'. It's more of a 'non-thing'. But it's not just friendship, not like me and Danny or Jeffers.

Don't get me wrong, Thailand is *amazing*. The people are so smiley and friendly, the food is delicious, the streets are buzzing and vibrant and the scenery is breathtaking. Yes, it's hot and humid but, hello, I'd rather be dripping with sweat over here than dripping with rain in England. No, Thailand's not the problem, nor is the amazing complex we're staying in. The fact is I can't do holidays like this anymore. The others don't know how to act around me and I've forgotten who I used to be. I can't relax. I've forgotten how to banter, and if I catch myself laughing, I immediately feel guilty. I might be seventeen but I feel like I'm a hundred years old.

'Miss Harper?' I jolt as Milo appears behind me. I was so caught up in watching Danny trying, and failing, to lift Honor above his head that I didn't notice him slip away

5

from the table he was sitting at with Meg. She's changed since we hit our teens. She used to be competitive, loud and outspoken. These days, if she does speak, it's usually to say something snarky.

'Mr Katsaro?' I shove my hands beneath the table and smile, tightly, up at Milo as my heart hammers in my chest. Like his sister he's got jet black hair but, while Meg's tumbles over her shoulders in dark corkscrews, Milo's is shaved around the sides and wavy on top. Their surname means 'curly' in Greek and their whole family has gorgeous hair.

'I'm going to the bar.' He reaches a hand towards me and, for one heart-stopping second, I think he's going to touch me. Instead he places his hand on the back of my chair and rests his weight against it. He glances towards my glass, most of my mojito mocktail long gone. 'Do you need a top-up?'

I glance across the pool, to Meg, sitting in her seat, hunched forward, her elbows on her knees, watching us. If Milo was interested in me, which these days he's not, she wouldn't approve and who could blame her? Who needs my kind of screw-up in their life? If you need me, I'll turn my back. If you want to talk, I'll run. And if you love me...

Something lurches inside me – like a bruise being pressed – and I twist the tender skin on the underside of my forearm until the feeling fades. I might not be a psychopath but I've got my own ways of switching off negative thoughts. My aim is to be in complete control of my emotions. I'm not there yet but one day I will be.

'No thanks.' I look back at Milo. 'I'm going to bed in a bit.'

Something in his gaze shifts. Did he just look disappointed or did I completely imagine that?

'Are you going to the bar?' Danny shouts to Milo from the pool as he launches Honor into the air. She shrieks for all of two seconds then plops back into the water with a splash. 'I'll come with you. I want a snack.' He pauses, waiting for Honor to resurface. 'Want anything to drink?' he asks her.

She runs her hands through her hair, slicking it back from her face. 'Lemonade, please.'

'You don't want a cocktail? This barman's not fussed about ID.'

'Nah. I'm good.'

As Danny swims to the side and heaves himself out of the water Milo drifts over to him. I watch as they saunter over to the bamboo bar that's surrounded by palm trees. When I look back at the pool, Honor has swum to the side nearest me. The top half of her body is out of the water, her blonde hair slicked back and her arms folded on the tiles.

'Are you OK?' she asks.

I stiffen. I can deal with people being kind on WhatsApp and social media but, in person, any kind of sympathy makes me want to cry. Thankfully no one's pushed me to open up. Other than a few awkward 'I'm really sorry, Jessie' comments on the day we arrived, no one's mentioned the reason my family didn't go on the group holiday to Norfolk last year. And I'd rather it stayed that way.

'Fine. Hot, isn't it?'

Honor takes the hint and changes the subject. 'Is Milo getting you a drink?'

'No. I said I didn't want one.'

'Oh right.' She shrugs lightly. 'I'm not sure why I asked Danny to get me one. I'm not even thirsty.'

Danny's always doing nice things for her. In the three days we've been here he's rushed up to their room to get things for her at least half a dozen times, given her countless shoulder rubs and, when she didn't like her fried snapper at lunch, he swapped with his own meal, even though he's not keen on fish.

Honor sighs loudly, prompting me to ask her what's up. She ignores the question and eases herself effortlessly out of the water and sits on the edge. 'Are you looking forward to going to the island tomorrow?'

I shudder, despite the heat. 'Not really, are you?'

She shrugs. 'Seven days with no 4G, no WiFi, no clean clothes and no soft beds. It's either going to be hell, or the best thing we've ever done.' She gestures across the pool to Jefferson whose got his face buried in a book. 'Bear Grylls over there is crapping himself with excitement.'

I can't help but laugh. Jefferson Payne, the youngest of the group by nine days, has been obsessed with camping, hunting and foraging for the last few years. He's small and wiry with oversized glasses but, in his head, he's some kind of action hero. If the WhatsApp group chats are anything to go by he spends every night after school whittling knife handles out of bits of wood and plaiting huge lengths of cord into bracelets. I'm not judging – how he spends his time is his own business – but it is a bit weird that a kid who lives in a three-bedroom house in north London and goes to private school is so obsessed with prepping for the end of the world.

I'm not sure if it's the prepper stuff or something else but he's changed since the last time I saw him. He was always the most reserved kid in our group, but he's got a real loner vibe going on now. We've chatted a couple of times since we arrived – small talk mostly – and I got the distinct vibe that he'd rather be anywhere than hanging out with us.

If our parents have noticed that we've all outgrown these group holidays, they've chosen to ignore it. They all seem as chilled and relaxed as they normally are. Well, maybe not my parents, not this year.

'I mean, it's only a week,' Honor says, 'and the guide will be doing all the hard work building us a shelter and stuff. It's not like we need to be fashioning spears out of bits of wood and killing fish for dinner.'

'I'm packing Pringles,' I say. 'Seriously, sod all the sensible stuff we're supposed to take with us. I'm filling my bag with—'

I'm interrupted by the slap, slap, slap of flip-flops as two lads – one about our age with a nose ring and the other a couple of years older with closely cropped hair – appear from between the palm trees and saunter towards us. Honor turns to look, flipping her wet hair over her shoulder. Inwardly I groan. I'm paranoid and self-conscious enough with people I know, never mind people I don't. I should have gone to bed while I still had the chance.

'All right, girls?' The shorter of the two boys looks me up and down dismissively before his gaze rests on Honor.

Behind him, the older boy smirks. With their blue eyes, fair hair and long, angular faces they're almost certainly brothers.

'How you doing?' The shorter boy with the nose ring plops himself down next to Honor, who immediately angles herself away from him. Her eyes dart towards the palm trees, anxiety written all over her face.

'Jesus,' the older one says, taking a seat next to me. 'Aren't you hot wearing that?'

Unlike me, in a long-sleeved top, linen trousers and flip-flops, he's barefoot and naked from the waist up.

'I'm fine,' I say, ignoring the fact my top is glued to my back with sweat.

'Each to their own.' He grins widely and sits back in the chair, blocking my view of Honor and his brother. 'I'm Jack by the way, and that's Josh, my brother.'

'Great.'

He laughs. 'Chatty, aren't you? How long have you been here?'

'Too long.' I give him a pointed look. I know what he's trying to do. He's trying to keep me distracted so his brother can crack on with Honor. I shift my chair to one side so I can see round him. Short-arse now has his arm around Honor's shoulders, his fingers denting the skin at the top of her arm. She's smiling at him but it's a fixed grin – the kind you use when someone's overstepping the line but you don't want to cause a scene. She's doing her best to wriggle away but he's tightened his grip, pulling her into his body. Over on the other side of the pool Jeffers still has his nose in his book and Meg has disappeared.

'Hey!' Honor says, whipping her face away as Josh dips his head to kiss her. 'Leave it out, I've got a boyfriend.'

'I heard you guys talking,' Jack says, shifting his chair towards me. 'You off on some kind of survival experience tomorrow or something?'

I ignore him. His brother has one hand on Honor's face now and he's angling her towards him, forcing her to look at him. The hand around her shoulders has slid under her arm and his fingers are plucking at the thin material of her bikini top.

Beneath the table I pinch at the only patch of skin on my forearm that's smooth and soft but the tight feeling in my chest remains. I don't want to get involved but someone has to. This has to stop.

'Hey,' Jack says as I stand up, still gripping the arms of my metal chair and carrying it behind me like a turtle shell as I walk to the edge of the pool. 'What the hell happened to your hands? Jesus, they look really—'

'Hi.' As I draw closer Josh releases his grip on Honor's face and rests his hand on the tiles. He feigns nonchalance, all cocky and chilled. 'Look at me just chilling by the pool late at night' – but he's moved his wandering hand back to Honor's arm and he's pinning her to his side.

'Where are you going with that chair?' he asks. 'Going to take it for a swim?'

Behind me his brother laughs.

'No.' I smile down at him. 'I thought I'd join you. Apparently you don't have a problem with personal space.'

He looks up at me in confusion but, before he can reply, I lower the chair so one of the metal legs is directly above his hand, then I sit down. His shout fills the air – a howl of surprise morphing into a scream of pain. He pushes Honor away from him and grabs at the chair leg but it doesn't move an inch. I'm too heavy for him to shift. He looks up at me and I feel a stab of satisfaction at seeing Honor's fear in his eyes. Nothing happens for what feels like for ever, then I hear Jack's chair scraping on the tiles and his roar of anger. A split second later I'm shoved so hard in the back that I tip forwards. There's no time to react. All I can do is hold my breath as I fall out of the chair and the lights of the pool rush to meet me. The last thing I hear before my ears fill with water is a single word.

It sounds a lot like 'psycho'.

CHAPTER 2

DANNY

Day one on the island

Danny Armstrong isn't sure what to make of Jessie Harper. There's a part of him that's grateful that she stopped that little creep Josh from manhandling Honor the night before, but there's another, bigger, part that feels awkward about spending a week alone on an island with her. The first few days of the NCT holidays are always a bit weird; these guys might be his oldest friends but, apart from Honor who lives a short train-ride away, the others are all spread around the country. They don't get to see each other much between holidays, and everyone's always a bit wary and awkward initially. But then the banter starts up and the group relaxes. It's like they haven't spent a day apart.

Only Jessie hasn't loosened up yet. She's so tense, so tightly coiled that it makes Danny nervous. That thing with the chair leg last night? There's no way she would have done something like that before. It's like there's an emotional bomb ticking away in her chest – at any moment she might go off – and that scares him. Scares the others too from the way they all seem to be tiptoeing around her, none of them daring to mention why her hands and arms are all scarred up. OK, so he won't be *alone* on the island with Jessie, strictly speaking. Honor, Meg, Milo and Jeffers will be there too, along with Anuman, their Thai survival guide who's currently sitting at the far end of the small motorized boat, guiding it through the crystal-clear water. But they're a hell of a long way from the mainland already. They've been on the boat for over an hour.

Danny tightens his grip on Honor's shoulder, pulling her into his body, and kisses her on the top of her head. Jessie, sitting nearest Anuman with Jeffers beside her, is staring out to sea, her long brown hair streaming behind her. Danny didn't expect her to show up for the trip. She wasn't waiting in the lobby of the hotel with the others when he traipsed down the stairs with his backpack at 6 a.m. She was too embarrassed, he assumed, about what had happened the night before. Or maybe her parents had been told about what she'd done and had banned her from the trip.

When it all kicked off the night before, he was at the bar with Milo – eating peanuts and talking crap. There was an anguished shout from the pool then Honor screamed his name. He knocked over his drink in his haste to get back to her and his blood ran cold as he rounded the palm trees and spotted her hugging her knees to her chest by the side of the pool. There were two lads crouched

14

together a couple of feet away – one of them screaming and nursing his hand to his chest – and Jessie, sopping wet and fully clothed, climbing the ladder at the far end of the pool. She didn't seem to be the slightest bit bothered by the commotion behind her. Instead she nonchalantly headed for the entrance to the hotel. As Danny gathered Honor in his arms one of the lads pointed over at Jessie and shouted something about payback, while the other lad, the smaller one, groaned about needing a doctor. As they headed off towards reception Danny asked Honor over and over again what the matter was. She was crying so much she couldn't speak, and it wasn't until he got her back into her apartment, after her mum had wrapped her in a blanket and given her a long hard hug, that she finally opened up. Danny was off like a shot then, speeding back down the stairs to reception, but it was deserted. The lads, whoever they were, were long gone.

Now, he stifles a yawn. He barely slept last night he was so angry. How dare that arsehole put his hands all over his girlfriend? He'll kill him if he ever sees him again.

A sudden squeal from Meg wipes the thought from his mind.

'Oh my God! Is that a squid?' She points over the side of the boat. 'It's enormous.'

'Don't touch it!' Milo shouts as Meg puts a hand in the water. 'It's a jellyfish. Remember when Tom stood on one on the beach in Cornwall and his foot swelled up so much he had to go to hospital?'

At the mention of Tom's name Danny inhales sharply and

a strange expectant silence fills the boat. Everyone stares at Jessie, waiting for a reaction. She doesn't say a word. Instead she continues to gaze out to sea, a muscle pulsing in her cheek, as though she's repeatedly clenching and unclenching her jaw. The tension is more than Danny can bear and he searches his brain for something, anything, he can say to lighten the mood but the best he can manage is:

'Aren't you hot wearing all that, Jeffers?'

Unlike the others, dressed in vests or T-shirts or light summery clothes, Jeffers looks kitted out to go to war in the desert in his black sunglasses, hat, sandy-coloured long trousers, bulky waistcoat and boots and a huge great rucksack propped up beside him.

He shakes his head. 'Not at all. Everything I'm wearing is either lightweight or breathable, or it wicks the sweat away.'

Danny shakes his head. How can one of his friends be seventeen years old and sound like a fifty-year-old man? Jefferson wasn't always so weird – tactless and insensitive definitely – but not weird. He was perfectly normal until two summers ago when he turned up to their holiday in Norfolk wittering away about a new group of friends he'd met on the internet who'd opened his eyes to how screwed-up we'd be in the event of natural disasters, petrol shortages, war or acts of terrorism and how important it is to prepare for such an event. Danny mostly uses the internet to access PornHub, not that he'd ever admit *that* with Honor in the same room.

'We are here!' Anuman announces as the boat creaks

and putts as it slows down and Danny looks around in surprise. They're in the shallows and stretched before him is a long, white beach framed with palm trees; beyond them, dense jungle and huge, jagged cliffs. They've arrived on the only privately owned island off the coast of Thailand – Ko Kār p̄hcy p̣hạy. His breath catches in his throat as he spots a couple of macaque monkeys jumping and playing at the edge of the forest. It's like they've just arrived in paradise.

'The island of adventure,' Anuman had told them as he'd shepherded them out of the hotel when Jessie finally rocked up, hiding her face behind sunglasses and an oversized hat. 'Not many people get to go, and not alone. You very lucky.'

Lucky, Danny thinks cynically as Anuman jumps out of the boat and into the sparkling, clear sea – or stinking rich. Thailand is by far and away the most exotic – and expensive – holiday they've had as a group since Milo and Meg's parents first mooted the idea that they should have an antenatal group getaway when they were all little more than a year old. They spent a week in a shared house on the Cornish coast. He's not entirely sure what Jefferson's dad does for a living but it's something to do with banking and investments. Enough, anyway, that he's rented Ko Kār p̄hcy p̣hạy, and a survival expert, for a week to celebrate Jefferson's seventeenth birthday. When Danny's dad heard where they'd be holidaying this year he went pale. Unlike some of the other parents, his dad isn't loaded. He's a freelance sound engineer and work is sporadic – a three-month tour here and there and then nothing for months on end. Danny hates the way his dad is always so stressed about money, and when the Thailand trip was mentioned he told him that he wasn't fussed about going. But then Honor voice-messaged him, squeaky with excitement, and his stomach twisted into a tight knot. He hadn't been apart from her for more than a week since they got together on the day of his fifteenth birthday and he couldn't bear the thought of being without her for a whole fortnight. He'd help pay for the holiday, he told his dad; get a job washing pots in a local restaurant after school, or working in a café at the weekend. He didn't have to do any of those things in the end; his dad was offered a gig and couldn't make the holiday and Honor's mum, Thea, stepped in to say she was happy for Danny to share their apartment. He'd be on the sofa, of course, but the offer was a godsend. It meant they only had to stump up enough money for one return flight.

Danny's grip on Honor's shoulder tightens as the boat rocks and Jeffers leaps into the water, holding his rucksack above his head.

Meg stands up next, clutching her belongings to her chest, and nervously stares down into the sea.

'Hold your backpack up in the air as you jump!' Jeffers shouts. 'You don't want to get your stuff wet.'

'Duh,' Danny says. He looks at Honor, expecting to see her smile, but there's the weirdest look on her face – it's like she's gone completely blank behind the eyes.

'Hey.' He nudges her. 'You OK? I thought you were looking forward to this.'

She shoots him a smile but it looks fake. 'Yeah, I am.'

18

'You thinking about what happened last night?' he asks. It's his fault that lad hit on her. He never should have left her alone in the pool, but nothing's going to happen to her on the island. He'll make sure of that.

Before Honor can answer, Meg jumps into the sea with a gasp and a splash, swiftly followed by Milo, who turns and offers a helping hand to Jessie. She shakes her head and, instead, hands him her bag then clambers over the side of the boat.

'Oi, Jeffers,' Danny shouts, waving at the diminutive figure trying, and failing, to relieve Anuman of the rope that's attached to the front of the boat. 'How about you help the girls with their bags instead of playing the big man. I think you've got your priorities a bit screwed up there, mate.'

He snaps back round as Honor mutters something and wriggles out of his grasp.

'What was that?'

She looks at him defiantly. 'Just leave him alone.'

Danny raises his eyebrows. He can never be sure when Honor's genuinely annoyed with him or when she's messing around. She's good at switching her emotions on and off, it's what makes her such a good actress. He went to see her in her school play in Brighton and couldn't believe how easily she was able to transform herself into someone else. She wants to go to uni to study drama after school but she's worried she's not good enough. Danny's pretty sure she is.

'I'm not kidding, Danny,' Honor says. 'You really need to—'

The rest of her sentence is lost to the breeze as she launches herself over the side of the boat leaving her bag, and Danny, behind.

CHAPTER 3

JESSIE

I have never been anywhere more beautiful in my life. When the boat pulled up at the island I felt like I'd arrived in another world. The beach was a white sheet, pulled tight between two towering limestone hills cloaked in greenery. As I walked up the powdery sand towards the forest, the gentle lapping of the waves faded away and the air filled with the buzz of cicadas, the chirp of birds and the low whoop of monkeys. Paradise. The only thing spoiling it was us. Ever since we got off the boat Jefferson's been buzzing around Anuman like a fly, commenting on what he's doing and offering 'helpful' suggestions. He's doing it now, while Anuman shows us which trees we need to chop down to make a shelter.

'We need to avoid this, don't we?' Jeffers says, resting one hand on a tree trunk whilst awkwardly flicking through the pages of his book with the other. 'Mai nhang. Termites love it, don't they, Anuman?'

'Yes, yes.' Our guide nods politely and gestures for us to

follow him further into the jungle. He told us in the boat that he's sixty-one years old and, whilst his face is as lined as a walnut, he's so strong and sprightly he could pass for a man twenty years younger.

Honor, walking to one side of me, has her eyes fixed on the ground as she takes tentative step after tentative step.

'Spiders,' she says, catching me looking. 'Tarantulas, black widows, giant orbs and huntsmen.' She chants the list as though casting a spell to keep them away.

I haven't got a problem with spiders but even I shiver. I'm pretty sure there are snakes in Thailand too, and God knows what else. All I spotted back at the hotel was a couple of shy geckos and some brightly coloured birds, but we're a long way from that clean, sanitized world now.

'Don't worry,' Jefferson calls back. 'The spiders here can't kill you but bites might hurt and could become infected if they aren't kept clean.'

'Thanks,' Honor mutters under her breath. 'Really helpful.'

Danny, following behind us with Meg and Milo, gives a strange, forced laugh. I'm not sure what's going on with him and Honor today but there's a weird vibe between them. They're not as touchy feely as they normally are, and when Honor jumped out of the boat before Danny, he looked really annoyed. I'm guessing it's got something to do with what happened last night. Not that anyone has mentioned it to me, although Danny did mutter an awkward, 'Thanks for looking after her,' as we left the hotel this morning and piled into the taxi.

'Dalbergia cochinchinensis,' Jeffers says so loudly he makes me jump. He's pointing at a weedy-looking tree with a thin trunk. 'Thai rosewood. We can't chop that down: it's protected.'

'Yes, yes.' If Anuman is annoyed he doesn't let on. 'This,' he says, resting his palm on a tree with a trunk the size of my thigh. 'We chop this.'

'That's a—' Jeffers begins then cries out in pain as Meg squeezes between me and Honor and cuffs the top of his head.

'Seriously, Jeffers? Are you going to be like this *all week*?'

'Like what?' He stares at her in astonishment.

'A know-it-all. Can't you just let Anuman do his job? He *is* the expert.'

'Yes but…' As Jefferson hangs his head and stares at his feet I feel a pang of pity, then immediately feel annoyed with myself. When I woke up this morning I felt numb, like nothing could touch me, but when I confessed to Mum that I was having second thoughts about the trip she brought out the emotional big guns.

'Tom would have loved an opportunity like this,' she said as she perched on the edge of my bed. 'You can't not go, Jessica.'

Tom. T–o–m. Those three letters are my kryptonite.

'Mum, don't.'

'Go on, Jessica. Do it for Tom. Go for him.'

As if I don't feel guilty enough! I wanted to scream.

'Jessie?' A swift, sharp nudge in my bicep snaps me back into myself and the sweltering heat beneath the canopy of leaves. 'Are you OK?'

Milo looks down at me, his dark brows knotted together. 'You just made a weird noise.'

The others are all staring at me too. Oh God. What did I just do?

I clear my throat. 'I'm fine… just um…'

I'm saved by the sound of a machete thwacking against wood. Anuman has started chopping down one of the trees. Within seconds it crashes to the ground and he hands the machete to Jeffers. He couldn't look more pleased if he'd just been gifted a lifetime subscription to *Preppers' Monthly*. An hour later, dripping with sweat and huffing and puffing, we drag the felled trees through the jungle and back towards the beach.

'Here we set up camp,' Anuman says, pointing to a small clearing among the trees. 'There is a waterfall nearby for fresh water and we are near food source.' He points upwards. There are coconuts high in the tree above us, and another tree with ripe coral-coloured mangos weighing down the branches, as well as a plant heavy with green bananas.

'It's amazing,' Honor breathes and I can't help but agree. Now, standing in the jungle, listening to the sweet songs of the birds and the frantic whooping of the monkeys, I can't believe I ever considered not coming. It's breathtaking.

'Mind you don't eat those,' Jeffers says, pointing at a tree near the beach. It looks like it's growing yellow apples with little green poops hanging out of their bottoms. 'Cashews,' he says, clocking the blank looks on our faces. 'If they're not ripe they're poisonous.'

'Yes.' Anuman nods knowingly. 'I tell you all what to eat later. First, we build shelter, then fire.'

For the first hour or so we work enthusiastically, laughing and chatting as we split the trees with axes, hammer them into the ground and then fashion a roof made out of banana leaves, but when Anuman tells us that this is our sleeping shelter and we have to make another one to store and prepare food, the excuses come thick and fast: Honor's got a splinter, Danny feels like he's got sunstroke and Meg's hurt her back. I watch, enviously, as they trail down to the sea, strip off their clothes and dive into the icy blue, clear water.

'It's all right,' Milo says, shooting me a look. 'If you want a swim go and have one. Jeffers and I can cope. Can't we, Jeffers?'

Jeffers looks up from the tree he's splitting, a look of grim determination on his face. 'Sure. Go have fun, Jessie.'

I pass a hand over my brow then push my fingers through my hair. It's absolutely soaking with sweat. I feel hot and heavy in my long sleeved linen top and cargo shorts and I can't think of anything nicer than peeling off my clothes and jumping into the sea.

'Jess,' Milo lowers his voice. 'You don't have to be self-conscious here, it's just us lot.'

'I'm not self-conscious. I just don't fancy a swim. OK?' I glare at him then stalk off into the jungle, hot tears pricking at my eyes.

Come after me, I think as I continue to stomp away,

25

annoyed, but not so angry that I don't check the ground for snakes and spiders.

But of course he doesn't and I feel like a dick for even hoping that he would. He's not a mind reader. He was right. I *am* self-conscious. He knows it. I know it. We all know it. For the first couple of days of the holiday Mum needled at me, telling me that no one would be able to see my burns unless they were standing right next to me, and that as soon as I was in the pool I'd look just like the other kids. But I couldn't bring myself to do it. I could imagine how they'd react – Danny would gawp, Honor's blue eyes would grow big and round and Milo would look horrified. But more than that, I was afraid of sympathy, silence and awkwardness. I was afraid that, whenever they looked at me they wouldn't see me anymore, they'd just see what I'd been through. I want to cut through all the bullshit and the softly-softly, the concerned looks and silence when Tom's name is mentioned and face it straight on. I want to sit them all down and tell them, in my own words, what happened. But I can't. I'm afraid that if I open the lid on my emotions I'll never be able to close it again. Now two fat self-pitying tears roll down my cheeks and I choke back a sob.

I stop walking.

So much for staying in control. I may as well try and tame a whirlwind.

'Stop it, Jessie,' I say aloud.

A loud whooping noise, high in the treetops above me, makes me freeze. What the—

I press my hands to my chest as a grey-brown macaque

26

monkey with pointy ears and a long, solemn face leaps from the top of one tree to another with its baby clinging to its belly. As it lands the air fills with the sound of beating wings as half a dozen multicoloured birds flutter out from the leaves and soar into the sky. It's such a beautiful, breathtaking sight that I instantly forget all the crap that's been bothering me and stare in wonder.

A hand on my shoulder makes me jump. It's Jeffers, his baseball cap pulled low over his eyes and his axe resting on one shoulder.

'You shouldn't go wandering around on your own. It's not safe.'

'I know... I...' I trail off and I turn to walk back the way I came but Jefferson touches my shoulder again.

'Jessie.' He gives me a searching look. 'It isn't my place to say this but I think you should keep away from Milo.'

'What?' I stare at him in surprise. Jeffers isn't big on heart-to-hearts and he's never commented on my friendship with Milo before. As kids they were as thick as thieves and, while they're not as close as they used to be, they still get on. 'What do you mean? Why?'

'I know you like him, but I think you'll get hurt.'

I'm so flabbergasted I don't know what to say. It's no secret to the others that Milo and I have a bit of a chequered history. Ever since we were twelve one of us has had a crush on the other – but never at the same time. I thought he was gross when he liked me – tall and gangly with bad skin, obsessed with computer games and sick jokes. I changed my mind on a group holiday the following year. He'd quietened down a bit and I found his aloofness really intriguing. Only he wasn't interested anymore. According to Meg, he was obsessed with a girl at school. Then the next year we met I'd started seeing someone at my school. And so it's continued. Milo and I aren't so much star-crossed lovers as two planets in entirely different universes.

'What makes you think that?' I call after Jefferson, but he's already disappeared into the thick green undergrowth.

CHAPTER 4

DANNY

Danny's heart jumps as the spark from the flint and steel he's rubbing together leaps onto the soft coconut matting and a tiny flame licks at one of the fibres.

'Gently, gently,' Anuman urges as he gathers the tiny bundle in his hands and blows on the flame. 'Too hard will kill it.'

Come on, come on, Danny prays as he blows softly. Apart from Jefferson, none of the others has managed to get a fire started and he can feel their eyes on him, urging him to fail. But he won't let that happen. He doesn't give up.

'Yes, yes,' Anuman says as the flames grow and spread. Danny looks at Honor victoriously as he gently places the tiny fire on top of the pile of sticks and kindling that sits between the sleeping shelter and the cooking shelter.

'Good man!' Jefferson slaps him on the back and Danny basks in his own sense of achievement.

'Proud of me?' He hooks an arm around Honor's shoulders and pulls her close.

''Course.' She turns her face up to his and closes her eyes as he kisses her.

Life, Danny thinks, as the sun slowly sinks over the sea, striping the sky orange, pink and red, couldn't get much better than this.

Danny dips his fingers into his metal dish then grimaces as he shovels piping hot fish into his mouth. It's full of bones, and each time he plucks one out of his mouth it makes him gag. His friends eat their fish too, only their murmurs of appreciation fill the air, cutting through the pop and crackle of the fire. It's dark and, other than the fire, the only light is from two flaming torches – one on either side of the shelters – that Anuman fashioned from coconut shells and thin tree trunks. The only thing slightly spoiling Danny's pleasure is the fact that he didn't manage to catch the fish they're all eating. He, Honor, Meg, Milo and Jessie dangled their rods off the rocks at the edge of the beach for what felt like hours but, despite a few nibbles, none of them landed a fish. Thank God then for Anuman and his net. He and Jefferson took the boat out and returned with a haul big enough for a feast.

'I've got a ghost story,' Danny says, swallowing his mouthful. 'Do you know the one about the hitch-hiker and the…'

'Yes,' the others groan.

They've been telling ghost stories since Anuman put the fish on tree-branch skewers above the fire, dropping their voices at the tense bits then shouting the punchlines to make each other jump.

'I know,' Honor says. 'Let's tell each other the scariest things that have ever happened to us.'

'Isn't that the same as a ghost story?' Meg asks.

'Well, no. You can be scared without ghosts being involved,' Jessie pipes up. Unlike Danny, who's sitting so close to the fire he feels as though his cheeks are glowing, Jessie is far away, practically sitting in the entrance to the sleeping shelter.

'We could go for a walk in the jungle,' Milo suggests, but he's immediately shouted down by Jefferson who only has to say the word 'dangerous' before the others all boo and then burst into laughter.

Anuman, sitting apart from the group, and sorting through the contents of his bag under the light of the food shelter torch, laughs too.

'So what do we talk about next?' Danny asks.

The air rings with suggestions as they all shout over each other, then Honor's voice rings out clear and loud.

'Let's talk about our worst phobias.'

'Are you kidding?' Meg, sitting on one side of Danny with her knees pulled up to her chest, shivers theatrically. 'Most of them are on this bloody island!'

They all laugh.

'Come on,' Honor cajoles. 'It'll be fun. We'll find out which one of us is the biggest weirdo.' She pauses for effect. 'Jeffers?'

Everyone, including Jefferson, laughs.

'Fine.' Jefferson shrugs. 'I've got a phobia of heights.'

'You do not!' Danny scoffs. 'I sat next to you on the flight over here and you were fine.'

'Not that kind of height. I'm OK when I'm sitting down surrounded by a metal box. It's sharp drops that freak me out. You know, when it's really steep?' He presses his fingertips together, one hand horizontal, the other vertical. 'If I get to the edge I get this really weird compulsion to throw myself off.'

'Why don't you?' Milo says and everyone laughs again. There's nothing malicious in Milo's comment, or our reaction. It's light-hearted banter, an easy togetherness formed over seventeen years of friendship.

'Be a bit weird if you were afraid of heights, Milo,' Jeffers banters back. 'You'd be scared every time you stood up!'

'Heights I can take.' He uncrosses his long legs and stretches them out towards the fire. 'Snakes, on the other hand…' He glances at Meg, sitting beside him. 'I blame you. When I was four she put a worm in my mouth when I was sleeping.'

'Didn't happen! You dreamed it.'

'I did not!'

'OK, OK,' Honor holds out her hands. 'Enough bickering or I'll put you both on the naughty step! Jessie, how about you?'

There's an awkward pause as all eyes turn to Jessie.

'I'll go next,' Meg says quickly. 'I'm afraid of—'

'No, no.' Jessie's voice cuts across her like a knife. 'Let me take my turn. I don't mind. I've got a phobia of vomiting. There, I said it.'

No one says a word.

'Seriously,' Jessie continues. 'It freaks me out. I can't stand the smell of it, the sound of it, the way people retch and I'm shit-scared of puking myself. I haven't been able to eat prawns for three years since I had a dodgy takeaway.'

There's a beat then Jeffers says, 'Don't blame you, vomit stinks! Did I tell you about the time that I—'

Honor holds up a hand. 'Yes, we know and we don't need to hear it again.'

Everyone laughs and Danny feels the tension ease from between his shoulder blades. Jefferson might be a know-it-all but, for once, he picked the right time to launch into one of his stories. Everyone sitting around the fire knows that Jessie just lied about her phobia. When Anuman asked for volunteers to use the flint and steel to start the fire she couldn't get away fast enough. She wanted to go beachcombing to find stuff that might be useful, she said. They all know what happened last summer – their parents told them and they've discussed it in a private WhatsApp group – but Jessie hasn't mentioned it once since she arrived and none of them has had the guts to bring it up. Danny wasn't sure who was more uncomfortable when she walked into the hotel lobby with her parents on the first night in Thailand – her or him. While Jessie's parents stood hand in hand, she stood apart. You could have fitted another person in the gap between Jessie and her dad. Her older brother hadn't been on one of the NCT holidays for years – preferring to stay at home instead – but he was there, in the mental scrapbook of Danny's memories: sitting at the head of the kids' table, deliberately swimming out to a buoy when they'd all been told it was too far out, laughing at Danny and calling him 'a little kid' when he was too scared to attempt a zipwire. And now there was a Tom-shaped space in the hotel lobby that would never be filled. Danny stared at it for a very long time.

'Anyway,' Meg huffs. 'My phobia's blood. No big deal, apart from to me. Honor?'

Danny glances at his girlfriend. He knows what her phobia is and she knows his. They've had this conversation before. There isn't a single thing they don't know about each other.

'I'm not going to say,' Honor says, giggling nervously, 'because I wouldn't put it past one of you bastards to try and scare me.'

'We wouldn't,' Jeffers says.

Milo laughs. 'I would.'

'You try it,' Honor says to him and Danny picks up on her flirty tone.

'No one's going to be trying anything,' he says pointedly.

'Dude.' Milo raises an eyebrow. 'I was joking.'

'As long as that's all it is.'

'Seriously, Danny?' Honor glares at him. 'You're going to do this now?'

'I'm not doing anything.'

'And I am?'

Danny tips his head to one side and mimes flicking long hair over his shoulders. 'You try it,' he mimics.

'Dan—' Meg stops tracing her finger through the sand and looks up at him. 'Leave it out.'

'Yeah, can we just get this done?' Jessie asks. 'It's getting boring now.'

'Well, sorry to bore everyone,' Honor says irritably. 'I was trying to share my phobia but *someone* wouldn't let me speak. Anyway, it's spiders.' She holds up her hands, palms face out. 'There, done.'

Danny watches as she crosses her arms over her chest and stares, sullenly, into the fire. He can't keep up with her mood swings this holiday. One minute she's playful and fun and the next she's quiet and prickly. Maybe he shouldn't have called her out on being flirty with Milo but she's never flirted with anyone in the group before and it creeps him out. He's going have to take her to one side for a chat. Find out what the hell is going on.

'Danny. Danny. Dan. Hello, Dan, is there anyone there?' He turns his head sharply as Meg shouts at him from across the fire.

'Your turn,' she says. 'You're the last one.'

'OK, OK.' He forces a laugh. 'If I must. I've got a massive phobia about small spaces. When I was little I got stuck in a bucket at nursery. You can all laugh and take the piss now.'

And they do. Everyone apart from Honor, who gives him a suspicious sideways look. She knows Jessie wasn't the only one who lied about her phobia. He did too.

CHAPTER 5

JESSIE

Day two on the island

Danny and Honor are arguing. They're pretending they're not, doing that low-pitched hissing thing my parents do when they don't want to cause a scene in front of me, but whenever the fire lights up their faces you can see how irritated they are with each other. I'm not sure what they're arguing about. It seemed to kick off after the discussion about phobias. That was awkward – the phobias topic. I could have told the truth about mine; it did cross my mind but I didn't want the others to pull sad faces at me or for there to be a weird silence. As it was there *was* an awkward silence but Jeffers broke it with his vomit story. I know Danny is wary of Jeffers – there's always been a bit of a weird tension between those two, even when we were younger – but he's clever and he tells it like it is. And he's more empathetic than he lets on. He didn't chime in with his vomit story because he likes the sound of his own voice, he just didn't want me to feel awkward.

It's so ridiculously dark now that the sea has become a long black strip of satin shimmering in the moonlight. There's no chance I'm going anywhere near the jungle. The birds have stopped singing but I can still hear the low whooping of the monkeys. There are other sounds too: clicks and whistles and buzzing. I can tell that they're freaking Milo out. He keeps twisting round and looking behind him as though he's expecting a huge great snake to slither out from the trees. His confession surprised me. I thought he'd say he had a phobia of something more physical like deep water or being buried alive. Snakes, no.

Maybe I don't know him as well as I thought I did. Why else would Jeffers warn me off him earlier? It's not because Jeffers has any kind of ulterior motive. He came out the summer we all turned fifteen. Milo and Danny were surprised, but it wasn't a shock to any of the girls. The boys held back while we all hugged Jeffers and, for a second, I wondered if things were going to be a bit weird between us all, but then Milo said something that made everyone laugh, Jeffers pretended to punch him round the head, and we were all back to normal. That was the summer that Danny and Honor got together. It had been on the cards for ages. They'd been really flirty in our WhatsApp group chats and Danny hadn't held back on commenting on Honor's Instagram photos. He blatantly fancied her and, when I took Honor to one side to ask if she felt the same, she admitted that she did. All we had to do then was set them up in the most unsubtle fashion ever. We were on holiday in Croyde. It was Danny's birthday and Milo arranged for us all to go to the beach one evening, to watch the sunset. One by one we made excuses to be somewhere else, leaving Danny and Honor sitting on the beach together. Next time we saw them they were holding hands and grinning like idiots.

They're not smiling now, though. They've given up the pretence that they're not arguing and Honor's voice cuts through the jungle sounds like a knife.

'Danny!' She twists away from him and throws her hands up in the air in frustration. 'I've been sitting next to you for the last two hours. How is that being off with you?'

'You've barely touched me!'

'Oh, I'm sorry. Did I miss the rule where we have to have our hands locked together, twenty-four hours a day?'

'No, but you did miss the rule about flirting with other people.'

'Who?' Honor physically recoils, anger lighting up her face as she gets to her feet. 'Who have I flirted with? Anuman? Jeffers?' She stares across the fire. 'Milo? You seriously think I've been flirting with Milo?'

Milo raises his eyebrows but doesn't say a word. Is this what Jeffers was warning me about earlier? Has something been going on between him and Honor?

'Sit down!' Danny grabs Honor by the wrist. 'You're overreacting.'

'*I'm* overreacting? You're the one acting all needy for no reason.' She yanks her hand from him and turns to face us. 'Am I right? Guys? Tell me I'm right.'

The silence that follows is painful. Not one person says a word and when I sneak a glimpse to my right, Meg and

Milo are both staring down at the sand while Jeffers determinedly whittles away at a piece of wood with his pocket knife. No good can come of getting involved with Danny and Honor's argument. It's a lovers' tiff and there's no point taking sides. They'll have made up and be all lovey-dovey again by the morning.

'Sod this!' Honor shouts. 'I'm not staying here. Anuman, first thing tomorrow I want you to take me back in the boat.'

Our guide looks up impassively. He doesn't want to get involved either. Honor doesn't wait for a response. She stalks off down the beach with Danny running after her, shouting that there's no way he's letting her go anywhere alone.

The others are asleep, lying side by side in the shelter; a row of multicoloured worms in their waterproof sleeping bags. Meg and Milo went to bed first, shortly followed by Jeffers. Anuman tried to convince me that I should go to bed too. When I said no, that I wanted to stay up for a bit longer, he shrugged, retired to the food prep shelter and crawled into his own sleeping bag. A few minutes later I saw the shapes of Danny and Honor wandering back towards camp. You could have driven a truck between them they were standing so far apart. As they drew closer the fire illuminated Honor's puffy eyes, her eye make-up striped down her cheeks. Danny was still raging; his eyes narrow, his jaw tight. Neither of them so much as looked at me as they rounded the fire and scrabbled around in the gloom, trying to find their stuff. Danny lay down first, taking a spot on the ground next to Jeffers. Honor stood with her back to me, clutching her sleeping bag, for the longest time. She looked like she was trying to decide where to sleep – next to Danny or next to Meg, on the other end of the row. Finally, she made her choice and lay down next to Danny, rolling onto her side so she had her back to him.

It's after midnight and the sweltering heat of the day can't have dropped more than a few degrees. When Danny started the fire earlier Anuman explained that, in a survival experience, it's vital to keep it burning all the time; that it's our only source of heat, cooking and water purification. He sent us all into the forest to collect wood, and there's a huge pile stacked up behind me. But that's not the reason I'm still awake. I'm not worried the fire will go out. I'm terrified it will get out of control. And if the whole island goes up in flames, so will we.

CHAPTER 6

DANNY

Danny groans and stretches as he wakes up. Every bone in his body aches, as though he ran a marathon the night before. Honor, beside him, is still asleep, her back curled away from him. He woke in the night and, forgetting their argument, snuggled up beside her and threw an arm around her waist. They haven't had sex all holiday. Back at the hotel he tried knocking on Honor's door when he was sure Thea was asleep, but Honor refused to let him in, claiming the walls were thin and her mum would hear. Last night, as he pressed up against his girlfriend on the cold, hard shelter floor, she curled into a tight ball. She didn't want him to touch her.

Danny looks down at her as she sleeps, his heart twisting in his chest. Honor has always made him feel so loved and safe, but she's losing interest, slipping away, growing more and more distant with every day. He crawls out of the low shelter and reaches for the empty bottle of vodka, half buried in the sand. He glances at Jessie, curled up on the sand beside the gently flickering fire. Like Honor, she's still fast asleep. No sign of Anuman, though. His sleeping bag, in the food prep shelter, is empty. He's not on the beach either. He's probably in the jungle, foraging for food.

Danny pulls the empty bottle out of the sand and throws it onto a haphazard pile of rubbish near the fire. As it strikes another bottle Jessie jolts awake, her eyes wide and fearful, one cheek smothered with sand and her hair sticking up at all angles. She props herself up on her elbow and stares at him. 'What... who—'

'Morning,' he says. 'We're on the island. Remember?'

Jessie stares blearily around, taking in the long stretch of beach and the sea lapping at the shore.

'Did you sleep out here all night?' He gestures at the small patch of skin between the hem of her trousers and her ankle bone. It's pricked with angry red dots. 'Looks like the sand flies had a feast.'

Jessie groans in despair and rubs at her leg. 'Great.'

'Someone's busy.' He points further down the beach where Jefferson is sitting cross-legged on the sand with a large green net spread out around him.

Jessie shields her eyes with her hand and blinks into the distance. 'That's the net I found yesterday. I think he's trying to fix it. Do you know if there's anything to eat? We finished all my Pringles last night and I'm starving.'

'I don't know. I think we ate all the fish yesterday. Anyway, look, Jess, I um... I need your opinion on something. Was I out of order last night? With Honor. Because, if so—'

He's interrupted by a rustling from the jungle. Anuman

appears between the trees, his arms loaded with bananas, mangos and coconuts.

'Oh my God!' Jessie leaps to her feet and charges over to their host. 'Talk about heaven!'

Danny trudges after her, stomach rumbling. An idea forms in his mind as he reaches out and takes a bunch of bananas, a mango and a coconut from Anuman's towering pile. Maybe he could prepare a fresh fruit cocktail for Honor. If he borrowed Jeffers' knife he could chop it all up and serve it to her in half a coconut shell. It would be worth it for a smile. She might even look at him the way she used to. He reaches for another piece of fruit but, as he does, Jessie lets out a little shriek of surprise.

'Jess?' He looks from her to their guide and immediately spots what's wrong. The whole right side of Anuman's face has suddenly sagged, as though his skin has melted, pulling down the side of his mouth and eye. Their guide's arms go slack and he drops the fruit. Danny jumps back as a coconut lands beside his foot.

'Anuman! Are you OK?' he asks as another coconut falls to the sand, then several bunches of bananas and half a dozen mangos. Anuman stumbles towards him, lips moving. Nothing he's saying makes sense. It's a series of nonsensical sounds.

'Anuman?' Jessie says, her voice high and tight. 'What is it? What's wrong?'

She leaps forward, grabbing the older man as he tips to the side. 'Help me!' she shouts but Danny can't move. He feels as though someone has screwed his feet through the sand and deep into the earth.

'Danny!' Jessie cries as she awkwardly lowers Anuman onto the sand. His eyes are closed and he's not moving. 'We need to get him back to the mainland. Now! I think he's having a stroke.'

Danny doesn't reply. He feels as though he's watching the scene before him play out on a movie screen.

'Danny!' Jessie shouts again. 'You need to help me carry him down to the boat. Now!'

Danny takes a step backwards. He can't do it. He can't even look at Anuman.

'Jeffers!' Jessie shouts. 'Jeffers, help!'

But Jefferson is already speeding down the beach towards them, his green fishing net abandoned and flapping and twisting in the breeze.

CHAPTER 7

JESSIE

Anuman is small and light but it takes for ever to carry him across the sand to the boat, tethered at the shore. The sand is dry and my feet keep slipping as I walk sideways, crab-like, bearing the weight of his legs while Jeffers holds him under the armpits. Meg speeds past us shouting something about looking for a medical kit. Honor and Milo are back in the shelter, arguing about what we should do. Milo thinks we should abandon our stuff and just leave, while Honor thinks we should pack it up and take it with us. Danny seems completely oblivious to their argument. He's still standing by the spot where Anuman fell, staring into space. Meg reaches the boat and clambers inside. It rocks back and forth as she slithers into it then she's up on her knees, scrabbling around looking under the wooden seats. As we draw closer she shouts something but I can't make out what she's saying. I'm worried about Anuman. He hasn't moved or opened his eyes since he collapsed and now his mouth is hanging open. We need to get him in the boat and back to the mainland as quickly as we can. There'll be a hospital there, and people who can help him.

'Is he still alive?' I ask Jeffers as we wade into the sea.

I'm too scared to look at Anuman's chest in case it's not moving.

'I don't know,' Jeffers says. And there it is, my worst fear, reflected back in his eyes.

Somehow, we manage to lift Anuman's limp body into the long, narrow boat, then Meg scoots over to the diesel engine at one end as Jeffers shouts instructions at her. I remain in the sea, watching. When Milo shouts my name I turn to see him and Honor sprinting down the beach towards us, waving their arms frantically. Back at the shelter Danny still hasn't moved.

Jeffers is watching him too. 'He needs to get a move on or we'll have to leave him behind. We need to get going *now*.'

I want to tell him that I'll go and get him but I'm shaking so much that when I open my mouth to speak, my teeth chatter together. Even my heart seems to be vibrating in my chest. And I can't breathe. I can't get enough air in my lungs. I feel hot and faint and like I'm going to die.

'Oh God,' Jeffers says under his breath then, louder. 'Jessie! Jessie, it's OK. Take deep breaths. You're having a panic attack. Meg, just pull the starter cord.'

'I can't find it!'

'Oh for God's sake. I'll do it. You look after Jessie.'

I hear a splash as Meg jumps out of the boat and then she and Honor peer into my face asking me if I'm OK and Milo's got his arm around my shoulder and I just want them all to go away. There's not enough air. I can't breathe. And I'm so hot. I'm so hot I feel faint.

'Um… guys.' Jefferson's shout cuts the incessant pounding of my blood in my ears. 'It doesn't look like we're going—'

He doesn't finish his sentence. Instead he drops to his knees and disappears from view.

'Jeffers?' Meg says. She takes a step away from me, heading back towards the boat.

'What's going on?' Honor breathes.

Milo, still holding me close, looks conflicted. He wants to stay with me but a bigger part of him wants to find out what Jeffers is doing in the boat.

'Try the pulse in his neck,' Meg says as she leans over the side of the boat.

'I've tried that.' Jefferson's disembodied voice floats back towards us. 'I've tried both his wrists too. I can't… I can't find a pulse.'

'Let me try.'

'I'm telling you, there's no pulse!'

'So we do CPR. We… we…' Meg's voice cracks. 'Jeffers, stop staring at me like that! We've got to do something. We've got to try.'

'It's too late.'

'No it's not. It's not. Do CPR! For God's sake, Jeffers. We can't let him die.'

There's a pause that seems to last a lifetime then Jefferson says, 'It's too late, Meg. Anuman is dead.'

'No,' I murmur. 'No. No. No. No.'

'Jessie?' Milo says as I pull away from him. 'Jessie, wait!'

My bare feet pound the sand and my lungs burn as I speed down the beach. I don't stop when I reach the rocks at the far end. I clamber up them, the sharp planes scratching my palms and the soles of my feet. *This can't be happening. This can't be happening.* The chant plays out in my head as I continue to climb. I reach the edge of the rocks and stare down at the sea, crashing and splashing below me. There's nowhere left to run. My chest's burning with the scream that's been building since Anuman's face drooped on one side but, when I open my lips, nothing comes out.

I sit on the rocks, staring out to sea until my breathing slows and my hands stop shaking then I scrabble to my feet and walk back along the sand to the boat. Someone's put a tarpaulin over Anuman but it's not big enough to completely cover him. The sight of his brown, worn boots, sticking out of the bottom, almost makes me turn back but I force myself to keep walking closer. Honor is sitting on the sand, her knees gathered to her chest, her head in her hands, sobbing quietly. Danny is beside her, his arm around her shoulders, his face chalky. Our eyes meet as he turns to look at me and something passes between us – shock, pain, disbelief – before he turns back and nestles his head against Honor's.

'Honor,' I say softly. 'Are you OK?'

She shakes her head mutely.

My gaze drifts back to the boat and the boots sticking out from the tarpaulin. I want to believe that Jefferson was wrong, that Anuman is just unconscious and in a second, a minute, an hour, he'll throw back his waterproof covering and ask us why we've abandoned the fire. But that's not going to happen. We're never going to hear his soft lilting voice again.

'It must. It must be so hard...' Honor looks up at me, her face streaked with tears. 'For you, Jessie. To see... to see what happened to Anuman, I mean... because...' she tails off, unsure how to finish her sentence. I'm grateful for her awkwardness. The last thing I want to talk about right now is Tom.

'I liked him,' Danny says and for a second I don't know if he's talking about our guide or my brother. 'He was really patient with me yesterday, when I was trying to start the fire. And he... he put up with all Jefferson's know-it-all shit too.'

The smallest of smiles creeps onto Honor's face. 'He was so nice. He was telling me yesterday about his wife Boonsri and how her name means beautiful and how, even at sixty-three years old, she's still the most beautiful woman he's ever met and—' her voice breaks and she presses her face into Danny's shoulder again, her body shaking as she sobs. I press a hand to my chest. I feel as though someone just slid a piece of glass into my heart.

As Danny hugs her close I wander over to Meg, Milo and Jefferson, huddled together beside the boat, up to their knees in seawater, talking softly. Jefferson turns as I approach.

'Are you OK, Jessie?'

'Yeah,' I lie.

'We think it was a stroke,' Meg says. The sun is beating down on us but she's got her arms wrapped around her body like we're in the Arctic.

'It happened so quickly,' Milo says. 'He seemed fine yesterday. He was whacking down trees and hoisting them onto his shoulder; he was fitter than all of us put together. It just... it doesn't make sense. How can someone like that just... just die?' He swallows and turns away, lightly shaking his head. He can't believe what's happened. None of us can.

'A man his age shouldn't have been chopping down trees and sleeping on the ground with a bunch of teenagers,' I say. 'He should have been at home, with his family, he should have been retired, enjoying life—' The word catches in my throat and I take a steadying breath.

Meg rests her hand on my shoulder and gives it a squeeze. 'You know there was nothing we could have done. Don't you, Jessie?'

She means well but her words send a shiver through me. I've heard that phrase before.

'Wasn't there?' I ask.

'If anyone should feel guilty it should be me,' Jefferson says. 'This was my birthday present. It was—'

'Stop it,' Meg says. 'Guys, please. It wasn't anyone's fault. It was a stroke. It could have happened anywhere, at any time.'

'We should bury him,' Jefferson says. 'It's the respectful thing to do.'

'No.' Meg shakes her head firmly. 'His family... they'll want to pay their respects.'

'Meg's right,' I say. 'He's got a big family – a wife, three children and seven grandchildren. We can't bury him, that's not our decision to make. We need to take him back with us.'

'My dad will help,' Jefferson says. 'He'll make sure his family are well looked after.'

'We'll all ask our parents to contribute,' Milo says.

Everyone nods and then we lapse into silence, lost in our own thoughts.

'Can we go then?' Meg asks.

'Go?' Jefferson looks confused.

'Back to the mainland. You can drive the boat, can't you?'

He shakes his head.

''Course you can,' Milo says. 'You just pull the starter cord and steer with the handle thing.'

'It's called a...' Jeffers shakes his head sharply. 'Doesn't matter. We're not taking the boat anywhere.'

'But why not?' I say. 'Do you think it's too dangerous? Or—'

'Jessie,' Jeffers says. 'We can't start the engine because the starter cord is gone.'

We've all been sitting around the fire for a good hour or so now: Danny and Honor locked together as they stare listlessly into the flames, Milo and Meg talking softly and Jefferson and I discussing what we do now. With no starter cord the boat's as good as useless. There are no paddles and, even if there were, this island is so remote it could take hours and hours for us to get back to the mainland, and that's assuming we didn't drift off course.

'Are you sure it was cut?' I ask Jeffers. 'It didn't just snap off?'

'There's no way. It wasn't worn or fraying. Someone cut it, probably with a knife.'

'What was that?' Milo breaks off from his conversation with Meg and leans round me to look at Jeffers. 'You think someone deliberately cut the starter cord?'

'Seriously?' Meg says. 'Who would do that and leave us stranded here?'

Jeffers shrugs. 'I've got no idea.'

Honor, sitting on the other side of the fire, pulls away from Danny and turns to look towards the jungle. She runs her hands over her arms then hugs herself tightly. 'Do you think there's someone else here? Other people on the island?'

Jefferson shakes his head. 'Unlikely. It's a private island. My dad rented it for the week on the proviso that we're the only ones staying here. The owner's security firm will have checked it out before we arrived.'

'But there's a chance we're not alone,' I say. 'If someone turned up after the security guys left and we arrived? We don't even know what the other side of the island looks like, never mind whether there are other people on it.'

'I'd be very surprised,' Jefferson says. 'My dad's a stickler for getting what he pays for. He'd be straight on the phone for a refund.'

'But what if it's not an official booking,' Milo says. 'What if it's randoms on a day trip? Or locals? Fishermen or something?'

'Nah,' Jefferson says. 'The owner has prosecuted trespassers before and no one wants to end up in a Thai jail. Besides, why would someone local or a fisherman cut the cord on our boat?'

'To freak us out? Maybe it's a message they want us to pass on when we get back – *if* we get back – stay away from this island or bad shit will happen.'

'Oh God.' Honor presses her hands over her face and leans into Danny's shoulder.

'Guys,' he says, 'can we change the subject? You're freaking her out.'

There's a beat as no one speaks. Meg takes a swig of her water and sets it back on the sand, then looks at each of us in turn.

'I think it's more likely that one of you guys did it.'

Milo swings round to look at her. 'What?'

She doesn't meet his gaze. Instead she focuses on Danny. 'You didn't want Honor to leave. You said so last night, we all heard you. You heard him, didn't you, Jess?'

Of course I remember but it's a bit of a stretch, imagining that he would cut the cord on the boat and leave us all stranded here. Although I'm not sure I like the alternative much – that there's someone else on the island with a vendetta.

'I don't know, Meg,' I say vaguely. 'I can't really remember.'

Her face hardens. 'No, that's fine,' she says. 'You sit on the fence. But you heard him, didn't you, Jefferson? He definitely said she wasn't going anywhere.'

'You did say that,' Jeffers looks at Danny.

'Whoa! Whoa!' Danny holds up his hands, palms out. 'Careful who you're accusing, buddy. You're the only one with a knife.'

'Me?' Jefferson's jaw drops. 'You don't honestly think—'

'It's your survival week. Maybe you wanted to add a bit of edge to the experience? See how we all coped when we're really stranded?'

'Jess was the last one up.' Honor points at me. 'Did you see anything?'

'Or maybe you did it,' Danny says before I can answer. 'Is that why you stayed up so late? Were you waiting for us all to fall asleep so you could creep down to the boat?'

I look from him to Honor and shake my head. This is ridiculous! Anuman is dead, we're stranded and they're arguing about who cut the starter cord? I look at Jefferson but he shrugs and raises his eyes to the sky. He looks as exasperated as I feel.

'What does it matter who cut the starter cord?' I ask. 'If it was even cut. We've got more important—'

'See,' Danny says. 'She's changing the subject. Obviously guilty.'

I stare at him. 'What possible motivation would I have for stranding us here?'

'Who knows how your mind works? The other night you nearly broke someone's hand with a chair leg!'

'To help Honor out. For God's sake, Danny. Would you listen to yourself? There's a dead man over there,' I point across the beach to the boat, 'who's never going to see his family again and you're… you're…' I scrabble to my feet and walk away from the group, hands crossed over my body, gripping my arms, the sand hot and scratchy against the soles of my feet.

'Jess.' Milo is behind me and touches me lightly in the centre of my back, making me jump. 'Are you OK?'

'No, not really.'

'I don't know what's wrong with everyone.'

'They're scared. I get it. It's not every day you see some-one… someone…' I can't finish my sentence and Milo puts an arm around my shoulder and pulls me into a hug. My cheek rests just beneath his collar bone and I can smell the suntan lotion and salt on his warm skin. My hands rest lightly on his back but I can't bring myself to close my eyes and lose myself in the hug. My muscles are tensed, my mind is racing and I can hear Meg and Jefferson's raised voices drifting over from the fire. They're arguing about what we should do now. Meg thinks we should sit it out while Jeffers thinks we need to get help.

'You know I didn't do it, don't you?' I pull away from Milo. 'I didn't cut the cord.'

'Of course you didn't.' His eyes search mine. 'But someone did. I saw the end of the cord. It didn't just snap off.'

'But why? Who'd want to leave us marooned here? Danny can be an idiot but he's not that stupid. And I don't buy that Jeffers would do it.'

'You think there's someone else here?'

'There could be. This island's massive. For all we know the owner could have rented the other side out to another group and we wouldn't have a clue. The owner pockets twice the cash and each group thinks they've got the place all to themselves.'

'But why would they sneak across the island and damage our boat?'

'For a laugh? Maybe they were pissed?'

'We can barely get through the jungle sober, never mind drunk.'

'Maybe they used a boat?'

'We'd have heard it and woken up.'

'Locals then? Fishermen? Someone who's pissed off with the fact it's a private island.'

I shake my head. 'That doesn't make sense either. Why would they cut the cord? It doesn't get rid of us, it keeps us here.'

'Maybe that's what they want? To teach us a lesson.'

I shiver as I stare at the thick throng of palms, bamboo and mango trees gently swaying in the wind. The idea that there might be someone in there right now, watching us, is terrifying.

'What do you think we should do?'

I break off as Jeffers speeds past us then launches himself into the water and starts swimming out to sea.

I look back at Milo. 'He's not trying to swim back to the mainland, is he?'

'He wouldn't be that stupid.'

We run back to the others. Danny has his arm around Honor, who's sobbing uncontrollably, and Meg's staring out to sea with her arms crossed over her chest.

'He wouldn't listen!' she says irritably. 'It took us over an hour to get here by boat. He'd have to swim for *hours* to reach the mainland. And he's not even that strong a swimmer.'

I shield my eyes from the glaring sun and follow her gaze. It can't be much after seven o'clock in the morning and it's already swelteringly hot. The sea's calm but there's a strong tide. Jeffers has only been in the water for a couple of minutes but he's already slowing down and his technique's terrible. He's craning his neck out of the water instead of breathing out below the surface and coming up for a breath every three strokes. There's no way he can keep that up all the way to the mainland.

'Jeffers!' I cup my hands around my mouth as I walk towards the shore. 'Jeffers, come back!'

Milo starts to shout too, so does Meg, but if Jefferson hears us he doesn't respond. Instead he continues to splish and splash through the water, his T-shirt billowing out around him like a big green life vest.

'We're better off trying to fashion oars out of some wood,' Danny says, Honor's face still nestled into his neck. 'Row the boat, and Anuman, back to the mainland.'

'It's not a bad idea,' Milo says begrudgingly but I shake my head.

'I don't think we should risk it. There are some pretty strong currents between here and the coast. If we get into difficulty and get swept off course we'd be in *real* trouble.'

'Since when were you Captain Ahab?' Meg snaps.

'Who?'

She rolls her eyes. '*Moby Dick*?'

I'm about to snap back that I used to go sailing with the swimming club but I'm interrupted by Milo shouting and pointing out to sea. Jefferson has stopped swimming and is flailing around in the water, one arm raised.

'He's in trouble!'

I react instinctively, pulling off my linen top and trousers. As I run into the water I can hear the others shouting and calling my name but I don't stop and I don't look back. I run until the sea is waist high then launch myself forwards and, head down, pull my arms through the water. It's like coming home, being in the water again, and I feel strong and powerful as I plough towards Jeffers. When I reach him he grabs at me frantically, wrapping his arms around my neck as though I'm a life buoy. We sink instantly, and my world turns a hazy shade of blue and green as I fight to break his grip. He's scared, and much stronger than he looks. No sooner do I loosen one of his arms, he tightens his hold with the other. My lungs burn as his pale, drawn face looms closer then drifts away as we wrestle underwater. I can't hold my breath for much longer. If I don't get away from him soon he's going to drown us both. I lift my knee to fill the space between our bodies then, leaning back as far as his grip will allow, push as hard as I can. His grip loosens around my neck and I kick my legs frantically, head craned towards the surface. I gulp air into my lungs but I don't tread water for long. Jefferson's still under the water, his body starfishing – arms and legs spread as he sinks towards the seabed – a metre or so below me. I take a deep breath and dive back into the water. I hook my hand under his chin and frantically kick my legs but he's a dead weight, and we're barely moving. Fear so powerful it's paralysing flows through me. We're both going to die. This is it. This is how our lives end. We're seventeen and we've barely lived. When the others go back to the mainland they'll have to tell our parents that their children are dead. Oh God, Mum and Dad. They'd have to mourn a second child.

Fear morphs into rage and I kick harder, reaching through the water with my free hand. I won't let the sea beat me. No one's going to die.

I hear the scream of a gull as my head breaks through the water. I choke back air, gulping and panting, my lungs burning and my limbs aching. I lean back, kicking hard with my legs, pulling Jefferson's head up and out of the water, my hand still clasped around his jaw. But his lips don't part and his eyes don't open and his weighty body remains below the surface of the water. He's not floating because his lungs have filled with water. Adrenaline and rage course through me and a silent chant fills my head: *get back to the beach, get back to the beach*. I stare up into the cloudless azure sky and it is as though time has stopped. It's just me, floating in the ocean, utterly alone in the world. And then I hear raised voices and bodies splashing through the water. Before I can turn to look round, strong hands hook me under the armpits and drag me through the sea, my heels catching in the rough sand. I try to speak, to shout for them to help Jefferson rather than me, but my voice has disappeared, replaced by a seal-like bark each time I inhale.

CHAPTER 8

DANNY

The relief Danny feels when Jefferson coughs violently and spews sea water onto the sand is overwhelming. He thought his friend was dead when he dragged him out of the water. Jefferson's head was lolling to one side and his eyes were closed. After Danny laid him on the sand he felt for his pulse, fumbling inexperienced fingers over his friend's wrist, and promptly recoiled when he found nothing but cold, slippery skin. Meg took over then, pushing Danny out of the way. She heaved Jefferson onto his back, clasped her fingers together and had just lowered her hands to his chest to start CPR when he lurched onto his side and began to cough.

Unlike Jefferson, who's still lying on the sand, Jessie is in a sitting position. She's further down the beach with Milo and she's trying to talk, but each time she opens her mouth she makes a weird rasping noise. Danny's eyes meet Milo's. They stare at each other – wordlessly sharing the horror of what they just witnessed.

Danny hadn't even realized that Jeffers had got into trouble. He was whispering in Honor's ear, reassuring her that everything was going to be OK, when Jessie suddenly stripped off her clothes and ran into the sea. She was a good swimmer. As kids she'd always win the races they held in various hotel pools, but she ploughed through the sea towards Jeffers like a woman on a mission. When she reached him Danny felt himself relax – everyone was going to be OK – but when they both disappeared under the surface of the water he felt as though he was trapped in a nightmare or a horror film.

He jumped to his feet and ran to the shoreline with the others and stared impotently out to sea, not knowing what to do. When Milo charged into the water Danny did the same. They half ran, half swam, side by side, to where Jessie was sculling through the water on her back, her hand cupped under Jefferson's chin. The water was shallow but she was too exhausted to stand. Milo dragged her to the shore while Danny did the same for Jefferson.

Now, as Jessie makes her way down the beach towards them, supported by Milo, hot tears fill Danny's eyes. She could have died. Her and Jefferson. Instinctively he reaches for Honor's hand but there's no one beside him.

He turns sharply and looks round, expecting to see her slim frame hovering uncertainly behind him. But she's not there. He spins around on the sand and scans the beach and the shoreline, but there's no sign of his girlfriend.

'Meg, have you seen Honor?'

She looks up, her dark head bent over Jeffers. 'Nope.'

'But she—'

He looks back towards the shelters and the jungle beyond them. Logically he knows she can't have gone far. She probably walked to the stream to have a cry in private, or found somewhere out of sight to have a wee; but his mind is still on high alert and he can't bear the thought of anything happening to her. They all need to stay together. They're safer that way.

'Is he OK?' Jessie crouches down on the sand beside Meg and Jeffers. She's stopped making that strange rasping noise but her voice is as thick as sandpaper. She sounds like a forty-a-day smoker.

'He'll be fine.' Meg smiles up at her. 'Won't you, Jeffers?'

Jefferson struggles to sit up, batting away Meg's hands as she tries to stop him. 'You saved my life, Jess. I thought I was dead.'

Jessie says nothing, instead she stares at him with the strangest expression on her face. Up close Danny can see the scars she's been trying to hide all holiday. The skin on her hands is lumpen and shiny and the burns twist up her wrists and arms to her neck like thick red snakes. She flinches, as though sensing his eyes on her body, and shrinks away from Milo so the arm he has around her shoulders falls away.

'You nearly killed me,' she snaps at Jefferson. 'The next time you do something idiotic try not to drown the person who's saving you. OK?'

Danny's shocked but says nothing. Neither do any of the others, and when Jessie announces that she's going back to camp to get some dry clothes, the only sound is the sharp cry of gulls circling overhead. As she disappears into the shelter Milo crouches down beside Jefferson.

'She didn't mean that. She's still in shock.'

'No, I deserved it.' Jeffers peels off his wet T-shirt and rests his arms on his knees. 'There's no way I could have swum all the way to the mainland, even if I hadn't got cramp in my leg.'

'And there was me thinking Action Man was invincible.'

'None of us are,' Meg says grimly. 'We need to remember that.'

Back at the camp, while everyone apart from Jessie – who's lying in the shelter with her eyes closed – congregates around the fire, Danny rummages in his rucksack for his bottle of water.

'Where are you off to?' Milo asks as he heads towards the jungle.

'Gonna look for Honor.'

'But she's—' Milo glances around, startled, as though he's only just realized she's missing. 'Oh. Where is she?'

Meg shakes her head. 'I haven't seen her for a while.'

'Want me to help you look?' Milo asks Danny.

'No, no. I'm sure she's just gone to get water.' Danny fights to keep his tone light. A new, unsettling thought had hit him as they walked back to the shelter. What if Honor hadn't run off because she was upset about Jessie and Jefferson getting into trouble in the sea? What if she just wanted to get away from him? Last night she'd screamed at him that she was sick of him accusing her of flirting with Milo and wanted to leave. And now she's stuck on the island with him for the rest of the week.

Danny heads for the waterfall first, certain Honor won't have ventured far into the jungle – not with her fear of spiders – but the only visitors to the waterfall are a couple of macaque monkeys who take one look at him, whoop with fear and leap into the trees and disappear. He heads left, along the rough path Anuman created by chopping at the plants and bushes with his machete when they had been looking for trees to fell.

Anuman.

Just thinking about his guide makes Danny's stomach clench. It was terrifying how quickly death had claimed him. One second he was walking out of the jungle with an armful of fruit, and the next he was staring at Danny with fear in his eyes as the stroke dragged at his face and twisted his lips. Had he known what was coming? Was he afraid? Danny stops in his tracks as his own mortality hits him full force. He doesn't believe in heaven or an afterlife. Death is final, a full stop. It's eternal darkness, nothingness, a void. When he was six years old he was told that his grandfather had died after he'd fallen into a deep sleep and never woke up. Years later Danny was told that his grandfather had suffered from heart failure and fallen into a coma, but Little Danny didn't know that. He became too scared to fall asleep in case death claimed him too. He spent night after sleepless night trying to imagine how it felt to no longer exist, winding himself up so much his breath would catch in his throat and he'd sit up in bed, gulping in air.

Just remembering it makes his chest tighten and he rests a hand against a tree, fighting to take a deep, steadying breath as sweat beads on his forehead and rolls down his face.

I'm not going to die, he tells himself. *It's just a panic attack. It's just a panic attack.*

Movement in the corner of his eye makes him jump, but it's just a large brown lizard, tongue extended, scuttling out of his way. The distraction, and flood of adrenaline, snaps him out of his negative spiral and he heads off again, focusing on the surrounding objects, saying their names aloud to stop the dark thoughts from creeping back in again.

'Honor!' As he reaches the small clearing and the circle of tree stumps that surrounds it, he shouts his girlfriend's name. 'Where are you?'

He hears the squawk of birds and the treetops above his head rustle as two beautiful blue and orange kingfishers make their escape. But there's no human reply to his shout. Honor's either ignoring him or she's further away than he thought. Danny pulls the bottom of his T-shirt up to his forehead and rubs it over his face, then swigs from his water bottle. It's not as hot in the jungle as it is on the beach under the constant glare of the sun, but it's humid as hell and his body is slick with sweat. He looks around the small space, searching for footprints or tunnels made through the undergrowth, any sign that his girlfriend has passed this way, but there's nothing. He'd have to battle through the thick foliage to find a way through. He turns and heads back towards the waterfall, pausing at the bottom of a small dirt track that leads up out of the jungle to the cliff tops above. Could she have headed up there?

There's only one way to find out, he thinks as he starts to walk.

The worry Danny felt as he set off to find Honor has morphed into irritation. It took him for ever to scale the rough, stony route to the cliff top and now that he's reached it, it's obvious that Honor's not up here. He sits on the edge of the brown rock, legs dangling, and stares down at the green-blue sea twenty metres below. He can hear voices on the beach, down to his right, but he can't see anything because his view is blocked by the green bushes that cling to the cliff face.

'Danny!' He hears his name being called but doesn't respond. Instead he lifts his foot and examines the sole. He slipped on the walk up the cliff and one of his flip-flops came off. He cut his foot on a sharp sliver of rock as he stopped to retrieve it. His foot's still bleeding. The blood rolls off his heel and drips, disappearing before it hits the water below.

'Danny! Where are you?' Honor's shout drifts up towards him. She's on the beach!

'Danny!' she shouts again. There's a note of urgency in her voice that makes him scrabble to his feet, wincing as he puts weight on his cut foot.

'Honor!' He cups his hands to his mouth as he shouts then waits, squinting into the sun, for her reply.

None comes.

'Honor!' he shouts again.

A dozen different thoughts flood his mind – a boat has turned up to save them? They've discovered a way off the island? Or maybe... Honor's hurt?

The thought makes his heart pound painfully in his chest. He's got to get back to his girlfriend but it will take him for ever to walk back down to the beach on his injured foot. He stares down at the sea – still, calm and clear below him – then, before he can change his mind, he steps off the cliff.

CHAPTER 9

JESSIE

'What the hell was that?'

I'm not the only one who freezes as a loud splash, like a rock – or a person – falling into the sea, cuts through the cawing of the gulls. Milo, wading through the shallows with one of Anuman's pointed fishing poles in his hand, snaps round, spear outstretched, pointing it in the direction of the sound. A second later his eyes meet mine. We're both thinking the same thing – is it the 'others' we speculated about? Another group living on the other side of the island?

Honor, clambering on the rocks to our left, freezes. Shortly after Danny disappeared to go and look for her she appeared at the far end of the beach, her arms full and gathered up to her chest.

'I've been beachcombing,' she said as she drew closer and deposited her treasure next to the fire. 'I found some empty plastic bottles washed up just past those rocks. I thought we could use them to keep water in. Until we're, you know, rescued.'

We filled them at the waterfall, then went through everyone's rucksacks to see how much food we had. It wasn't much of a haul, just a couple of packets of crisps and biscuits, a few sticks of gum, some sweets, two bottles of vodka (one in Danny's bag, one in Meg's) and a bottle of rum Milo had nabbed from his parents' duty-free allowance. Jeffers was a bit weird when we asked him if we could go through his bag. Instead of letting us have a rummage he took himself off into the jungle and came back with three packets of dried meat, a can of mixed beans and a can of tuna. Milo joked that he probably had a massive bar of chocolate and a Victoria sponge hidden in the bottom of his rucksack too, but, when he tried to grab his rucksack off him, Jeffers snatched it away and moved to the edge of the camp. That didn't go down well with Milo, who shouted that he wouldn't be alive to eat whatever he was hiding if I hadn't saved his life. Then he stomped off to look for Danny, muttering something about Bear Grylls and how sticking together was the first rule of survival.

I've got no idea how long Milo was gone – none of us wear a watch and all our mobile phones ran out of juice last night – but when he returned his hair was slicked back and his T-shirt was clinging to his body. No sign of Danny, he said. God knows where he'd gone. We all got worried then, everyone apart from Honor, who was sitting on the sand by the fire with a strange, glazed look on her face. Meg pulled her to her feet, reassuring her that Danny would be fine and he couldn't have gone far.

'It's Danny!' Honor shouts now, waving frantically from the rocks. 'He just fell off the cliff.'

I feel sick with fear. The cliffs must be at least twenty metres tall and if Danny landed into the shallows or on the rocks then—

'He's OK!' she screams. 'He's swimming. He's still alive.'

'Bloody hell, Danny!'

'Are you OK?'

'What happened?'

'Was it an accident?'

'Did you fall?'

'Did someone push you?'

The questions come thick and fast as Danny reaches out a hand and Milo pulls him out of the sea and onto the rocks. Unlike Jeffers and I – who could barely breathe when we came out of the sea – Danny seems totally fine. Never mind broken bones, there isn't a scratch on him and the smallest of smiles pricks at his lips as he looks up at us all crowded around him.

His smile fades. 'Where's Honor?'

Meg and I move apart from each other so he can see his girlfriend, standing behind us, sobbing softly.

'Hey, hey.' Danny gets to his feet and pulls her into his arms. 'It's OK, I'm fine. Honor, I'm fine.'

'What happened?' I ask as she nestles into his chest, her

hands covering her face. 'What were you doing up on the cliffs?'

'Looking for her.' He strokes the back of her head, smoothing down her blonde hair. 'I heard her calling my name and thought she was in trouble. Jumping was the fastest way to get back down.'

Honor moans in torment and mumbles something I can't make out. Danny cranes his neck to listen.

'What was that, babe? It wasn't your fault. You know that, don't you?'

She raises her voice but keeps her hands clamped over her face. 'You could have died!'

'But I didn't, did I?' He kisses the top of her head. 'It looks like you're stuck with me, babe.'

'That's why she's crying,' Milo says and everyone, apart from Honor, laughs with relief.

It's a warm night, and the black sky is dotted with twinkling stars, but there's a strange, strained atmosphere as we pass Milo's bottle of rum and one of the bottles of vodka between us. Jeffers isn't joining in. He's holed himself away in the shelter and is lying on his back with his head on his rucksack and his arms crossed over his chest. When I go over to check on him he opens his eyes then closes them again.

'You all right?' I crouch down on the pile of banana leaves that serve as a very thin, very uncomfortable mattress. 'You know Milo was only joking earlier, about going through your bag. If you want to keep whatever's in there private, that's cool.'

'It's not that.' He opens his eyes to look at me. 'I just… you all think I'm a joke, don't you?'

'No! God no. It's cool that you're into all this. Honestly. No one thinks you're a joke. I know the banter can get a bit much sometimes but no one wants to upset you.'

'But it is a joke, isn't it? All this?' He gestures towards the beach. 'Dad showing off how rich he is by renting an island for my birthday. I didn't even want this. I asked for a book and some pieces of equipment. And now Anuman's dead we're all alone and there's nothing I can do to put things right…' He turns his head away but not so quickly that I don't see the tears glistening in his eyes.

'That's why you tried to swim for it, isn't it? Because you felt responsible for what happened.'

'And I couldn't even do that properly. I nearly drowned us both.'

I rest my hand on his arm. 'I'm sorry. For what I said earlier. I… I was in shock.'

'No.' He shakes his head. 'I deserved it.'

'You didn't, Jeffers. You were freaking out and you didn't realize what you were doing. We'll get through this. It's going to be OK.'

He sits up and reaches out his arms. 'Hug?'

I smile and lean in towards him. He holds me tightly, his hands gripping my shoulder blades. He really is scared. I can't remember the last time he gave anyone a hug.

After I leave Jeffers in the shelter I head down to the beach, rather than return to the fire. So much has happened today

73

that I need some time alone to clear my head. Danny shouts after me, demanding that I take my turn with the vodka, but, from the way his words slur together, it sounds as though he's had his turn, my turn and then some. Honor, on the other hand, has barely said a word all evening. I've never seen her as tearful as she's been this holiday. She's always been a bit funny about showing a vulnerable side. She's like a YouTuber, all smiles and fun when she's the centre of attention, but I've seen sneak peeks of the other side, when I've stumbled across her and Danny, sitting alone. She speaks quietly and there's a brittle tone to her voice that isn't there when we all hang out together.

When we were twelve she turned up to our group holiday in the Lake District with just her mum. I wasn't surprised. There had been a few holidays when one or the other of us had arrived with just one parent because of work or other issues. But it wasn't until the very last day of the holiday, when I overheard my parents talking in their bedroom in hushed voices, that I found out that Honor's dad had met someone on the internet and moved to Australia to be with her. You'd never have known that Honor's dad had abandoned her, the way she behaved that holiday. She'd seemed the same as ever, maybe even happier and chirpier. Overcompensating, I guess.

Years earlier, when we were nine, it was Danny's mum who didn't show up. Even before the holiday I knew something was up because I heard my parents talking about her and Danny's dad, and the minute I walked into the living room they swiftly changed the subject. They told me what had happened the next day and said I should be extra nice to

Danny the next time I saw him. I could tell he'd changed the second he stepped out of his dad's car. Instead of grinning widely and bouncing over to the rest of us as normal, he crossed his arms over his chest and glowered at us from across the car park. When we asked him how he was he said he didn't want to talk about it. The rest of us let it drop but Jefferson refused to. I don't know if he thought he was being funny, or if he was revelling in the fact that he'd finally found a button to push which would wind Danny up, but he wouldn't stop asking him about his mum. When he said, 'My mum says it's good to talk about your feelings, why won't you talk about yours?' Danny went white and threw a punch. The next thing I knew they were on the ground, fists flying. I was terrified that one of them was going to die, but when they were pulled apart by Meg and Milo's dad, their only injuries were a split lip and a bloody nose. Jeffers hasn't mentioned Danny's mum since. Neither has Danny.

As I reach the sea I can see the boat on the other side of the beach, gently bobbing on the waves. I don't turn to get a better look. No one's mentioned Anuman since Danny fell off the cliff, even though we had to walk straight past his body to get back to camp. I tried not to look at the boat but it was like telling myself not to breathe: I couldn't help it. The sound of laughter from the camp drifts across the beach. Instinctively I pull the sleeves of my top down over my hands even though they've all seen my burns now. I saw Danny's eyes roam across my arms as I sat on the beach with Milo, gasping for breath. I saw his reaction too – shock, then revulsion.

'I don't care what he thinks of me,' I tell myself as I pinch the thin skin of my forearm until it smarts. 'I don't care what anyone thinks.'

I lie on my back, staring up into the inky black sky, listening to the sounds of the jungle and the gentle lapping of the sea, until my breathing starts to slow and my eyelids grow heavy. There's a part of my brain needling at me to go back to the camp where it's safe, but my limbs are heavy and leaden and the bigger part of my brain is adrift, thoughts muddling as I slip closer to sleep. Images appear and disappear behind my closed eyes – the sea, the glare of the sun, my parents' faces, school, a packet of cigarettes, a bottle of cider, Tom.

And then I see the fire.

I sit up with a jolt, sand slipping between my fingers and stare, confused by darkness that surrounds me and the gentle lapping of the waves.

'Jessie! Shit, sorry. You were asleep.' Milo is crouched beside me, a bottle of rum in his hand. 'You were so still and, after everything that's happened today, I was scared you were...' he tails off, shaking his head and takes a swig from the bottle. 'Never mind.' He passes it to me. 'Want some?'

'Sure.' I reach for it. The rum warms my throat, then I feel it hit my stomach. I haven't eaten much today, none of us have. That's why everyone's so pissed on a few swigs of vodka.

'You doing OK?' Milo props himself up on one elbow and looks at me. 'I still can't get my head around what's happened.'

My gaze drifts towards the boat, gently bobbing near the shoreline, and Anuman's boots sticking out from beneath the tarpaulin, casting a dark shadow onto the sea. 'I know what you mean.'

'I just… I keep expecting someone to pop out from the jungle and shout, *Surprise! You're on a new reality TV show. Anuman isn't really dead and you're not really marooned.*' He reaches for the rum and takes a swig. His eyes meet mine as he lowers the bottle. I feel sick, knowing he saw me in my underwear earlier, my skin all twisted and red.

A frown creases Milo's brow. 'You sure you're OK?'

'Yeah, just um… just worried about Jeffers. He's blaming himself for what's happened.' I lie back in the sand and stare up at the stars.

Milo shuffles onto his back and does the same. 'It's not his fault. But I still want to know what's in his bag!' He laughs and, out of the corner of my eye, I see him turn his head to look at me. 'Do you think he's hiding something?'

'What like?'

'I dunno. A severed head.' He laughs again. 'This island would be a pretty good place to dispose of body parts.'

'That's sick.'

'I wasn't suggesting we actually do it. Unless, you know, you fancy offing Meg.'

'Why would I want to do that?'

'She keeps giving me evils.'

I laugh. 'She's your sister. She's always done that.'

He doesn't say anything for several seconds then he sighs heavily. 'She's pissed off with me and I'm not sure why.'

I turn to look at him. I want to tell him about the way Meg was watching me by the hotel pool the other evening but I don't want to shit-stir for no reason. Meg and Milo are for ever falling out and, because they're both as stubborn as each other, they can go for *days* without talking. But then one of them will finally relent, there'll be a raging row and they'll make up again.

'Have you talked to her?' I ask.

'Yeah, no, sort of. Sorry. I'm talking shit. I'm a bit drunk.'

He smiles and closes his eyes. I watch as his body relaxes and he inhales deeply, breathing in the salty sea air. I've looked at his face a thousand times and I still think he's the best-looking boy I've ever seen. His eyelashes are ridiculously thick and long and, beneath his closed lids, his eyes are the warmest brown. His nose is long and straight, his lips full and—

Urrgh. I roll onto my back and cover my face with my hands.

What am I doing? Why do I do this to myself?

I just had the strongest urge to lean over and kiss him, which is ridiculous because Milo isn't interested in me. If he was, something would have happened between us years ago. He's just a friend, one that likes a bit of a flirt occasionally, but there's nothing more to it than that. I reach the fingers of my right hand over to my left forearm and I'm just about to pinch my skin when I sense that I'm being watched.

'Why do you do that?' Milo's brown eyes bore into me.

'Do what?'

'Pinch yourself. I've seen you do it a few times over the last couple of days. You never used to do it before.'

'I'm not pinching myself. I'm just… itching.'

There's a pause and my stomach clenches as I brace myself for an onslaught of questions. But Milo doesn't push the subject. Instead he sighs and says, 'Do you really think there's someone else on the other side of the island?'

'I don't know. Do you think we should look? Tomorrow, when it's light?'

'What if they're bad guys?'

Now it's my turn to laugh. 'Bad guys, Mr Katsaro? How old are you? Five?'

'Six. Nearly. It's my birthday tomorrow. We're going to Laser Quest. Want to come? Oh, look at that!' He sits up and points up into the sky as something white whizzes overhead. 'What do you reckon? Meteorite, UFO or plane?'

'It could be a shooting star.'

'Yeah, one with wings and two hundred passengers. I'd wave for help but I can't be arsed to move.' He slumps back onto the sand, arms spread wide. His right hand lands so close to my left that our little fingers touch. I don't snatch my hand away. Neither does Milo.

'If it had been a shooting star,' I try to keep my tone light, but all I can think about is the fact that his finger is touching mine, 'what would you have wished for?'

He snorts softly. 'If I told you I wouldn't get my wish, would I?'

I sneak a glance at him but he's not looking at me, he's staring up at the sky. I don't know if it's my imagination or not but he looks more tense than he did a couple of minutes ago, and he's breathing more shallowly.

We lapse into silence. My heart's thudding and every time I inhale my breath seems to catch in my throat. I try to focus on the sounds of the jungle – the soft honking of a bird, the cracks and snaps of branches breaking, the whooping of the monkeys – but all I can think about is the centimetre of skin where our bodies are touching. It's nothing, something I wouldn't even notice normally but now, lying on the beach with Milo, it feels like everything.

My heart sinks as Milo moves his finger, lifting it away from mine, and I curse myself for being so ridiculous, but a split second later he lowers it onto my finger again and, with the smallest of movements, gently moves it back and forth over my skin. I don't react, I don't speak, I barely breathe, but inside I feel a rush of excitement and longing that journeys up from my stomach to my chest.

I can hear Milo breathing, quickly, shallowly and I know I'm not imagining what's happening between us. This isn't two friends flirting anymore. The air between us is loaded with tension but I can't bring myself to turn my head to look at him. I don't want to break the spell.

But I want him to kiss me. Right now, I want that to happen more than anything else in the world.

Still staring up into the dark sky I lift my little finger and slowly, gently curl it around his. I hear him inhale sharply, then he moves his hand over mine, sliding his fingers between mine, moving them slowly back and forth and he rubs his thumb over the back of my hand. As I turn my head to look at him his eyes meet mine and there's an intensity to his gaze that makes my stomach clench.

Neither of us smiles or says a word. We just look, as though seeing each other for the very first time.

Milo shifts onto his side, closing the space between us, and my heart beats so fast it's as though it's pulsing in the base of my throat. He's going to kiss me. He's finally going to—

'There you are, you loser!' Danny appears from nowhere and dives onto Milo, spraying me with sand. 'Oh! You're here too, Jess. Meg and Honor have gone to bed and I'm bored. Who fancies skinny dipping?'

CHAPTER 10

DANNY

Day three on the island

There's a distinct tang of sick in the air as Danny wakes up, sweating in the clothes he's been wearing for three days, his sleeping bag pushed down around his hips. He smacks his dry lips together and investigates the unpleasant taste in his mouth with his tongue. Yep, as he suspected, he was the one who was sick. Vague, blurry memories of the night before drift across his mind as he wriggles out of the shelter and crawls over to a bottle of water, covered with sand. He remembers sitting with Honor and Meg at the fire and playing what seemed to be a hilarious game of thumper. He also recalls stumbling along the beach, seeing Milo sitting alone and then jumping on him, only to realize too late that Jessie was lying beside him. Then he remembers stripping off his clothes and running into the sea with Milo. After that? Not very much.

'All right, guys!' He winces as Jeffers' strident voice cuts straight through him. He blinks up at him, shielding his eyes from the sun as Jeffers strides out of the jungle, his 'travel rucksack' slung over his shoulders. 'Now that everyone, or nearly everyone, is awake, I thought we should come up with a plan of action.'

Danny glances back at the shelter. Honor is sitting up, squinting as she runs her hands through her knotted hair. He feels a jolt of hope as she flashes him a smile. He just wants her to love him the way she used to.

Now, Danny feels someone else's eyes on him and turns to see Meg walking up from the sea in a black bikini, her dark hair a thick wet rope that hangs down one shoulder. Unlike Milo, who's always been an open book, his sister's always been more reserved. Danny and Meg have never been particularly close. She tolerates him in front of the others, and occasionally laughs at his jokes, but he's seen the looks she gives him when she thinks he's not looking – like she thinks he's a dick. She likes Honor, though. Out of the girls, they get on the best, but they couldn't be more different. If Honor is sweetness and light then Meg is darkness and shade. It's weird how much they've all drifted apart since they were kids. They were all born in London but, while Jessie, Meg and Milo still live there (on opposite sides of the city), the other families all moved away. Jeffers lives in Edinburgh and Danny and Honor live in the South-East – a seventeen-minute train journey away from each other (him in Lewes, her in Brighton).

He slumps back on the sand, propping himself up on his elbows as Jeffers approaches.

'The first thing we need to do,' Jefferson says, nudging

the charred remains of the fire with his boot, 'is to keep this going. I did say yesterday that we should take it in turns checking on it through the night but someone,' he raises his eyebrows at Danny, 'obviously forgot.'

Danny grins. 'I checked on the fire, it said it was fine so I went to sleep.'

Meg, walking past, snorts in amusement then quickly stifles the sound with her hand.

'I'm not joking,' Jeffers snaps. 'We need this fire.'

'But it's boiling hot!' Danny snaps back. 'Even at night. We're not going to freeze to death.'

'Maybe not but the fire cooks the food, sterilizes the water and keeps animals away. You're welcome to get bitten by a cobra if you want but I'd rather not take my chances.'

'Oh God,' Milo's voice rings out from the shelter. 'Do we have to talk about snakes?'

'They exist.' Jeffers crosses his arms over his chest. 'So do vipers, kraits, tarantulas and black widows. They're not locked away in zoo cages and we need to be careful.'

'OK, OK.' Danny holds up his hands in surrender. 'I get it, I'm sorry. I won't let the fire go out again.'

'Good. Now let's get organized. We need to decide who does what. We need one person to collect firewood, one to replenish the water, one to scavenge for food, one to go fishing on the rocks – or in the sea with the spear – and one to mend the net.'

There's a brief silence, then Jessie raises her hand.

'I don't mind what I do.'

'Nor me,' Meg says.

As everyone else joins in Jeffers holds up both hands. 'OK, OK. I'll decide. Milo, you're on fruit collecting. Danny, gathering wood. Jessie, you can fish. Honor, mend the net and Meg, you can do water.'

Danny raises his eyebrows. 'And what are you going to do?'

'Supervise!'

'Seriously?' He starts to laugh then stops when he clocks the irritated look in Jefferson's eyes. 'Nope, that's fine, dude. Whatever you say.'

'Stick together!' Jeffers shouts as Milo and Danny traipse into the jungle, carrying an empty rucksack, Anuman's machete and an axe. 'We can't afford for anyone to get lost.'

'No worries, mate!' Danny raises a hand in goodbye and then turns to Milo and lowers his voice. 'He's getting right on my tits.'

'Ah, give him a break,' Milo says, then he runs his tongue over his lips. 'He's loving this. God, I feel like crap. I think I'm dehydrated.'

'You and me both,' Danny says. 'I don't think I've puked as much since Jack Foster's party in Year 9.'

'I don't know who that is, but given how much camp stinks this morning I don't think I want to know.'

Danny shifts the axe up and onto his shoulder as Milo leads the way through the tight corridor of trees, hacking at the bushes blocking their route to the clearing. 'What was going on with you and Jessie on the beach last night?'

Milo continues to swing the machete. 'Nothing.'

'You sure about that? You two were lying pretty damned close to each other.'

'Says the guy who was so drunk he fell over us.'

'I didn't fall, I jumped on you.'

'Dick.'

They both laugh.

'So?' Danny asks, refusing to let it drop. 'Spill.'

'Nothing to spill, man. We're just friends.'

'Are you sure about that? You looked pretty cosy from where I was standing.'

'Leave it, mate.' There's a curtness to Milo's answer that makes Danny raise his eyebrows. Milo's definitely fancied Jessie in the past. They had a chat about it one night when they were thirteen, over their first, and last, cigarette. While Danny was coughing his guts out Milo confessed that he'd had a thing for Jessie for a while but thought she wasn't interested. The next day Danny did a bit of digging via Meg but Milo struck out; Jess wasn't interested. The last time they all went on holiday together when they were fifteen it all switched round; it was Jessie who had a crush, but Milo was seeing someone from school and was absolutely infatuated with her. It was still going on last summer, when Jessie and her family didn't show up, although Milo's not with her anymore.

'Anyway, how are you doing after you dumped whatsher-face... Bella?' Danny asks Milo as they step into the clearing.

'I'm doing fine, thanks.'

'Meg said you want to get back with her.'

'Meg doesn't know shit.' Milo shoots him an annoyed

look. 'I'm going a bit further in for fruit. We've pretty much cleared all the trees round here.'

Before Danny can object, or make a joke about Jeffers telling them off, Milo is gone, ploughing through the jungle, swinging the machete this way and that.

Danny swipes at his forehead with the back of his hand. It slides across his skin. There doesn't seem to be a single part of his body that isn't slick with sweat. After an enthusiastic start – his first few trees felled with half a dozen strokes of the axe – his energy has drained faster than a cheap battery. He feels sick and his head aches and all he wants to do is lie down. Only there's no way he's going anywhere near the jungle floor with God knows how many creatures and creepy crawlies hiding under the leaves and moss. He rests his forehead against the nearest tree instead and closes his eyes. It's ridiculous, really, how much trouble they're going to when they only have to survive for another four days before their parents send out a search party. Even if they don't eat another thing between now and then they'll be fine as long as they all drink enough water.

But the water needs to be sterilized on the fire.

He imagines the look on Jefferson's face if he returns to camp without any wood and, sighing, opens his eyes and reaches down for his axe. As his fingers wrap around the handle he hears a yell, the sound of branches snapping and then a loud thump that shakes the birds from the trees and sends them swooping up into the bright blue sky.

'Help!' Milo's yell reaches him from deep in the jungle. 'Help! Someone, help!'

Danny, panting and sweating, swipes branches out of his face as he crashes through the jungle, following the sound of Milo's voice, then gasps in shock as an arm appears from nowhere and smacks him straight in the stomach.

'Careful!' Jeffers shouts. 'Or you'll fall in too.'

Inches away from Danny's feet is a huge muddy crater in the jungle floor. It's at least four feet across in both directions and eight feet deep. Slumped in the bottom, surrounded by broken branches, leaves, moss and jungle vegetation, is Milo. He's clutching his ankle and breathing shallowly.

Stepping carefully, Jefferson rounds the hole then crouches down. He shuffles onto his stomach and reaches an arm into the pit. The tips of his fingers graze Milo's hair, making him yelp in terror.

'It's OK, it's OK,' Jefferson says. 'It's just me. Twist round and I'll pull you up.'

As Milo turns awkwardly Danny spots something on the other side of the pit that makes him clamp a hand to his mouth. Writhing and twisting against the muddy wall is a cobra. Danny holds his breath as the snake moves part way up the wall then drops back down again. The angle is too sheer but on the other side, where Milo's hobbling onto his feet, it's less steep. The snake seems to sense this and slowly slithers its way across the pit.

'Quick, quick,' Danny mutters as Milo reaches a hand up to Jefferson.

Jefferson and Milo's hands meet and Jefferson leans back, taking Milo's weight. He's heavier than Jeffers, taller too. 'You've got this,' he puffs as Milo puts a foot to the wall of the pit.

As Milo takes another step, with his bad ankle, he cries out in pain and drops back into the pit, almost pulling Jefferson in with him.

As he lands the snake senses the vibration and slithers closer, leaving an S-shaped imprint in the soft soil.

Danny presses his other hand to his mouth. The urge to shout, to warn his friend, is almost more than he can bear. He knows how Milo will react. When they were eleven they all went to a zoo and Milo wouldn't even enter the snake enclosure never mind put one around his neck like everyone else. Danny looks across to Jefferson who waves at him.

'I could do with a hand here!'

'Sure, sure, of course.'

Keeping his eyes on the snake, Danny carefully navigates the edge of the pit.

'We'll take a hand each,' Jefferson says. 'And pull him out, OK?'

Danny nods. Standing on this side of the crater he can see why Jefferson isn't freaking out. You can't see the snake with Milo in the way.

'Ready?' Jefferson asks, as he grabs Milo's right hand and Danny grabs his left. 'Three, two, one…'

Danny digs the heels of his flip-flops into the ground and leans back, pulling with all his strength. He can hear Milo's feet scrabbling against the side of the pit and then *boomf*, all three of them collapse in a heap on the leafy jungle floor.

CHAPTER 11

JESSIE

Meg is glaring at us. 'Could everyone *please* stop crowding my brother!'

We are all gathered around Milo, who is sitting by the fire with a wet towel wrapped around his ankle.

'I was picking some mangos,' he says, looking around the group, 'and heard this whistling noise. I ignored it at first, I thought it was a bird, but it was… it was very distinct, like someone whistling a tune.'

'It could have been a mynah bird,' Jefferson says. 'If there've been a lot of visitors here they might have learnt to imitate a human whistle. There was a bird in the market that could speak Thai and—'

'OK, OK,' Meg says. 'We get it. You're an expert on the local flora and fauna. Could you just let him finish his story?'

'I was just looking for a logical explanation and there is one, so…' Jeffers tails off and shrugs.

'Anyway,' Milo says, 'I shouted hello but no one replied,

so I headed in the direction of the noise. Next thing I knew I was falling and…' He spreads his hands wide. 'Hello, massive great hole.'

Honor looks puzzled. 'How did you not see it?'

'Because there wasn't one! It wasn't there.'

'How can a hole just appear?' I ask. Milo turns to look at me. It's pretty much the first time we've made eye contact all day and I feel my cheeks warm. Neither of us has mentioned what nearly happened last night. After Danny interrupted us and suggested skinny dipping, Milo leapt to his feet, ripped off his clothes and ran into the sea without so much as an *Are you coming in, Jessie?* Not that I would have. As Danny joined him, his naked bum glinting in the moonlight as he ran into the water, I headed back to the camp. I was still awake when they came back, laughing and chatting and generally dicking about, but I kept my eyes closed and pretended to be asleep.

If he likes me Milo will lie down next to me, I told myself as he and Danny shuffled around, grabbing clothes and sleeping bags, but Milo didn't take the space beside me. He lay on the other side of the shelter, beside Danny and Honor.

'There wasn't a hole,' Milo says. 'It didn't look any different to the rest of the jungle, it was leaves and branches and moss and stuff.'

'It was a trap,' Jeffers says, closing the book he's been studying for the last five minutes.

We all stare at him.

'That hole wasn't freshly dug. It had probably always been there but someone covered it over.'

'How do you know?' Meg asks.

'No fresh soil, plants growing in the sides and the base—'

'No, how do you know someone covered it?'

'I had a look after Danny helped Milo back here. There were a load of branches in the bottom and around the sides, all snapped. When I matched them up they were long enough to cover the diameter of the hole. I imagine whoever placed them there covered them with leaves and moss.'

'Maybe it was left by the last lot of guests,' I say.

'Or,' Milo catches my eye, 'we were right and there *are* other people on the island.'

'What other people?' Meg looks from her brother to me.

'It's just speculation,' I say. 'We were talking earlier. The island's so big we thought there might be other people doing the same thing as us, but on the other side of the island.'

'I don't like that.' Honor shuffles closer to Danny, who puts an arm around her shoulders and pulls her close. 'It freaks me out.'

'So we go and see if we can find them,' Danny suggests. It's pretty much the first thing he's said since he got back from the jungle, supporting a limping Milo. Considering Milo was the one who fell into the pit, Danny looked as though he'd seen a ghost.

Meg raises a hand. 'I'm up for seeing if there's anyone else here.'

'And me,' I say.

Jefferson shakes his head. 'There are jobs that need doing.'

Danny raises his eyebrows in disbelief. 'You're kidding? There could be another group of people on this island who are setting traps for us and you think we should stay here and mend nets and chop firewood?'

'I do, yes. Our survival is paramount.'

'Which is why we need to find out if we're alone here or not! Look how freaked out all the girls are.'

'Hello?' I point at myself. 'Not this girl.'

Meg glares at him. 'Me neither.'

'Fine. But if there are other people here they've obviously been listening to our conversations, like the one about our phobias the other night.'

'Why obviously?' I ask.

'Well, not obviously…' Danny corrects himself. 'We don't know what they've seen or heard.'

'Oh God, Danny, don't.' Honor digs herself further under his arm.

Jeffers rolls his eyes. 'Now who's freaking her out?'

'I just think,' Danny sighs, 'that that we need to check.'

'And we can do it tomorrow, when we've got some water to take with us.'

Danny glances at the empty water bottles lying in the sand and shrugs. 'There's nothing to stop us getting water en route. Fine, fine,' he adds as Jeffers' lips part in objection. 'We'll go tomorrow.'

Jeffers turns to look at me. 'I don't suppose you managed to catch any fish before all this,' he waves an arm in Milo's direction, 'kicked off?'

I glance back at the rocks, where I abandoned my spear. But there's nothing there.

CHAPTER 12

DANNY

Danny waits until Jeffers – who's walking along the beach towards the rocks, berating Jessie for leaving the spear there – is out of earshot, then he beckons Meg closer.

'I vote we just go and explore,' he hisses. 'I don't know who Jeffers thinks voted him Camp Commander but it definitely wasn't me. I say we do what we want.'

Meg glances at Milo, still sitting on the sand by the fire. 'Someone needs to look after him.'

'I don't mind staying with him.' Honor wriggles out from under Danny's arm and drops to the sand opposite Milo.

Danny falters. He's not sure about leaving Honor alone with Milo. But if he changes his mind and stays in the camp it'll look like he's accepted that Jeffers is their leader and there is *no way* he's letting that power-hungry idiot feel like he's got one over him. Leave it is, then.

'See you later, dude,' he says to Milo, who's staring out to sea with his hands wrapped around his ankle and a pained expression on his face.

'And you, behave yourself!' He shoots Honor a look, then, seeing Meg raise her eyebrows, he softens his tone. 'Love you.'

When Honor doesn't reply his heart twists in his chest, but he doesn't say anything. Instead he leans down to kiss Honor goodbye then scoops a water bottle up out of the sand. 'Let's go to the waterfall first,' he says to Meg. 'This could be a bit of a trek.'

'What was that all about?' Meg shoots him a look as they kneel by the spring, screwing the tops back onto their water bottles. They've only been trekking through the jungle for ten minutes and they're both knackered. There was a moment when they first set off when he considered telling her about the cobra, and how close Milo had been to being bitten – and possibly dying – but he decided against it. Jefferson obviously hadn't seen the snake. If he had he'd have made a big song and dance about it when they got back to camp, pointing it out in his guide book and scaring them all half to death. No, Danny had decided, better to keep quiet and not add to the hysteria. And besides, he liked knowing something Jefferson didn't. For a change.

He presses a hand to his stomach as it rumbles angrily. All he's had to eat since Anuman cooked them the fish is a handful of crisps and a few boiled sweets.

'What was what all about?' he asks Meg.

'Your comment to Honor about behaving herself. What's going on?'

He stiffens. Has Honor said something to her? They have been hanging around together a lot this holiday.

'Nothing.' He shrugs. 'Why?'

'Why tell her to behave herself? What do you think she's going to do – stick her tongue down Milo's throat?'

'No,' he says. Honor wouldn't do something like that. And there's no way Milo would kiss her back. 'Nothing like that. I just…' he says uncertainly. 'Sometimes I get the feeling she has more fun when I'm not around.'

Meg shrugs. 'Maybe she does. A different kind of fun,' she adds before Danny can respond. 'You can't live in each other's pockets all the time. It's not healthy.'

'Has she said something to you?'

'No, it's just…' She pauses. 'It's just an observation. From an outsider.'

So he's not imagining it, things aren't right between them this holiday, but it's weird that Honor hasn't mentioned anything to Meg. Normally she'd be the first person Honor would turn to. Unless… he tries to push the thought away but it remains firmly lodged in his head… unless she was too scared to say anything in case it got back to him.

'*Is* everything all right?' Meg asks.

'Everything's fine between us,' he lies. 'Honor would have told you if it wasn't.'

They set off again, trudging uphill, following the path of the waterfall, neither of them speaking, both of them searching the jungle floor for any more hidden pits. Danny looks up into the thick green canopy above and mentally shakes himself. It's beautiful in the middle of the jungle with the birds singing in the trees, the cicadas chirping and the geckos and lizards speeding across his path and hiding under frond-like leaves. He thinks of his dad, sitting on the sofa at home with Sarah, his new girlfriend, and wonders how they're getting on. They've only been together a few months. His dad's crap at dating. Since his mum, he hasn't been able to hold on to anyone for more than six months. They all leave him eventually. He definitely doesn't want to end up like his dad.

'What do you reckon?' Meg says as they reach the top of the waterfall. 'I figure if there's a beach on this side of the island we'll find the other one if we keep walking in a straight line.'

Danny swigs at his water bottle. 'That makes sense.'

'Crap,' Danny says, stopping suddenly and resting his hand on the gnarled trunk of a palm tree. 'I think we've walked in a circle. I swear we've been here before.'

Meg, panting, puts her hands on her hips and stares around. 'Do you? It all looks the same to me.'

'Yeah, look, there's that branch we said looked like an elephant's trunk.'

'Oh God, you're right.' She sighs heavily. 'Which way did we go last time, can you remember?'

Danny checks for a break in the leaves or footprints on the jungle floor but there's nothing. It's as though whenever they force their way through the jungle the plants fold themselves back over the path.

'We should have left a breadcrumb trail,' Meg says.

Danny gives her a look. 'Didn't Hansel and Gretel end up in a witch's lair when they did that?'

'Can we stop for a bit? I'm knackered.'

Danny pauses to look back at Meg. She's bent double, her hands on her knees, her empty water bottle swinging from her fingers. He's not sure how long ago they ran out of water but his mouth's so dry he could use his tongue as a pumice stone on his scabby feet.

'Yeah, sure.' He drops down and rests his back against a palm tree. After a pause Meg does the same.

They stare at each other for a couple of seconds then Danny sighs heavily. 'We're lost.'

'Should we shout? If the others are close by they might hear us?'

'Jeffers would love that, us needing to be rescued.'

Meg plucks a wide, flat leaf from a bush and uses it to fan herself. 'What's your problem with him?'

'Other than the fact he's been an annoying dick all holiday? I just don't like being told what I can and can't do.'

'But you're happy telling Honor what to do.'

He raises his eyebrows. That came out of nowhere. Or did it? He's seen Meg taking enough swipes at her brother this holiday. But then they're all getting a bit snippy with each other because everyone's tired and hungry and fed up. The only person who hasn't had a go at him is Milo, although even he was a bit off when Danny asked him how he felt about Jessie. Being disliked isn't something Danny's ever really experienced before. As a kid at primary school he had a massive gang of friends. Other kids would always shout hello on the walk home, prompting his mum to nudge him and whisper, 'Say hello back, Danny.'

'Never mind me and Honor,' he says now. 'What's going on with you? I've seen the way you look at Milo and Jessie.' He imitates Meg's narrow-eyed glare.

'Wow.' She raises her eyebrows. 'Deflecting your own issues with a bit of stirring, are we?'

'No. Are you?'

She laughs. 'Touché! For what it's worth I haven't got a problem with Jessie. I don't want her to get hurt, that's all. Milo's playing with her. He thinks he's being the nice guy, giving her loads of attention because of what she went through, but he's leading her on. If he carries on the way he is she's going to get her heart broken. And anyway...' she tails off deliberately.

Danny gives her a long look. 'Anyway what?'

'He's in love with someone else.'

'Who?'

Meg's lips part as though she's about to reply then she holds up a hand and presses a finger to her mouth, gesturing for him to listen.

A slow smile forms on his face and he punches the air. 'It's the waterfall. Thank God for that!'

Silence greets them when they return to camp. Milo, Honor and Jessie are lying in the shelter, eyes closed, seemingly asleep. The fire is blazing but there's no fish roasting above it, just a pan full of bubbling water. Sitting next to the fire, resting on his rucksack and hacking at the end of a long branch, is Jeffers. He raises an eyebrow at Danny and Meg as they glug at the water bottles they refilled at the waterfall.

'Well?'

Danny wipes his hand over the back of his mouth then screws the top back on the bottle. 'We didn't make it across to the other side of the island.'

'Get lost, did you?'

'No,' Danny says as Meg says, 'Yes.'

'Find anything interesting?'

'Not particularly,' Meg replies, 'but we had to look. It's suspicious, isn't it? First the boat cord...' Danny looks over at the boat, gently bobbing at the edge of the sea, 'and then the trap. Didn't Jessie's spear go missing, too?'

Jeffers shrugs. 'Probably got swept out on the tide.' He nods at the piece of wood in his hands. 'I'm making another one. Someone has to if we want to eat.'

'For God's sake,' Milo's voice rings out of the shelter. 'Stop being such a bloody martyr, Jefferson. We're all doing our bit.' He inclines his head towards Jessie and Honor snoozing beside him. 'They haven't eaten either and you didn't hear either of them bitching and moaning when they got back from setting up the fishing net.'

Danny exhales softly. He can't remember Milo ever snapping at Jeffers before. Or anyone really, other than his sister. He's not sure if it's the sun, hunger, worry or if something else is bugging him.

'We know you've got more food in your rucksack but did you offer it to the girls?' Milo adds. 'Did you hell.'

'They're emergency rations,' Jefferson snaps, 'and we're not there yet. You'll thank me when we are.'

'What do you mean "we're not there yet"? I'd say we're absolutely bloody there. Everyone's hungry, Jeffers. They're tired. *I'm* tired.'

'I get it. But there's food for the taking on this island. We can scavenge, fish and hunt. A few pieces of biltong aren't going to fill you up.'

'No? I bet you take some with you when you sneak off into the forest when the rest of us aren't looking. I wouldn't be surprised if *you* set the trap. Hoping to land yourself a boar, were you, so you could lug it back on your shoulders like some kind of action hero?'

'Milo.' Meg gives him a sharp look. 'Dial it down.'

'No, no.' Jeffers holds his hands up then gets to his feet. 'Carry on venting, Milo, but I'm sick of listening. You guys obviously think I'm a joke. So do what you want. I've given up caring.'

Danny stares after him as he storms off down the beach, spear and knife in one hand, machete in the other, his rucksack slung over his back.

'Jefferson!' Meg shouts after him. 'Jeffers, come back!'

It's dark when Meg returns to the camp and plonks herself down on the sand next to her brother.

'Well done,' she says. 'He's not coming back. He's set up his own camp.'

Milo groans. 'I shouldn't have had a go. I was tired but I couldn't sleep because my ankle was hurting and the sand flies were doing my head in. I'll go and talk to him and say I'm sorry.'

'No. Don't. He wants to be left alone tonight. Go and find him in the morning. He's over by the rocks.' She points to the right. 'There, but further back, in the jungle.'

Jessie gets to her feet. 'I'm going to find him. Seriously, no one should be alone out here.'

Honor gets to her feet too. 'I'm coming with you.'

The guilt Danny's been feeling ever since Jeffers left builds to boiling point and he reaches for her hand.

'I'll come too. Part of the reason I went into the jungle with Meg was to wind him up. I'll talk him into coming back.'

'Oh my God!' Meg starts to laugh. 'You lot are such a bunch of divas. Sit down! Seriously, Jeffers is fine. He just wants a bit of headspace. A few hours alone. He'll be fine in the morning.'

Danny frowns. 'I dunno.'

'Seriously, Dan, if you go over there you'll just piss him off. He wants to be alone for a night. Guys, he'll be fine, honestly. Now, is there any fruit at all, anywhere? I'm starving.'

Danny is so tired he feels sick but, no matter how much he shuffles around in the shelter, he can't get comfy. The banana leaf mattress that was such a novelty on the first night now feels thin and unwieldy. His sleeping bag smells of smoke and damp and he's sweating his arse off. He'd be cooler if he slept in his clothes but the bag is the only protection he's got against the sand crabs that scuttle across the beach in the night and the flies, mosquitos and midges that buzz in his ear when he's trying to sleep.

Three more nights, he tells himself as he tightens the toggles of his sleeping bag around his face. Just three more nights and then a boat will speed across the sea and whip them off the island and take them back to a comfortable hotel, breakfast buffets, warm showers and clean clothes.

Honor's scream rips through Danny's dream, jolting him awake. He sits up, heart pounding and stares into the darkness, confused and disorientated. The fire is out and all he can see is moonlight, dancing over the dark waves. He blinks, caught between a dream and reality, trying to make sense of his surroundings, but the screaming doesn't stop. If anything it intensifies, filling his ears and piercing his brain, making him squint in pain. Something hits him clean in the chest and he recoils, twisting his body away as he's hit again and again and again. The pain makes the fog in his brain clear and he raises a hand, shielding himself from his girlfriend's whirring arms. She's lying on the ground beside him, eyes closed, lips moving, but nothing she's saying makes any sense.

'Honor! You're having a nightmare. It's OK, I'm—'

Danny's breath catches in his throat. Scuttling all over his girlfriend's body are dozens of tarantulas the size of his hand.

'What's going on?' Jessie asks groggily from behind him. 'Why's Honor screaming? What's happening?'

The others are awake too and shouting out in confusion. As Danny desperately swipes at his girlfriend's body, knocking the spiders off her sleeping bag, he hears Milo crawling out of the shelter and fumbling in the dark.

'What are you doing?' Danny hisses.

'Trying to find a torch.'

'I think Jeffers took it.'

'Oh for God's—'

Adrenaline courses through Danny's body as he continues to push, shove and flick spiders off his girlfriend as she thrashes about, still trapped in her nightmare. When they're all gone he wraps his arms around her and pulls her close. Her eyelids flicker and she blinks up at him.

'Danny, why are you looking at me like that? What's happened? What's going on?'

He shakes his head wordlessly.

'Tell me!'

'Dude,' Milo says from the just outside the shelter. 'You looked like you were beating her up.'

'I... I...' Danny shakes his head. 'I was getting rid of...' He pauses. If he tells Honor the truth she'll refuse to sleep in the shelter again.

'Tell me!' She pulls herself out of his arms and sits up. 'Tell me what's going on.'

He shakes his head, closes his eyes tightly, trying to block out the image of the fat hairy spiders with their bulbous bodies and their long, furry legs, scuttling and creeping and crawling all over her.

'Danny, tell me or we're over.'

'Spiders,' he breathes. 'They were all over you and—'

The rest of his sentence is obliterated by her scream.

CHAPTER 13

JESSIE

Day four on the island

The next morning, watching carefully where we step, we search every inch of the shelter and the surrounding area.

'Nothing here,' Milo says decisively, standing straight and rubbing at his lower back. 'Dan, you must have scared them away.'

Honor, standing about as far away from the shelter as she can without actually straddling the dead fire, is hugging herself tightly. She's wearing one of Danny's sweatshirts, the hood pulled up over her head and fastened tightly under her chin. None of us have slept. I'm not particularly afraid of spiders but I was out of the shelter like a shot when Danny said the word 'tarantula'. Meg scrambled after me, swiftly followed by Honor, Danny and Milo. The fire and torches had gone out and we couldn't see a thing. No matter how much Danny tried to reassure Honor that he'd got rid of all the spiders she refused to go back to bed. Milo offered to go and find Jeffers, to see if we could borrow one of his torches, then changed his mind when Meg reminded him that he wouldn't be able to see if there were any snakes on the forest floor. We tried to sleep, curled up on the sand around the dead fire, but there was no way that was going to happen. We waited for the sunrise instead, leaning against each other, knees gathered up to our chests, no one saying a word.

Danny pauses as he rounds the shelter and stares down at the sand.

'What is it?' Milo asks. 'What have you seen?'

Danny crouches down. 'Were these always here? These boot prints?'

We all move closer. None of us are wearing boots. We've all been living in flip-flops since we arrived four days ago.

'Were these here yesterday?' Danny asks again, touching the sand. 'Can anyone remember seeing them?'

A shiver runs through me. I was wrong about us all wearing flip-flops. There's one of our group who turned up on the island wearing very different footwear.

Danny reads my mind. 'Jeffers wears boots, doesn't he?'

I exchange a wary look with Meg. I can tell by the look on her face that she's thinking the same. There's no way Jeffers would have crept up on us in the night to drop spiders all over Honor. Absolutely no way.

'What are you saying, man?' Milo asks.

Danny gets to his feet. 'I'm not saying anything, but I think we need to talk to him, don't you?'

I can't let this happen. 'Milo,' I say. 'Can I have a word?'

We move away from the others, trailing down the beach in our bare feet. When we're far enough away that we won't be overheard I gesture for him to sit down.

'What's up?' He turns to look at me. His face is sleep-crumpled and there are dark circles under his eyes, but his lips curve upwards into the smallest of smiles.

'Something's missing from camp.'

'Huh?'

'There were two axes lying on the sand near the shelter last night. I remember thinking I should pick them up in case anyone stood on them but I… I got distracted.'

Milo shrugs. 'I wouldn't beat yourself up.'

'You don't get it. They're not there anymore. They've been taken.'

He glances over towards the shelter where Meg and Honor are deep in conversation and Danny is sitting alone by the fire, staring into the ash. 'Are you sure?'

'One hundred per cent.'

His eyes widen. 'Oh my God. You think whoever put the spiders on Honor also took the axes?'

'Not necessarily, but if they were Jefferson's boot prints and he took the axes, he might have seen someone else creeping around.'

Milo picks up a small stone and flings it towards the sea. It bounces over the surface three times then disappears. 'We need to talk to him, as soon as possible.'

'I know, but we can't tell Danny about the axes. He'll put two and two together and—'

'All hell will break loose.'

It takes us a while to find Jefferson. We spot his camp first – a hammock, strung between two trees, a rolled sleeping bag sitting in it, his rucksack hung from a sturdy branch and a huge fire, with an axe lying on the ground beside it, an axe he must have taken from our camp – but it takes some searching to locate him. We're guided by the sound of an axe thwacking against wood and eventually stumble on to him a good ten- or fifteen-minute walk into the jungle. He jumps as we approach, then looks back at the tree and takes another swing at the trunk.

Milo hobbles towards him. His ankle's a lot better than it was yesterday but it's still sore.

'Hey, Jeffers… I don't suppose you heard anyone creeping around the jungle last night? Or spotted someone walking along the beach?'

Jefferson lowers his axe. 'A stranger, you mean?'

'Yeah. Something weird happened in camp, the original camp, last night and we're just… we're trying to figure it out.'

'Weird how?'

'Jeffers,' I say. 'We know you came back to the camp last night and took the axes.'

The base of his throat colours and he swallows.

'It's cool,' Milo says. 'We don't care but if you saw anyone then you really need to—'

'You need to fess up!' Danny bursts through the trees behind us, making me jump. 'You know exactly what happened last night. You were pissed off and decided to get your own back by chucking spiders all over Honor.'

Jefferson's jaw drops.

'I wouldn't put it past you to rig up that pit trap either.' Danny's face is flushed red and his T-shirt is so damp with sweat it's clinging to his body. 'Is this some little game you're playing? Trying to freak us all out by making our phobias come true? A power trip so we all look to you for leadership and—'

'Danny, stop it.' I touch him on the shoulder but he shakes me off angrily.

'What's going on with you guys?' He looks from me to Milo. 'Earlier on you were crapping your pants about the tarantulas and now what? The sun's come up and you don't care? Well, Honor does.' He turns and points at his girlfriend as she walks out from the jungle with Meg. Danny walks over to her, puts his arm around her shoulders and pulls her close. 'She doesn't want to sleep in the shelter anymore. She said she'd rather chance swimming to the mainland than spending another night here.'

'It's true.' She looks pained as she wriggles out from his grasp. 'I don't want to stay here another night. I'd rather swim for it or make paddles out of bamboo and try and row Anuman's boat back to the mainland.'

'We can't do that,' Meg says. 'I know how freaked out you are, Honor, seriously, I do. But it's too risky. What if the paddles break or there's a storm or a strong current and we drift off course? We've only got three more nights left and then our parents will raise the alarm and send someone to look for us.' She looks to the group for support.

'I agree with Meg,' I say. 'Sorry, Honor, but I'd rather

take my chances on the island. At least we've got water, shelter and fruit.'

Milo holds up his hand. 'Another vote for staying. It's more dangerous on the water than it is here...' He smiles wryly. 'And I was the one who fell in a massive great hole.'

Danny shakes his head irritably. 'This is all very lovely but it wouldn't even be a conversation if Jeffers hadn't been a dick last night. If he just admits what he did we can all relax. Seriously, man, I've never seen Honor that scared. If you'd have been there I'd have swung for you. And I still might.'

Jefferson's derisive laugh makes Danny clench his right hand into a fist. I share a look with Milo. The last thing we need is for these two to start fighting.

'Dan,' Honor says warningly.

'Fine, fine.' He holds up his hands, palms out. 'I'm not going to do anything. I just want him to admit what he did.'

We all turn to look at Jeffers, waiting for his reply. My gaze flicks to the axe in his hand. There's no way he's going to admit to being in our camp. He wouldn't give Danny the satisfaction.

'Seriously?' he says. 'You all think I'd do something that petty and vindictive?'

'No!' the word escapes from my mouth, loud and forceful in the small, sheltered space. 'Not all of us.'

Danny glares at me. 'Thanks for the support, Jessie.'

'Of course I didn't bloody do it,' Jeffers spits. 'Jesus, Danny. I know you've got a problem with me being gay but seriously, man—'

'Screw you!' Danny stares at him, aghast. 'I couldn't give a crap about that. Don't even go there. I'm not homophobic, man.' He looks at the rest of us. 'Am I?'

I'm pretty sure he's not. I've never heard him say anything homophobic but he's kept his distance from Jeffers – physically and emotionally – since we were nine, and they had a fight. When we were little, properly little, like six or seven, we all got on so well that we'd cry at the end of the holiday and say we didn't want to go home. But now there are so many divisions in our weird little ragtag group that I'm not entirely sure who likes who anymore.

'Jeffers, this has nothing to do with your sexuality. Nothing!' Danny says. 'It's to do with you telling the truth. Did you or did you not creep over to our camp and scare Honor?'

'For the last time,' Jeffers' grip on his axe tightens as he looks Danny straight in the eye, 'I had nothing to do with it.'

'Can I have a quick word, Jessie?' Danny grips my elbow.

We're traipsing back through the jungle towards camp – without Jefferson, who refused to come with us or speak to anyone after his argument with Danny, including me.

'Jessie,' Danny says again. The look in his eyes puts me on the defensive. He's going to have a go at me for keeping quiet when he asked us to back him up on the homophobia thing. 'What is it?' I keep my voice low. We're far enough away from Jefferson's new camp that he can't see us but – if he stopped his chopping and listened hard – he would be able to hear.

111

When Danny doesn't reply I turn away. 'I haven't got time for this.' I want to catch up with the others; the jungle has closed around us and I've already lost sight of them.

'Jessie, wait. We need to stick together.'

'Stick together?' I point back towards Jefferson's camp. 'How is this sticking together, exactly?'

'You can judge me all you want but there's something you don't know.'

'About what?'

'About this island.'

'What about it?'

'Honor isn't the only one whose phobia has come true.'

'Go on...' I say wearily.

'Milo's did too. You know when he fell into the pit the other day? There was a snake in there with him.'

I stare at him in disbelief.

'He didn't see it,' Danny says, reading the shock in my eyes. 'And I haven't told him.'

I push my hair away from my face and sigh. I don't know if it's the heat or the argument I just witnessed still ringing in my ears but I'm not sure why he's telling me this.

'What does Jeffers think? He was there, wasn't he?' Even as the words leave my mouth I realize how stupid they are. Danny and Jeffers have barely said two words to each other all holiday, other than the snarky ones.

'I don't know if he saw it or not,' Danny says, his eyes not leaving mine, 'but if he did he's keeping it quiet.'

I consider this. 'Maybe he doesn't want Milo to freak out?' I venture.

Danny raises an eyebrow.

'What? You think he put the snake in the pit?'

'I think someone is making our phobias come true. Someone could have dug the pit out during a jungle walk, and whistled to get Milo's attention and—'

'It was a bird. Jeffers said as much.'

'Or someone pretending to be a bird. The fact is Milo ended up in a hole with a snake and Honor woke up covered in spiders. Jeffers was near the pit and his boot marks were found in our camp. Still think I'm an arsehole for having a go at him?'

I swipe at a mosquito buzzing around my face and swear under my breath. 'Why, though? What possible reason could he have for doing something like that? He likes Milo, and Honor, he wouldn't want to scare them.'

'Wouldn't he? You saw him last night. You heard how pissed off he was. He knows we find him annoying.'

'Speak for yourself.'

'It's not just me. Not by a long shot.'

I slap at my arm then peel back my hand to reveal a small bloody mark and the remains of a mosquito. I still don't think Jeffers would do something so vindictive. Sure, he'd creep back in the night to take the axes because they're useful, but he wouldn't deliberately screw with us.

'There's no way he's behind it. It's someone else. A stranger.'

'Meg and I went into the jungle. There's no one else here.'

'How can you be sure? Milo reckons there's another group on the island. Over on the other side.'

Danny sighs heavily. 'You've been spending a lot of time with him this holiday, haven't you?'

'What's that supposed to mean?'

'He's my mate, Jessie, but he can be flaky and I don't want you to get hurt. Not after what you've been through.'

'What do you mean?'

'You know…' He rubs a hand against the back of his neck. 'What happened to T—'

'Not that.' I feel a sharp stab of irritation. I don't want to think about Tom and I don't want Danny's sympathy. 'Why do you think Milo would hurt me?'

'I'm not saying he'd do it deliberately but he's still in love with Bella. He wants her back.'

'What?' My stomach lurches horribly. 'How do you know?'

'Meg told me.'

'What did she say, exactly?'

He shakes his head. 'It doesn't matter.'

'No, really. It does.'

'Oh God.' He runs a hand through his hair. 'Can't we just leave it at this?'

'No, we can't.'

'She said Milo was gutted when Bella dumped him and he's using you to make himself feel better.'

The words hang in the air between us, like a knife aimed at my heart.

You're a distraction to get over his heartbreak.

He doesn't really care about you and he never has.

You're making a fool out of yourself.

Give up now before you make it worse.

That's what he's implying. And it's what Jefferson had been hinting at the other day. They all know Milo's been playing me and I fell for it, hook, line and sinker.

'I'm not interested in Milo.' I look Danny straight in the eyes. 'So I don't know why you think this is of any interest to me.'

'I was just…' He looks crestfallen, just for a split second. 'I was just looking out for you, Jessie.'

'Well, don't. I can look after myself.'

I traipse behind Meg and Milo, listening to their conversation but not contributing. Meg's crying. I would be too if I wasn't so angry.

'I can't stand this,' she sobs, pulling away from Milo as he attempts to put an arm around her shoulders. 'It's so horrible. Jefferson's been ostracized from the group and he hasn't done anything wrong!' She raises a hand and points into the distance where Danny has caught up with Honor and they're walking hand in hand.

'I could have punched Danny myself back there,' Meg says. 'The way he waded in like that, pointing his finger and shouting. I don't blame Jefferson for not wanting to come back with us.'

'I feel bad…' Milo says. 'I shouldn't have had a go at him the other day, about the fish.'

'Yeah but, unlike Danny you apologized.'

'It didn't make any difference, though, did it?'

Meg side-eyes her brother. 'Would *you* come back to camp? After everything that's happened?'

'Nah. I guess not.'

'What a bloody nightmare.'

They lapse into silence and as we walk through the last of the trees and reach the beach I pause to take off my flip-flops.

'You guys go on without me,' I say as Milo looks questioningly back at me. 'I'm going to have a swim.'

'Want company, Miss Harper?'

'No thanks.'

'Oh, right.' His smile falters and he gestures to Meg to keep walking. 'See you in a bit then, Jess.'

I wade into the sea fully clothed then take a deep breath and dive deep into the water. Within seconds I'm in a quiet, blurry world where all I can feel is the ache of the air in my lungs and the weight of the water. I reach out my arms and pull myself down, down, down. A shoal of orange fish with white stripes and black-tipped fins swerve around me and it's all I can do not to shout, 'Nemo!' as they dip down and disappear into a waving mass of white-fingered coral. Other fish – their bright blue scales glinting in the light from the sun – glide warily away from me. I spot a sea turtle and swim excitedly towards it but it speeds away, becoming a distant brown blur within seconds.

I swim until my lungs ache, then I tip back my head and kick my legs until my face breaks through the surface and I gulp down warm, salty air. I flip onto my back and float, face turned up to the sun, arms and legs wide, barely sculling. The thoughts that magically disappeared when I was underwater reappear in my brain and buzz angrily like wasps.

Milo's a dick.

Why am I such an idiot?

I'm so embarrassed I could scream.

Now the tears fall, rolling towards my ears and disappearing into my hairline as I screw my eyes tightly against the sun. The sea cradles my body, gently lifting me this way and that. I *told myself* I wasn't going to let myself care for anyone. After Tom died I swore I'd never let myself love anyone that much again. Love means pain. That's the truth no one teaches you. I flip over onto my front and power through the sea, slicing at the water with my hands and kicking at it with my feet.

I swim until the anger drains from my body and I'm too tired to lift my arms above the waves. I let my legs drop and I scull with my hands as I look back, surprised at how far I have travelled. I've made it past the rocks and another small patch of jungle and, stretched in front of me, is another beautiful white beach. My breath catches in my throat as something I'd mistaken for a rock suddenly moves across the sand. A sea turtle! We were told there were loads on this island but there aren't any near our camp. The fire and our shouting and screaming must have scared them away. As I watch I spot another turtle and another.

I glide effortlessly through the water until my palms touch sand then, keeping low, I creep out of the water and onto the beach. The turtles don't pay me the slightest bit of notice as I stand stock still, hands on hips, watching them. Instead they scoop at the sand with their flippers and hump their bodies over the sand as they head for the sea. It's one of the most magical things I've ever seen.

As the turtles slip effortlessly into the sea and disappear under the waves I drop down onto the sand and lie spread-eagled, eyes closed, breathing the warm air deep into my lungs. All the anger and fury that squeezed at my chest has gone, but my heart still feels tender. Prod it too hard and it'd hurt. I don't think Milo was leading me on the other night, when our fingers entwined. I think he was trying to tell me that he was there for me, as a friend.

Sighing, I sit up and gather my knees to my chest. I should go back and tell the others about this beach but I like that it's just mine, for now at least. My stomach rumbles and I press a hand to my belly. Jeffers was right about us gathering food. I can't remember the last time I ate, and I'm going to struggle to swim all the way back unless I can find some fruit. I scan the trees at the edge of the jungle. I can't see any coconut palms, fruit trees or banana plants but that doesn't mean there aren't any a little way in. As I get to my feet a low humming sound makes me pause. It's not animal or human. It's—

I turn sharply and stare out to sea. And there it is, cutting through the water like a hot knife through butter and headed straight for me.

A boat.

CHAPTER 14

DANNY

Danny stands by the dead fire, staring out to sea, his hands in the pockets of his shorts and his heart twisting in his chest. It had hurt, Jefferson implying that he was homophobic and none of the others sticking up for him, when all he was trying to do was find out who'd scared his girlfriend. Honor had looked so bloody uncomfortable, standing beside him, watching him flounder and fail. He'd been trying to protect her, not embarrass her. He'd taken Jessie to one side to try and explain why he'd gone after Jefferson, but there was no convincing her. In her view Jeffers could do no wrong, and the snake and the spiders had been down to some 'other group' that no one had seen and probably didn't exist. He hadn't planned on telling her about Milo, but then he'd seen how much her eyes shone whenever she mentioned his name and how much she valued his opinion and he knew he had to set her straight.

Milo was a good friend, the best, but he and Jessie were never going to get it together. They'd been at it for years – flirting then pulling away then flirting again – and, as far as Danny could see, nothing was ever going to change. The moment they got back from holiday they'd find someone else to hook up with.

He realized he'd made a terrible mistake the second he told Jessie about Milo's ex-girlfriend. Her face fell and she looked gutted. Absolutely heartbroken.

'Banana?' Meg says now as she wanders out from the jungle with an armful of fruit.

'Sure. Thanks.' He takes a banana, peels away the skin and shoves it into his mouth.

I'll make it up to Jessie when she comes back from her swim, he tells himself as chews. He's not entirely sure *how* he'll make it up to her but he'll do something to put the smile back on her face. Milo's too. He's hiding it well but he must be gutted about Bella not wanting to get back together with him. Danny can't even begin to imagine how broken he'd feel if Honor ever left him. He finishes the last of the banana and chucks the skin at the dead fire. Pieces of burnt wood scatter over the sand and Honor, sitting about as far away as she can get from the shelter, weaving something out of banana leaves, shakes her head disapprovingly.

'Hey, Dan!' Milo waves a hand from further down the beach, beckoning him to the shoreline.

'What's up?'

As he walks towards him Milo points into the distance

where an empty Coke bottle is bobbing on top of the sea. 'Fancy helping me check the nets? Jessie isn't back from her swim yet and Meg says she's too knackered.'

Danny glances back towards the shelter and the remains of the fire with a banana skin lying in the centre.

'If we find any fish we're not going to be able to cook them.'

Milo raises an eyebrow. '*Someone* should have been nicer to Jeffers and then we'd have a flint and steel.'

Danny sighs heavily. Milo is right. He shouldn't have gone wading in the way he did, not when Jefferson has most of the things they need to survive. He should have confronted him *after* they'd asked for a flint and steel. *Why* doesn't he *think*? He's such a short-sighted idiot. If this was the island of arseholes, he'd definitely be king.

All thoughts of dead fires and being the biggest loser on the island go out of Danny's head as he swims out to the home-made Coke bottle buoy, Milo gliding effortlessly through the water beside him.

Please, Danny prays as they draw closer to the fishing nets. *Please let there be fish*.

Six fat, healthy fish would put everything right. There'd be one each to fill their aching bellies and one to take to Jefferson as a peace offering in exchange for the flint and stone. He might even offer to start the fire for them if they brought him a fish.

'Ready?' Milo bobs in the water beside him. They're quite

a long way from shore now. Fair play to the girls for laying the net. Danny's out of breath and he hasn't even dived under the water yet. But he's not going to let his lack of fitness get in the way of them eating something good tonight.

'Ready.' He nods at his friend.

A second later he's underwater, squinting as his vision blurs and the net looms in front of him, an indistinct green blur. He grabs hold of it and works his way along it, his heart sinking the further he moves. Where are the fish? It's been in place for a full forty-eight hours. They have to have caught something! The air in his lungs runs out and he bobs back up to the surface. A split second later Milo joins him.

'Anything?' Milo asks.

Danny shakes his head.

'We need to dive a bit deeper. I couldn't get right down to the bottom on the last go.'

'Me neither.'

'OK. Ready? Three... two... one...'

Danny dives down again, not taking so much air into his lungs this time, weaving his fingers into the net to pull himself deeper. His heart leaps in his chest as he spots something grey and silvery a foot or so away and he frantically kicks his legs. His lungs ache as he reaches out a hand to grab it but... damn it... he's still too far away and his fingers only graze the tip of its tail. He *needs* this fish. Not because they're starving, there's more fruit on the island than they could ever eat, but to prove to the others that he's not a complete loser. He imagines the delight on Honor's face as he walks, victoriously, out of the sea with the fish held aloft, his finger hooked through its gills. *It's for Jeffers*, he'd say and she and Meg would give him admiring nods. *Danny isn't such a dickhead after all.*

His pulse pounds in his ears as he passes one hand over the other, dragging himself closer, inch by inch, to his prize. Jeffers will be so surprised that he, Danny, is the first to bring home some fish. He'll nod begrudgingly then hand over the flint and steel in return for a share of the haul. Then Danny would return to their camp, start the fire and they'll have a good night, eating tiny portions of fish and finishing off the vodka.

His lungs start to burn as he pulls himself the last few inches towards the fish. Every cell in his body is telling him to let go of the net and swim to the surface, to take a breath, but he grits his teeth and grabs at the fish with fumbling fingers. The sea pulls at his body, trying to snatch him away, but he fights back, keeping one hand entwined in the net as he wraps the other one around the fish. Even under the water it feels slick against his palm and his hand slides away as he pulls. He tries again, squeezing it tighter and yanking it harder until, finally, it comes free. Jubilation then relief course through him as he tips his head up towards the sky, lets go of the net and kicks as hard as he can. He breaks through the water, hand held aloft, the fish a shimmering prize, and sucks the warm sea air deep into his lungs.

'Yes, man!' Milo, already bobbing beside him, shoves his

hands in the air too to show off his spoils. 'That's three fish for tea!'

Danny looks towards the shore, hoping Honor's left the shelter and is waiting for him on the sand, but there's no one on the beach. She must still be resting.

'Race you back!' Milo's eye sparkle with excitement and satisfaction. 'Three... two... one...'

He's off before he says go and Danny feels a surge of adrenaline. There's no way he's going to let his mate show off his winnings to the girls before he does. He powers through the water – or as powerfully as he can given his sloppy front crawl technique. He can see Milo, taller and stronger, pulling away so he puts his face into the water and concentrates on curving his arms through the air. All his concentration is focused on getting back to shore and across the beach as quickly as possible. He feels the fish shift in his right hand as his fist hits the water and he tightens his grip. But he squeezes too hard and it slips out of his hand.

No! He stops swimming and stares desperately around. Where's it gone? He twists to his right and stares into the water. He catches a glimpse of something grey and silvery drifting away and ducks back under the water. His fish, his prized trophy is sinking, one dead eye staring accusingly up at him as it plummets towards the murky depths of the sea bed. Danny swims desperately after it, cupped hands pulling, legs kicking. He can't go back to the others empty-handed. He just can't. But the fish is too far away. There's no way he can recapture it.

As he resurfaces, his heart heavy and his dreams dashed, he sees Milo splashing out the sea, arms aloft, fish dangling from his fingers.

'Loser!' Milo shouts. 'Loser!'

Danny raises a hand and gives his friend a middle finger salute.

CHAPTER 15

JESSIE

A boat! I can't believe someone's already sent one to rescue us! How did they know? Was this always part of the plan, that part way through the week they'd send someone else to the island to join us? Could it be another instructor? Maybe another group of kids? A hundred thoughts fly through my head as I hold a hand across my eyebrows and squint into the sunlight, trying to get a better look. There are two people in the boat, one driving, the other sitting on the side, but I can't make out more than their silhouettes. I'm guessing they're male but I can't be completely sure. Not a new group of kids then, they have to be instructors. Although… I squint more… that's not an old, battered Thai boat they're in. It's modern, the sort tourists rent for day trips. I feel a sudden stab of worry. What if it's bad news? What if something's happened to one of our families?

Oh God. I press a hand to my chest. *Please don't let anything have happened to Mum or Dad. Please. Please.*

I wait, heart pounding, blinking under the shield of my hand as the boat draws closer. There are definitely two men in the boat but they don't look like anyone's parents. There's something familiar about them though. They're young, topless, tanned and...

I take a step backwards as they jump out of the boat. They're the two lads from the pool. The older one, Jack, who was talking to me at the table and Josh, who tried it on with Honor. Josh, whose hand I nearly skewered with the leg of my chair. I take another step back.

'Hey!' Jack waves one arm above his head as he walks through the waves behind his brother. 'Fancy seeing you here! Long time, no see.'

There's a friendly tone to his voice but it does nothing to slow the thump-thump-thump of my heart. As they walk closer, bare feet slapping against the sand, their flip-flops in their hands, I am frozen by indecision. They've got a boat, big enough to fit all six of us in. We could get off this island and go back home. We wouldn't have to worry about any more phobias coming true. I wouldn't have to worry about *my* phobia coming true.

The small one with the nose piercing is close enough that I can see his face now. He's smiling, but there's something dark glittering behind his eyes and I glance to the left; to the rocks that separate me from my friends. They're so high there's no way I'd be able to scale them. And no way Jeffers would be able to reach me quickly, even if he heard me scream. The fastest way to get from this beach to the other is to swim and I can't get to the sea, not with Jack and Josh in the way. My only escape route is the jungle.

'Hello, hello.' Josh draws to a halt a couple of feet in front of me. He hooks his thumbs into the belt loops of his cargo shorts and tilts his head to one side. 'Well, look who it is!'

'What are you doing here?'

He shrugs. 'We heard you guys talking about this place the other night and we fancied a little... getaway. Seeing as you didn't invite us we decided to invite ourselves.' His eyes glitter menacingly.

'Where's blondie?' his brother calls from the shoreline.

'Honor,' I say, before I can stop myself.

'I'd take her honour,' Josh says. 'Where is she?'

'Why do you want to know?'

He raises his eyebrows. I'm not the only one who can hear the tremor in my voice.

'We just thought we'd say hello.' He rubs the fingers of his left hand over his right. There's a huge, lumpen black and green bruise on the back of his right hand. I glance away quickly.

'Yes, it does hurt, thank you for asking.' He looks me up and down, his gaze resting on *my* misshapen hands. 'What's your name?'

'J-Jessie.' I feel a stab of anger towards my own voice. It's betraying me, letting him know he's got the upper hand.

'Have you ever had a broken bone, J-J-Jessie?'

'No.'

'Want one?' He steps towards me.

'No.' I take a step back, closer to the jungle.

'Are you religious, Jessie?'

I shake my head.

'Me neither, but there's some good stuff in the Bible. You ever read it?'

I shake my head again. My whole body is shaking now. The air between us is thick with menace.

'I've read it.' He raises his eyebrows, still staring right at me. 'I like that bit about an eye for an eye, a tooth for a tooth. But I'm…' He frowns, as though considering something, 'I'm wondering if that also applies to hands?'

Before I can answer he turns to look at his brother, walking along the sand towards us. 'Jack, I'm having a philosophical with Jessie here. We're wondering if—'

I don't wait for him to finish asking his question. Instead I run.

CHAPTER 16

DANNY

Danny traipses down the beach, Milo's fish hanging from his fingers. Milo said that as he'd caught it, he was the one who should take it to Jefferson. But then Meg stepped in, telling her brother that getting Jefferson back into the group was more important than him showing off.

'Danny's the one who needs to put things right,' she said sternly. 'Can't you just let him get on with it?'

Milo huffed and puffed a bit then shrugged his shoulders and patted Danny on the back. 'Good luck, mate. I hope you can talk him round.'

He turned then, to follow Honor into the jungle to collect water and fruit. Danny watched her go, her blonde hair tied into a messy bun on the top of her head, her short denim shorts barely covering her bum. She hadn't wished him good luck. She'd barely even looked at him when he'd walked out of the sea.

She's just tired, he tells himself as he finds the gap between the trees that leads to Jefferson's camp. *She barely got any sleep last night. None of us did. We all just want to go home.*

He spots Jefferson through the trees, lying in his hammock, eyes closed, and for a moment he feels the strong urge to run at him and shout, 'Boo!' They used to get on well, before the fight when they were nine, and, although Jeffers' dad forced them to make up and shake hands afterwards, the incident left Danny feeling shaken. What Jeffers had said had been like a bullet to his heart, ripping through the emotional armour he'd put up to protect himself. Afterwards he was wary of going anywhere near Jeffers in case he said anything else. The fight was years ago and, logically, Danny knows he's got nothing to fear but age hasn't made Jefferson any less tactless and, if anything, he's even more likely to speak his mind.

As Danny noisily clears his throat Jeffers sits up sharply, arm extended, a knife in his fist. He's lost weight, Danny thinks, staring at his friend's taut, sinewy arms. It's only been four days and he looks skinnier than ever.

'Who's there?' Jeffers shouts.

'Just me,' Danny replies. 'It's Danny. You're good.'

As he emerges from between the trees and steps into the tiny camp, Jeffers slips out of his hammock and faces him, the knife still in his hand. Danny rubs his dry lips together. This isn't going to be easy. Jeffers is staring at him, his face impassive, his pupils huge behind the sheen of his glasses. He barely seems to be breathing he's so calm. Danny, on the other side, feels like his heart is about to beat out of his chest. The air between them is thick with tension. He needs to play it cool. He's still pretty sure that Jeffers is behind the snake and spider scares but he needs to be clever, play him at his own game. Going in all guns blazing was a mistake. He needs to pretend that he got it all wrong, get Jeffers back on side and then keep a very close eye on him. And to do that he's going to have to persuade him to move back to the original camp.

'I'm sorry,' Danny says, forcing himself to look the other boy straight in the eye, his arm still outstretched with the fish dangling from his fingers. 'I was out of order.'

Jefferson raises a blonde eyebrow. 'What for?'

'Everything.' Danny looks down at his feet. 'Taking the piss out of you, having a go, accusing you of the phobia stuff. Basically…' He shrugs. 'Basically everything. Everything I've said. I'm sorry.'

'Are you? Or are you just saying that because your fire's gone out and you've got no way to cook those fish?'

Danny looks up at him, fighting the smile that's pricking at the edges of his lips. 'Bit of both.' As he says the last word he bursts out laughing.

Jeffers laughs too and the atmosphere between them eases.

Danny proffers a fish. 'Want one?'

'No, thanks.' Jeffers shakes his head then points up into one of the trees where a dead snake is hanging over a branch.

Interesting, Danny thinks. *Someone's obviously not scared of them.*

'Did you kill it?' he asks.

''Course.'

'What does… um…' Danny eyes the snake warily. 'What does it taste like?'

'Like fish, apparently. I'll find out later.'

He looks back at his own dinner. The eyes of the fish are starting to cloud. Anuman said that, in the Thai heat, they need to be eaten quickly or they'll go bad. 'Um… Jeffers, will you come back to camp? It's not right, you being here on your own. This trip was your birthday present from your dad. I'm sorry we've… I've… made it so crap.'

Jefferson smiles. 'It's fine. And I owe you an apology too, for throwing the homophobia grenade.'

'You know I really don't have a problem with you being gay. But it does piss me off when you tell me what to do.'

'Someone has to. You're a bloody liability.'

They both laugh.

'I've got so many chips on my shoulder,' Danny says, 'I'm going to start calling myself Harry Ramsden.'

Jeffers raises an eyebrow. 'Poor, very poor.'

'So will you come back? To our camp?'

Jefferson shrugs. 'Someone's got to cook those fish for you! Mind helping me pack up my stuff?'

'Sure.' Danny glances around the small camp, looking for somewhere he can put the fish without them getting dirty then freezes as a piercing scream echoes through the jungle. Birds fly from the trees, wings beating frantically. Danny listens. He can hear the rustle of leaves in the light wind, monkeys whooping and the soft chirping of some kind of insect. But what he heard wasn't an animal, it was a girl's scream.

133

He continues to wait, holding himself very still.

A second scream, louder than the first, rings out from somewhere to their left. The only girl on that side of the island is Jessie.

CHAPTER 17

JESSIE

My foot catches in something – a tree root or a vine – and I pitch forward, the brown-green jungle floor rising up to meet me. I land heavily and all the air is knocked from my lungs. I can hear Josh and Jack behind me, shouting and swearing and striking at plants as they crash through the jungle. Josh managed to grab the back of my T-shirt as I turned to run but I hit out at him, my fist connecting with his cheek bone. My flip-flops slid and slipped as I ran across the sand to the jungle so I kicked them off, not caring what I stood on as I swiped at banana plants and vines, trying to get away.

Now, as I scrabble to my knees, the palms of my hands throbbing, I risk a glimpse behind me. There's a flash of tanned skin, about ten metres away, incongruous against so much green. The boys have gone quiet. They're moving slowly and quietly between the trees. They're listening, trying to work out where I am.

I don't know what to do. They're near enough that if

I get up and run they could easily catch up with me. But if I hide then I run the risk of them discovering me. Blood pounds in my ears and sweat rolls off my forehead and drips off my eyebrows, making me blink. The nearest safe place is Jefferson's camp. But I've got no idea how much further I need to run to get there, or how thick the jungle gets. If it's impenetrable then I'm trapped.

I crouch low, tucking myself behind a huge fern, and try to slow my racing thoughts. Is that why they came out to the island? To get revenge for what I did at the pool side? No one's ever stared at me with so much hate in their eyes as Josh did just now. I glance left and right looking for something, anything I can use as a weapon, but there's two of them and one of me. There's no way I could fight them both off.

If they can't find me they'll have to give up and go back to the beach. But what then? If they get back in their boat and drive round the island they'll spot our camp. Even without the fire burning brightly they'll see our shelters and the mess of our belongings. I can't just hide. I need to warn the others. Jeffers will know what to do.

Keeping low I creep onwards, stepping as lightly as I can on the rough jungle floor. Frightened lizards skitter away, hiding on flat green leaves the size of my head. I can't hear Jack and Josh crashing around behind me but the silence is unnerving. They could be close. So close that at any second a hand could shoot from between the bushes and grab me. As I glance behind, one of the trees sways violently to the left, and my heart thunders in my chest. But it's just a monkey swinging off a branch.

Heart pounding, legs quivering, I raise myself up to full height. I'm just going to run for it.

Three…

A bird squawks to my right, a shrill, trilling warning sign.

Two…

A green metallic beetle scurries across a leaf.

One…

As I lunge forwards someone grabs my ankle. Deep male laughter rings out as my leg is yanked, hard, and I tumble to the ground.

CHAPTER 18

DANNY

Danny frantically searches for the source of the scream. It was close. Very, very close.

Jeffers presses a finger to his lips, motioning him to be quiet. Like Danny he is standing stock still, eyes wide and scared.

Danny passes a hand over his face, slicking back his sweat-drenched hair. He hears branches snapping, the low rumble of male voices and smothered grunts and squeals. He looks back at Jeffers, who's gripping his knife so tightly his knuckles are white. They're not alone on the island. Danny looks desperately around for a weapon of his own but none of the sticks littering the jungle floor are very big, and when he tries to snap a branch off a nearby tree Jeffers shakes his head sharply. They can't risk making any noise.

Danny's stomach cramps violently and, for one terrible second, he thinks he might be sick. Other than his scrap with Jeffers when they were nine he's never been in a fight in his life. And what if the men have guns? What if they are local criminals who've come to rob them, or worse? He pushes down his fear and tries to steady his breathing. Something awful must have happened to Jessie to make her scream like that and it's down to him and Jeffers to... to... so many terrible thoughts fill his mind that he screws his eyes tightly shut.

A sharp nudge in his side makes him open them again. Jeffers gives him a look as though to say, *Everything OK?* and Danny nods. He's bigger than his fear. He can do this.

Jeffers inclines his head to one side, gesturing which direction to head in and beckons for Danny to follow him. They set off, stepping lightly, moving slowly, following the muffled sounds deep in the jungle. They both freeze as they hear a man shout out in pain. A split second later the same voice says, 'I've changed my mind. Maybe we should just let her go, she's a complete psychopath!'

When Jessie screams again adrenaline surges through Danny and he springs forward, all thoughts of guns and criminals eclipsed. But he doesn't take more than two or three steps before Jeffers grabs the back of his T-shirt and halts him in his tracks.

'Not yet,' Jeffers hisses. 'We need to get closer, see exactly what we're dealing with. They're on the move again – listen.'

Danny holds his breath, his pulse pounding in his ears against a backdrop of undergrowth being trampled, branches being snapped and birds shrieking. His whole body is shaking. It's taking every ounce of self-control he has to stand still as Jessie and her captors move further and further away.

'They're heading to the beach,' Jeffers says. He indicates that they should squeeze through the bushes to their left and Danny nods.

They move quickly but carefully through the jungle. The further they walk the thinner the trees get and the easier it is to navigate their way through without being scratched by stray branches and prickly plants. Danny spots a flash of blue through the green. They're nearly at the beach. Jeffers gestures for him to duck down. They crouch together, arms touching, slick with sweat.

Jefferson nudges him gently then points towards the beach. Danny was right about there being two men. They're both white, late teens or early twenties. One's taller and leaner, the other shorter and broader and they both have the same light-coloured hair, shaved close to the scalp.

'Who are they?' Danny whispers.

'They were staying at our hotel,' Jeffers hisses. 'They're brothers. See the one with the nose ring? That's the one Jessie skewered with her chair leg.'

Danny's mouth drops. They're the guys from the pool who tried it on with Honor.

But it's not thinking about his girlfriend that make his heart ricochet off his ribs – it's the sight of Jessie, strung between them. One is holding her feet, the other holding her under the armpits. She's twisting and wriggling and scream-ing, clawing at the older guy, forcing him to lurch from side to side to avoid her flailing fingers scratching his face.

'Boat,' Jeffers hisses under his breath, pointing across the beach.

Danny follows his gaze and spots the large white motor-boat bobbing gently on the sea, several metres out. That's where they're trying to take Jessie.

'I think we've only got one option,' Jeffers whispers, sweat rolling down his temples and disappearing into the fair stubble on his chin, as the two lads struggle to manoeuvre Jessie across the sand to the sea. 'We burst onto the beach and make a lot of noise. With any luck they'll drop Jess and she'll run. But it does...' He lifts his T-shirt and wipes his face. 'It does mean they'll probably come after us.'

Danny swallows. Jeffers is a pretty fast runner, and he's still got his boots on. He, on the other hand, was always near the end of the pack on school sports day.

'Are you OK?' Jeffers shoots him an urgent look. The two brothers are feet away from the surf. 'If we do it, we do it now.'

Danny nods. 'I'm ready if you are.'

CHAPTER 19

JESSIE

I don't know if they're going to drown me in the sea or throw me in the boat. All I know is if I don't get away something terrible is going to happen. Jack's jaw and neck are bleeding from where I've scratched him, but my blows seem to be glancing off him now. Josh was the one who grabbed my ankle in the jungle. As I fell I saw him dart out from the bush he'd been hiding behind. I kicked out with my free leg, smacking him in the chest and he reeled backwards, his grip on my ankle loosening. I scrabbled frantically away on my hands and knees, the jungle floor scratching my palms and the humid air catching in my parched throat. I couldn't have crawled more than a couple of feet before strong arms gripped me around the shoulders. When I screamed a hand was clamped over my mouth. I wriggled and twisted and kicked out then tried to bite the fingers that were digging into my cheek.

'We've got a tiger here,' Jack said, panting heavily.

Josh got to his feet, red in the face, his lips curled back in a snarl. 'Tigers get skinned, and I've got a knife. Stupid bitch. You need to be taught a lesson.'

'No!' Jack growled. 'Grab her legs. Let's get her out of this bloody jungle first.' He swore under his breath. 'There are flies *everywhere*.'

I kicked out as Josh tried to grab my legs but he was ready for me and snapped his hands around my ankles, gripping them so tightly my skin throbbed.

As they roughly manoeuvred me between the trees I alternated between relaxing all my muscles to make myself as heavy as possible and twisting and squirming to try and break free. When a branch snapped somewhere behind us I turned my head sharply, hoping to see Jeffers, but it was just a macaque monkey. It tore off through the bushes and disappeared.

'God,' Jack growled at one point. 'I've changed my mind. Maybe we should just let her go, she's a complete psychopath. We'll find their camp and torch it instead!'

'I'm not letting her go anywhere.' Josh shook his head. 'I'm covered in bruises thanks to this bitch.'

Now, as they carry me across the sand, I use every last ounce of energy I have to try and escape but they've both tightened their grips. I raise my eyes to the sky and try to look beyond the endless stretch of blue.

Please, Tom, I pray. *If you're up there, please help me.*

A roar of anger fills the air. For one heart-stopping moment I think it's my brother, but then Jack twists his head towards the jungle and fury flashes across his face.

'Who are those losers?'

'Her friends. Get them!'

One second I am three feet in the air, the next, WHOOMPH! I've been dropped. I land half on the shore, half in the sea as they sprint towards the jungle. I only catch a glimpse of Jeffers' and Danny's startled faces before they turn and disappear into the dense green foliage. As Josh and Jack pelt after them I scrabble to my feet. I don't know whether to run and hide, help my friends or swim for it. No, the boat! I splash through waves towards it, haul myself over the side and drop into the belly like a landed fish. Then I'm quickly up on my hands and knees and crawling to the front. Anuman's boat had a petrol motor on the back but this one's got dials and switches on a control panel, a steering wheel and… my heart sinks as I touch my fingers to the metal keyhole. Where are the keys? I run my hands under the benches then open the first-aid box and search inside. But there's nothing in the boat other than a couple of bottles of water, two small rucksacks, a case of beer, some suntan lotion and a pair of sunglasses. I glance back towards the jungle, half expecting to see the two brothers speeding across the sand towards me, shouting in anger. But the beach is quiet and still.

Ankles and shoulders still throbbing from where I was held, I step up onto the seating area of the boat and jump back into the sea. Adrenaline pulses through me as I power through the water and round the rocks. I need to warn the others and get them to move the camp.

By the time I drag myself out of the sea my legs are so

weak I wobble, rather than walk across the sand. Milo, Meg and Honor come rushing towards me, their faces tight with worry.

'What happened?' Milo's the first one to reach me. I hold out a hand to steady myself on his shoulder, but before my fingers can graze his skin my legs give way and I collapse onto the sand.

'Jessie? What is it? What's wrong?' Fear is etched into the tired, tanned skin of Meg's face as she crouches beside me.

'We... we...' I try to struggle back up onto my feet but it's as though all the muscles in my legs have atrophied.

'Don't get up,' Honor says, appearing on my other side. 'Rest. Tell us what happened. If you can...'

I shake my head, struggling to catch my breath. I can't stop staring at the jungle, certain that, at any second, Jack and Josh are going to burst from between the bowed fronds of the banana plants.

'What is it?' Meg asks again. 'Jessie, where are Jeffers and Danny? Has something happened to them? Did something happen to you?'

I gesture beyond the rocks. 'They... they...'

'Deep breaths. Take nice, slow deep breaths.'

I exhale heavily then fill my lungs.

'Jack and Josh.' The words come out in a rush. 'They're here, they came after me... they tried... they tried...'

Honor's eyes widen. 'Those two boys from the hotel?'

I nod.

'They're here?'

'And they've got a knife and they tried to get me into their boat.' I try and get up. We're wasting time talking. We need to gather up our stuff and get as far away from the beach as we can.

'My God,' Milo breathes. 'There are finger marks – bruises – round both your ankles. And here—' He gently touches the side of my neck, making me flinch. 'Jesus, Jessie. Did they hurt you? I swear I'll…' He stands, the tendons in his throat as tight as piano strings. 'I'll kill them.'

'Where's Danny?' Honor asks as Milo stalks off towards the jungle. She touches the back of my hand. 'What's happened to him?'

'I don't know,' I say. 'He and Jeffers distracted the boys so I could escape. They ran into the jungle and Jack and Josh ran after them. I don't know where they are now.'

Honor gasps in horror and covers her mouth with both hands.

'How the hell did they know *we're* here?' Meg asks me. 'And how did they get here?'

'They overheard me and Honor talking by the pool. They've got a boat, I've seen it. Please.' I raise my arms, gesturing for her and Honor to help me up. 'We need to get out of here. We need to move the camp. They want to torch it.'

Honor shakes her head. 'We can't leave without Danny and Jefferson.'

'I'll go into the jungle and find them,' Milo says.

'No.' Meg grabs his arm. 'Not on your own. If Jack and Josh find you first…' she tails off but it's enough to make Milo pause.

'I can take them,' he says.

'No you can't. Not when they've got a knife.'

He looks from his sister to me to Honor, indecision etched into his face. If he charges into the jungle he'll be leaving the three of us behind.

'They've got a boat,' I repeat. 'If they give up chasing Danny and Jeffers and sail round the rocks they'll see us. We need to get out of here.'

'And go where?'

'To the cliff top.' Honor points to the jagged cliff beyond the rocks to our right. 'Danny told me there's a decent-sized clearing up there with no sand flies. He said it was a better place for a camp. Plus we'll be able to see if there's anyone looking for us on the beach, and we can see the sea.'

'No,' Meg says. 'If they find us up there we're trapped.'

'Not if we jump into the sea,' I say.

Milo raises his dark eyebrows. 'What about Jeffers? He hates heights!'

'He'd jump if his life depended on it,' Honor says. 'And anyway, he's not here.'

'Do you think Danny would think to look for us up there?' I ask as I struggle onto my feet.

Honor shrugs. 'Possibly. Like I said, he did say it was a good place for a camp. Or we could leave him a note.'

'Too risky,' Meg says. 'Anyway, Jeffers knows how to follow tracks. He'll work out where we've gone. Let's do it.'

'Just pack the essentials,' Meg hisses as Milo and Honor scurry around our messy camp, grabbing up discarded flip-flops, water containers, bottles of sunscreen and items of clothing. Most of my stuff is piled up beside my rucksack in the corner of the shelter but I can't bring myself to grab it. All I can do is stand and watch as the others buzz like flies. There's one part of my mind screaming that I need to move, to flee, and another part that's running through what just happened to me, like a film played at triple speed. I've never felt as vulnerable or as violated as I did being carried through the jungle like a piece of meat. Now I'm back with the others and shock has worn off, my emotions are morphing – vulnerability has been replaced by rage, and violation by a desire for revenge. I don't want to run from Jack and Josh. I want to find the sharpest, pointiest, deadliest weapon and run it straight through them. As I stare into the jungle, anger roiling in my belly, the others chat among themselves.

'What do we do about food?' Honor asks. 'We've stock-piled loads of coconuts.'

'We'll worry about that later,' Milo says as he hoists his rucksack onto his back then hefts Meg's rucksack into his arms. 'We need to get this stuff shifted.'

She reaches for it. 'I'll take that.'

'No. We'll take it in turns.'

'Do you think we're doing the right thing?' There's uncertainty in Honor's voice. 'Maybe we should all go and look for them. If we find Danny and Jeffers it'll be six against two.'

'Jessie said they've got a knife,' Milo says.

'We can overpower them,' Meg says. 'Like Honor said,

it'll be six against two then we grab the keys to the boat and we get the hell out of here.'

'You're assuming we'll find Danny and Jeffers before we run into them,' Milo says. 'What if they hurt one of you guys before we overpower them? What if someone gets knifed and they take off in the boat? Jefferson's little first-aid kit isn't going to do shit.'

'We need weapons so we're not going in unarmed.' Meg looks around the camp. 'Where are the axes?'

I share a look with Milo. 'Jeffers has got them,' I say. 'They're in his camp.'

'I'll go and get them,' Honor says. 'I can get there and back in five minutes.'

'No!' Milo and I say simultaneously.

'And why is that?' Honor raises an eyebrow. 'Because I'm female? You can stick that sexism right up your arse, Milo.'

This is the Honor we all knew and loved before she and Danny got together.

'You can't go alone,' I say. 'It's not safe. They nearly got me into their boat. I wouldn't have got away if Danny and Jeffers hadn't distracted them.'

'Then I'll go with her.' Meg moves to stand beside Honor. 'We'll get the axes and meet you two back here.'

'No.' I shake my head. 'We're not splitting up. If one of us goes we all go.'

We creep along the beach, staying close to the jungle and make our way to Jefferson's camp. As we leave the beach and edge through the trees every snapped twig makes me turn sharply, every whoop and warble makes me freeze.

'Are you OK?' Honor mouths as we silently pick our way through the undergrowth. I nod but it's taking every ounce of courage to keep walking. Now I'm back in the jungle where I was attacked my rage has deserted me.

'Crap,' Meg breathes as we draw closer to Jefferson's camp. 'They've trashed it.'

She isn't kidding. All Jefferson's neatly arranged kit has been strewn across his camp, trampled into the ground, ripped, crushed or burnt.

'They've burnt the axes.' Milo points at the fire, and the thick wooden handles poking out from the flames.

Honor creeps from between the trees, crouches near the fire and picks up something red, crumpled and singed. 'They've tipped everything out of Jefferson's rucksack and burnt most of it. I'm pretty sure this used to be a packet of beef jerky.'

Meg swears under her breath. 'He's going to be gutted when he sees what they've done. This is his kit, his best stuff.'

'They missed these.' I move a T-shirt with my foot and duck down to pick up a packet of water purifying tablets. 'And this.' I shove the flint and steel into my pocket. 'We can still purify water and make a fire.'

'No knives.' Milo looks around then kicks at the ground. 'They're probably carrying an arsenal.'

'Not this one.' Meg holds up a knife. It's small, the type you'd use for peeling an apple.

'Well, we can't protect ourselves with *that*,' Milo says.

'We can use it to whittle spears,' I say, 'up on the clearing that Honor was talking about. Come on, let's go. This place is creeping me out.'

We make our way back along the beach then head into the jungle and take the path that leads up to the right of the waterfall. We move quietly and carefully, placing each foot gently on the jungle floor. Sweat's pouring off me and the soles of my feet are throbbing, my flip-flops long abandoned. I block out the pain. The jungle is noisier than I've ever heard it – it's as though every animal, insect and bird has woken up and is whooping or squawking to make itself heard. But there are no human sounds among the cacophony of creature cries. Not a single scream or shout.

'This must be it.' Honor gestures towards the rough patch of dirt about ten metres to our right. 'The clearing Danny found.'

I lead the way to the centre of the space then shrug off my rucksack and roll my shoulders forwards and backwards. Every muscle in my body aches. The others follow, dumping their rucksacks next to mine. Honor swigs from her water bottle while Meg just collapses onto the ground. Milo paces back and forth, a movable barrier between the edge of the jungle and us.

'Milo,' Meg hisses at him. 'Save your energy.'

He shakes his head. 'I'm fine.'

He reminds me of a caged tiger, waiting for something to get close enough that he can attack. I've never seen him like this before but I've got a pretty good idea why he's so restless; he feels bad that he's not out looking for Danny and Jeffers. He's imagining them fighting with Josh and Jack and wishes he were there to back them up. It's got nothing to do with 'being a man' or trying to be an alpha male. I feel exactly the same way.

Honor wipes her mouth with the back of her hand then screws the lid back on her water bottle and glances across at me. 'What do we do now?'

I point across the clearing to a dense patch of bamboo. 'We cut that down then we sharpen the ends.'

It's dark now and, without the light from a fire, Meg, Honor and I are sitting in pitch black around the small pile of our belongings. I managed to whittle two bamboo poles into spears before the sun set. The knife was so blunt it took for ever. The jungle sounds have changed now – the whoops and squawks have disappeared and, instead, the air is filled with buzzing, chirping and the clicking of cicadas. There's still no sign of Jeffers and Danny. It's still warm, although cooler up here than it was on the beach. But it's not the temperature that makes me shiver. It's fear. Jack and Josh could come bursting out of the trees at any second.

Milo is still refusing to sit down. He paced for what felt like hours then announced that he was going back into the jungle to look for the boys.

'You can't,' Meg said. 'What if you disappear too?'

'They're my best mates. What if something's happened to them?'

'What if you leave and something happens to us?'

That stopped him in his tracks.

152

Logically I know that, even if Jeffers and Danny *are* OK, the chances of them finding us up here tonight are slim. Jeffers won't be able to track us in the dark and there's no fire to alert them to our new camp. All I can hope is that they've got away from Jack and Josh and they've found somewhere safe to hide for the night.

'Why do this?' Honor asks again. It's a question she's asked at least half a dozen times since we sat down. 'I mean, I get that you hurt Josh's hand, Jessie, but it's not like you broke any bones. Why terrorize us like this?'

'Because they can,' Meg says flatly. 'And because they're arseholes.'

'It's my fault,' Honor says. 'If I'd have just pushed that little squit off me none of this would have happened.'

'No.' I hold out a hand. 'Don't you dare. This is *not* your fault. He shouldn't have put his hands on you in the first place. He deserved what he got.'

'I could kill them.' Milo's voice drifts through the darkness. I can barely see him, just the vaguest of shadows when he moves.

'What's the plan of action for the morning?' Meg asks, keeping her voice low. 'Assuming nothing else happens tonight.'

'We look for Jeffers and Danny,' I say. 'If we don't have any luck, or if we run out of energy, we come back here, rest, then go out again.'

'And what if we run into the brothers?' Honor asks.

'They're not going to kill us,' I say. 'They're cowards. Look at the way they acted at the pool – divide and conquer – one of them tried to distract me so the other one could crack on with you. If all four of us confront them they'll back down.'

'You think?' Meg doesn't sound convinced.

'Yes.' I try to hide the doubt in my voice. 'I do.'

'They might have left,' Honor says hopefully. 'We could creep along the edge of the beach again and climb over the rocks to see if their boat is still here.'

'Sod that,' Milo says. 'I'm done with creeping about. This is our island, not theirs.'

I wake with a start and for one terrifying second, as my nails scrape against the rough dry ground, I have no idea where I am. It's still dark, apart from the tiniest streak of light on the horizon, and the low rumble of the jungle fills my ears. There's another sound too, the low bassy tones of a male voice. Milo, I think instinctively. But Milo's asleep. I can hear the gentle rumbling of his breathing from beyond the pile of rucksacks. Could it be Danny or Jeffers? But they would have woken us up. One of the brothers then? Have they found us?

As I peer into the darkness a shadowy, male silhouette moves towards the cliff face. As he approaches the edge he twists back and circles us, stepping around the periphery. Fear floods through me as he disappears from view. What is he doing? Waiting for someone else? Penning us in? A terrifying image jumps into my head, of petrol being spilt from a can, dripping onto the ground as he walks. A full circle, a dropped match and then... BOOM, we're trapped within a wall of fire.

The figure walks past me and then pauses. I just heard the same thing he did – a rustling sound from the bushes to the ledge of the cliff edge. I glance left and right but I can't see Honor or Meg on either side of me, it's too dark and they're obscured by the pile of rucksacks.

The dark figure moves away from me towards the bush. Below the sharp drop of the cliff, the sea is quiet. It feels like the whole world is asleep apart from me and the man – teenager? – I can't be sure – walking slowly away from me.

Is it Josh? Is his brother hiding in the bush? Are they about to ambush us? I slide my hand along the ground, fingers spread wide as I search for the spear or the fruit knife. My fingertips brush against something firm and wooden and I close my hand over it. A knife this small isn't going to do much damage but it might be enough to scare Josh off. That's if he's not about to set the island alight. I sniff, subtly, pulling the warm night air into my nostrils, examining it for traces of petrol or lighter fluid, but all I smell is salt and the musty tang of our rucksacks and my own body.

Josh is stepping closer and closer to the edge of the cliff. The bush rustles again and I shift up onto my hands and knees, priming myself to run, to shove, to send him hurtling over the drop and into the sea. On the other side of the rucksacks Honor snorts in her sleep. I want to say something, to wake her and the others, but I'm scared Josh will hear me. Right now he thinks we're all asleep and I've got the element of surprise on my side. I'm going to have to push him off the cliff. It's the only way to keep the others safe.

The dark figure stumbles towards the bush, hands out-stretched, blindly waving them through the air. He's six feet from the edge of the cliff...

They made me feel so defenceless earlier, swinging me between them like a slab of meat from the butcher's yard. They made me feel weak and afraid. I'm never going to let them make me feel that way again. Let's see how much they enjoy the tables being turned.

Five feet...

I jump up onto my feet, put the knife in my pocket and ready myself to run. Pushing Josh into the sea won't kill him – Danny survived that fall. I'll just be buying us time to deal with Jack.

Four feet...

I stand up. Josh is mumbling to himself but I can't make out what he's saying, it's blocked out by the sound of the bush rustling.

Three feet...

I start to run.

Two feet. As I raise my hands to chest height ready to push, Josh speaks again.

'Danny, is that you?'

My breath catches in my throat. I know that voice. And it's not Josh. It's Jefferson!

One foot...

I make a desperate grab for the back of his T-shirt but it's slick with sweat and my fingers slip away as he steps off the cliff.

CHAPTER 20

DANNY

Day five on the island

Danny is crouching on the large bough of a tree, fast asleep, his arms loosely wrapped around the trunk, his hands and feet scratched and bleeding, when a shout wakes him. He jolts, then tightens his grip on the tree, suddenly realizing where, and how high up, he is. It was pitch black when he fell asleep, but there's the tiniest glimmer of light on the horizon where the sun is slicing its way through the dark curtain of night. A loud splash makes him turn sharply to his left. The sound came from beyond the rocks; the small patch of sea he plunged into, feet first, when he jumped off the cliff a couple of days ago. He holds himself still and listens, anticipating a second shout or another splash. None comes.

Could it be Jeffers? They were separated in the jungle hours ago. Josh and Jack were chasing them and Jeffers leapt the fallen tree that blocked their path and kept on running. But there was no way Danny could get over it with his bleeding foot. He peeled off to the left instead, his pulse pounding in his ears as he continued to run. He headed away from the beach, charging deeper and deeper into the jungle, adrenaline and fear fuelling each painful step. He ran until his chest burnt and he couldn't pull another breath into his lungs, then he dropped to his knees, panting, sweating and crying with exhaustion. He didn't care if Jack and Josh caught up with him. He couldn't take another step.

He lay on his back on the jungle floor, panting and gasping, staring up at the canopy of leaves above him, not caring whether a tarantula crawled over his face or a snake slid up the leg of his shorts. He ran his tongue over his dry lips but it didn't wet them. His mouth was bone dry. Slowly, painfully, he dragged himself to his feet and began to make his way back in the direction he'd just come from, jumping at every sound, freezing whenever a twig grazed his ankle or arm. He needed water. Without it, and in such insufferable heat, he'd die within twenty-four hours. Anuman had drummed that into them on the boat on the way over.

Arriving on the island felt like another lifetime. He'd been so excited, apprehensive too at the thought of spending a whole week with the others. It all seemed so ridiculously childish now, when their tour guide was dead and two absolute psychopaths were charging through the jungle trying to hurt his friends.

When he finally arrived at the waterfall it was all he could do not to fall head first into the swirling pool. Instead he looked cautiously around then dropped to his belly and scooped the cool water into his mouth. When he couldn't drink any more he dunked his head into the pool, gasping with pleasure as the cold water soothed his parched skin. He didn't enjoy it for long. Josh and Jack hadn't caught up with him yet, but his luck wouldn't hold out for ever. He had to find the others.

Ten minutes later, covered in sweat again and limping, he crept out of the jungle to find the camp had been deserted. All that was left were a couple of empty plastic bottles, a few sweet wrappers and several discarded T-shirts. He looked up and down the beach for his friends but the only sign they'd ever been there were the footprints to and from the sea. He felt sick with fear. Had Josh and Jack discovered them and taken them away in their boat? Was he alone on the island with Jefferson? Or worse, the only one left. He dismissed the thought. If Jack and Josh had kidnapped his friends they wouldn't have allowed them to pack up their stuff first. Milo, Meg, Jessie and Honor had to be hiding somewhere. But where?

Beyond the sea the sun was sinking low in the sky: orange, red and purple fingers creeping into the wide stretch of blue. It would be dark soon. If he ventured back into the jungle to look for the others he would risk getting lost in the dark or stumbling into Jack and Josh. No, he decided as he grabbed a coconut and a screwdriver from the pile next to the shelter, he'd find a tree to hide in and stay close to camp.

Now he stares out warily from between the branches. It's so dark he can't see more than a few feet in front of him. If he stays in the tree he's safe. The splashing could be a trap – designed to lure him out. But what if it's not? What if, right now, one of his friends is thrashing around in the inky water, desperate for help? He puts the screwdriver between his teeth and bites down on it. As weapons go it's not great but it's better than nothing.

He carefully clambers down the tree, listening for the sound of human voices, searching the darkness for danger, then he runs down the short stretch of path that leads to the camp. There's no one there, no one on the beach either – or at least, not on the tiny sliver of beach he can see. He moves carefully over the sand, slowing his pace as the rocks rise up to meet him; huge, black, jagged boulders, slippery with seaweed and wet from the spray of the sea. He climbs slowly, carefully, trying to remember the route they'd taken to go fishing, gripping the slimy surface with his fingers and toes.

As he reaches the highest point of the rock he blinks into the darkness. He can see the small stretch of sea that fills the tiny cove but there's no sound of splashing and no one calling for help. Terror reaches its dark fingers into his heart and squeezes. Silence isn't good. Silence means that whoever fell into the water isn't going to make it out.

Please, he prays. *Please don't let it be one of our group.*

Shaking with fear he carefully slides down the rocks, feet first, feeling around for flat planes.

Maybe it wasn't a person who fell, he thinks as he eases himself onto the next rock. *Maybe whoever shouted threw something off the cliff?*

He extends his leg again, the screwdriver clamped between his teeth.

And someone grabs hold of his foot.

'Bloody hell!' Danny breathes, up to his chest in water. 'Did you have to pull me in too? I nearly shat myself.'

'I couldn't risk you yelling.' Jeffers, dripping wet and shivering, eases himself out of the water and onto the rock and then reaches out a hand.

Danny takes it, then, breathing shallowly in short, sharp bursts, his heart thudding against his ribs, clambers up onto the rock beside him. He studies Jefferson's pale, pinched face and feels an unusual rush of affection, all thoughts of the phobias gone. He's never been so glad to see him. 'I thought they'd got you.'

'Same.' Jefferson breaks eye contact and rubs his hands over his face. 'Sorry, man,' he says as he looks back at Danny.

'For what?'

'Leaving you behind.' He shakes his head ruefully. 'The first rule of survival is to stick together but the adrenaline was pumping so hard I just... I...'

Danny touches his wet sleeve. 'It's cool. Don't beat yourself up.'

'I am, though. What I did was cowardly. I tried to find you, once I'd shaken them off, but it was dark and...'

'Honestly, man. It's fine. We're both OK. For now anyway.'

They both sigh heavily and neither of them says anything for a couple of seconds. Danny stares out to sea. The sun is creeping over the horizon and there's the tiniest sliver of orange light where the sky meets the sea.

He glances up at the cliff face. 'What happened up there?'

'I'm not entirely sure.' As Jeffers runs a hand through his wet hair Danny notices there's something different about him.

'You've lost your glasses.' He glances down into the dark sea. 'I'd offer to look for them for you but…'

'You wouldn't find them anyway. I got whacked round the face by a branch as I was running and they came off. I didn't have time to stop. I had to keep running.'

'Why'd you jump? Off the cliff, I mean.'

'I didn't. After I gave those twats the slip I climbed a tree and—'

'I did that too!'

Jefferson grins then raises his hand for a high five. Danny slaps it.

'So anyway,' Jeffers continues. 'I was camped out in a tree for a bit but I couldn't sleep, so I thought I'd head back to the camp to see if the others were there.' He shakes his head. 'It had been trashed.' He swears under his breath. 'I grabbed some water and headed up to the cliff top instead, to wait it out until the sun came up. I had no idea the others were already there.'

'Honor's up there?' Danny scrambles to his feet, puts a hand to his eyes to shield them from the sun and squints up towards the clearing.

'I assume so. I could just about make out a big lump of bags and what looked like four people lying around them, I was going to wake someone up but I heard a noise, a rustling from a bush near the edge of the cliff. I thought it might be the brothers, preparing to ambush us so I went to investigate. I didn't realize how close to the edge I was and I…'

'Fell.'

'I just…' He shivers. 'I plummeted into darkness. I thought I was going to die. I really thought that was it.'

Danny's blood runs cold as a memory of the first night on the island flashes up in his mind – Jefferson talking about heights and sharp drops and how much they scared him. That's three now. First snakes, then spiders and now heights. Another phobia has come true. And whoever, or whatever, was rustling in the bushes made it happen.

CHAPTER 21

JESSIE

Milo's forearm presses against mine. His skin is warm and sticky with sweat. 'Can you see anything?' he asks.

Honor, beside him, turns to look at me. 'Are you sure it was Jefferson?'

Meg sighs noisily. 'There's no one in the bush.'

The questions and comments come thick and fast as I stare down from the cliff edge into the dark sea, searching the water for any sign of Jefferson. I'm lying on my stomach with Meg, Milo and Honor crowded close.

'Are you sure you weren't dreaming?' Meg asks, on her hands and knees beside me. 'I didn't hear anything and I'm a light sleeper.'

'No.' I look at her. 'Definitely not. There was someone up here, walking around the clearing. They heard the noise in the bush too. I thought it was one of the brothers and I was going to push him over the edge but then he spoke.'

'Who spoke?'

'Jeffers. It was him. I'm sure of it. I tried to grab him but he... I couldn't. It was too late.'

'But why would he jump off the cliff?' Honor asks. 'He hates heights.'

'There!' Milo hisses, pointing downwards. 'I just saw movement. There are two people down on the rocks.'

'Where?'

I squint down at the dark mass that seems to loom out of the sea. There's nothing there. Milo must be—

'I see them!' As the weak dawn sun lights up the edge of the rocks two shapes emerge from the gloom. 'There! Right on the edge of the rocks, one standing, one sitting.'

'Is it Jeffers and Danny?' Honor asks.

'Shout out their names!' Meg says.

'No!' I hiss. 'No one shout anything. We don't know for sure that it's them.'

'I thought you said you were sure it was Jeffers.'

'I was. But...' I squint into the darkness, 'what if I'm wrong? What if we shout and it's Jack and Josh?'

Milo makes a dismissive noise. 'Screw it, I'm shouting.'

But before he can, one of the people on the rock turns towards us and waves both arms.

'It's Danny,' Honor breathes. 'It's definitely him.'

Twenty minutes later we all crowd around Danny and Jeffers and hug the hell out of them as they emerge, puffing and panting, from the jungle.

'Why are you wet too?' Honor asks Danny.

'Someone pulled me in with him!'

165

'Sit down, sit down.' Milo shepherds them towards the centre of the clearing where our bags are stacked. Jeffers hangs back.

'Are you OK?' I touch a hand to the damp sleeve of his T-shirt as he stares past the rucksacks to the cliff edge. 'I'm so sorry. I tried to stop you, but by the time I realized it was you, it was too late.'

'I thought I was going to die.' He looks at me, his pupils huge and black despite the light creeping over the horizon.

'Oh, Jeffers.' I reach out and hug him, feeling his body trembling in my arms. Neither of us says a word for several seconds then he pulls away and runs his hands through his hair.

'Are *you* OK?' he asks. 'They didn't hurt you, did they? The brothers. They didn't…' he tails off.

'No.' I shake my head. 'Josh made some pretty nasty threats but Jack warned him off.'

'Are you talking about who I think you're talking about?' Danny sidles up to us, his arm around Honor's waist.

'Do you think they've always been here?' Honor asks. 'Do you think they cut the boat cord and…?' She shudders, 'Did the thing with the spiders?'

I shrug. 'I don't know. When I searched their boat all I found were little rucksacks, the sort you'd use for day trips. And they both looked really fresh – clean clothes, clean hair – they definitely didn't look like they'd been here for a while.'

Milo walks over to us too. He rubs a hand over the back of his neck then moves his head to the left then the right, stretching out the muscles at the top of his shoulders. He looks as tense and exhausted as I feel. 'I think we should do what Meg suggested and take their boat.'

'We can't. I've already told you, they've got the keys.'

Milo looks around our small group. 'There's six of us and we're armed now. Jeffers, have you still got your knife?'

'Yep.' He reaches down and pulls it out of the top of his boots.

'I've got a screwdriver.' Danny reaches into the deep pocket in his cargo shorts.

'And we've got a fruit knife and two spears,' Honor says.

'Guys,' I say. 'I'm not sure about this.'

'No one's suggesting we kill anyone,' Milo says. 'We just want to scare them into handing over the keys.'

'That's assuming they're still here,' Jeffers says.

We all look at each other. There's only one way to find out.

'It's gone.'

I don't know whether I'm relieved or disappointed as we step out of the jungle onto the 'new beach' and stare out to sea. There's no boat bobbing on the water. Other than two pairs of footprints that lead from the jungle to the sea, there's no sign that Josh and Jack were ever here.

'Well, I guess that's that.' Milo sighs heavily then drops onto the sand and stretches out his arms and legs as he stares up the sky. 'We're stuck here for another two nights.'

Meg nudges him with the edge of her flip-flop. 'At least no one got hurt.'

As Honor and Danny wander towards the sea, and Meg makes noises about looking for fruit and heads back into the jungle with Jefferson, I plop myself onto the sand next to Milo. He turns to look at me.

'Are you OK?'

'Are *you*?'

He smiles. 'I asked first.'

The truth is I don't know how I feel. I'm glad there wasn't a fight, but I can't relax. I still feel on edge.

'I just want to get off this island, Milo. I feel like something bad's going to happen. First you fall into that pit, then Honor gets covered in spiders, then Jefferson falls off the cliff. He was lucky he landed in the sea, not on the rocks.'

He flips onto his stomach and watches Meg and Jefferson as they disappear into the jungle. 'Do you think my sister's OK?'

I follow his gaze. 'I don't think anyone's OK.'

'I just… I dunno. One minute she's sniping at me, the next she's acting all concerned.'

'Isn't that always the way it's been between you?'

'Well, yeah, pretty much. But something's bugging her and she won't tell me what it is. Whenever I try and talk to her she shrugs me off. Has she said anything to you?'

'Not a word.' This is probably where I should tell him what Jeffers and Danny told me, about Meg saying he's still in love with his ex, but I don't feel ready to have that conversation. Particularly not now, after the night we've all had.

Instead I look towards the sea where Danny and Honor are walking hand in hand through the shallow water. 'Honor's so different when she's with him.'

Milo sighs. 'He can't see it but he's smothering her.'

'Yeah, he's been very overprotective this holiday. Was he like this last year?'

Milo nods. 'Yeah, not quite this bad though.'

'I keep seeing flashes of the old Honor,' I say, 'like when she wanted to play water polo back at the hotel, and earlier at the old camp, when she told you to shove your sexism up your arse.'

Milo laughs.

'But the rest of the time, when she's with Danny, she's irritated, quiet or weepy. Something's not right but she won't talk about it.'

'Seems like we're all keeping quiet about something.'

'Are *you*?'

He meets my gaze, his dark eyes serious and intense. His lips part, as though he's about to say something then looks back at the sparkling sea. 'Nah.'

We lapse into silence for a few seconds then Milo says, 'Are you sure that Jack and Josh haven't been here the whole time?'

'Pretty sure. Their clothes were really clean. They looked like they'd just arrived.'

'But most of us have still got clean clothes in our rucksacks. We just haven't been arsed to change into them. For all we know Dick One and Dick Two could have been camped out on the other side of the island.'

'But we'd have seen them, wouldn't we? If they'd arrived at the same time as us. Our camp was right on the beach. We'd have seen their boat.'

'Not if we were in the woods with Anuman collecting fruit and chopping down trees for the shelter.'

I consider it. We were probably setting up camp for a good two or three hours on the first day, but it does seem like a bit of a coincidence that that's when they chose to arrive – in that tiny window of time when we couldn't see them.

'OK,' I say. 'Say we go with that theory, that they camped on the other side of the island on day one. How do we know that's not where they are now? With their boat?'

'We don't.'

'Oh God.' I sit up and rest my head in my hands. 'So they could come back.'

Milo props himself up on one elbow. 'There is one way to test my theory.'

'What's that?'

'How much energy have you got?'

I laugh dryly. 'None. Why?'

He nods his head towards the trees as Meg and Jeffers reappear with armfuls of coconuts, mangos and bananas. 'What if you fill yourself up with some fruit?'

'Milo! Stop being so obscure. What are you suggesting?'

'That we go for a swim.'

CHAPTER 22

DANNY

Danny throws an arm across Honor's shoulders as they walk, side by side, along the shore, the waves lapping at their feet. Honor hugs herself tightly, but she doesn't shrug him off.

'Are you all right?' he asks.

She sighs deeply. 'I just want to go home, Danny. I can't take much more of this.'

He squeezes her shoulder. 'I know, but we'll get through this together. Two more nights and they'll send someone to look for us.'

'Two more nights?' She laughs dryly. 'I don't think I've slept properly since we got here. None of us have. I feel like a zombie.'

'A beautiful zombie, though.'

'Yeah. I really must get a selfie of my spotty, mosquito-bitten face for Instagram.'

Now it's Danny's turn to sigh. He knows better than to argue the point, but it hurts to see her so utterly miserable.

There was a time when just knowing she was going to see him in the evening was enough to stop her worrying about an exam or forget about a friend she'd fallen out with. But on the island nothing he does, nothing he says cheers her up. She's by his side but, emotionally, she's completely unreachable.

'One day,' he says, casting an arm wide, 'all this will just be a memory. We've just got to get through the next forty-eight hours.'

Honor stops walking and rubs a hand over her forehead. She moans softly.

'What's up?' Danny asks.

'I've got the most horrible headache. I left my sunglasses in the first camp and the sun's killing my eyes.'

'I'll go and get them for you, if you want.'

'Would you?' She smiles gratefully up at him.

'Of course. Come on, let's get you into the shade.'

He feels something inside him lighten as they walk, hand in hand, over the hot sand towards the shade of the trees. She still needs him, she still appreciates him and he's pretty sure she still loves him. Getting her sunglasses is nothing. He'd walk over hot coals if it made her smile.

Danny stands waist deep in the sea and steadies himself. According to Jessie, the swim round the rocks to their first camp isn't too arduous but he's still nervous. He needs to swim far enough out that his feet won't touch the floor. That wouldn't worry him in a pool, or if he was surfing back in the UK, but there aren't man-eating sharks off the coast of Cornwall. Anuman reassured them, on the boat over, that although bull and tiger sharks had occasionally been spotted in the Thai waters they preferred to stay at depth. But how deep was deep?

'Danny!' Jeffers comes running towards him, waving an arm. 'If you're going back to our old camp could you have a look in the boat to see if you can find any fishing hooks or twine?'

'The boat? *Anuman's boat?*'

'Yeah. I'm going to set some animal traps and Meg's up for a bit of fishing.'

'But… but Anuman's still in there.'

Jeffers shrugs. 'I know. Dan, it'll be fine. There's a sheet over him.'

'But he'll…'

'Hold your nose then. Come on. Do it for her if no one else. She needs a decent meal.' Jefferson inclines his head towards Honor, sitting with her back against a palm tree and her eyes shut.

'OK, OK. I'll do it.'

'Good man.'

As Jeffers ambles away Danny thumps himself on the chest with a clenched fist. *Come on! You can do this*, he tells himself. He thumps himself again then again, then he wades deeper into the water and begins to swim.

He has to fight against angry currents that threaten to hurl him into the rocks but he makes it past successfully then swims his way into the shallows and lowers his feet onto the soft, fine sand and walks out of the sea and onto the beach.

He heads for their old camp first. Where once there were

rough timber frames, palm roofs and banana leaf mattresses, now there's just two piles of wood and scattered greenery. Josh and Jack have trashed the place. Danny grits his teeth, rage burning in the pit of his stomach. Stupid bastards. He never should have run. He should have faced up to them and to hell with the consequences.

He scans the camp looking for any sign of Honor's sunglasses then spots something glinting in the sand. He crouches down. The glasses are broken: one arm snapped off and one frame smashed. He chucks them back down again.

He takes a steadying breath and forces himself to look at the boat, at the sleeping bag covering their dead guide and the rough soles of Anuman's bare feet peeking from beneath the tarp.

His feet?

He blinks, frowning as he searches through his brain, trying to work out why his guide's feet are making him feel so unsettled. A memory flashes back, of Anuman driving the minibus, shouting advice back at them.

'Don't go *anywhere* in bare feet.'

When they'd congregated in the hotel lobby in shorts and flip-flops Jefferson, in his sandy-coloured boots and long beige trousers, was the only one who'd received an approving nod.

Anuman was definitely wearing boots when they'd been cutting wood because he'd told Danny off for wielding an axe wearing flip-flops.

'What if the axe cuts off your toes?'

'Then I'll buy smaller shoes!'

It had raised a laugh from Milo but Anuman had tutted and shaken his head. It was then that Danny had clocked his footwear: boots, old and worn but sturdy as hell.

But there aren't any boots on Anuman's feet now, and Danny can't remember him ever taking them off, apart from to sleep. A dark thought forms in his mind. He'd assumed the boot prints were Jefferson's and he was responsible for the spiders. But it wasn't him, he knows that now. Jefferson's phobia came true when he fell off the cliff edge and there's no way he could have faked that. Had someone else taken Anuman's boots off and traipsed around in them to make it look like Jeffers was responsible? But why do that? Unless they were trying to get them to turn against each other, deliberately ripping their already fractured group apart.

CHAPTER 23

JESSIE

'Are you sure you're up for this?' I side-eye Milo as we wade into the sea. Our swimming stuff is back at the clearing, crammed into our rucksacks, so I'm in my bra and knickers while Milo's wearing knee-length khaki shorts. My stomach feels heavy and bloated from the fruit we've just gorged on but I'm buzzing with adrenaline and nerves. 'It's a long way to swim and it's going to be exhausting.'

He flings one tanned arm across his body and holds it there, stretching out his right shoulder. 'I think you'll find I'm in pretty good shape for someone who spent the first half of the holiday doing laps of the pool on an inflatable flamingo.'

That makes me snort.

'Ready?' I ask.

Milo doesn't miss a beat. He plunges into the water and starts to swim. I leap in too, relishing the coolness of the water on my skin. After five minutes or so of steady crawl around the perimeter of the island Milo lifts his head and treads water.

'You OK?' I ask.

'Yeah.' He grins. 'Just slowing down for you to catch up.'

'Catch up? I've been swimming alongside you the whole time. I'd be halfway round the island by now if I went at my own pace!'

'Seriously.' He presses a hand to his chest. 'I don't know how you used to do this for fun. My heart's on overdrive.'

'So we take it a bit slower. There's no hurry, is there?'

'I guess not.'

We swim in silence for a couple of minutes, the hot sun beating down and the gulls circling and squawking overhead. The island looks beautiful from the sea, the white gold of the sand framed by the emerald green of the trees. Anuman told us the owner rents it out for weddings too. Weird, though, imagining a bride in a white dress holding hands with her smartly dressed husband on the beach instead of a handful of teens in sweat-soaked clothes.

'Milo?' I glance at him as he switches from swimming on his back to a lazy breaststroke. Being in the water makes me feel more relaxed than I have in a long time. Braver too. 'Can I ask you something?'

'Sure.'

'Do you miss your girlfriend?'

'What?' He shoots me a sideways glance.

'Bella. Do you miss her?'

'She's not my girlfriend.'

'Potato potatoe. You haven't answered my question.'

He stops swimming and turns to look at me, his brown eyes shining in the hot, midday sun. 'Why are you asking?'

'No reason.' I drop my face into the water and break into a crawl, speeding away from him.

Why did I just ask him that? Is that what I'm about now – torturing myself? How did I expect him to answer?

Of course I don't miss her. I'm in love with you.

I mentally shake myself. It was a stupid thing to ask and I only did it because there's a part of me that refuses to believe that what happened between us on the beach on day two wasn't just friendship. A stupid part of me. A very, very stupid part.

I power through the water until I'm too tired to swim another stroke and then I flip onto my back, close my eyes and let the sun warm my face. If there's another group holiday after this one I'm pretty sure our parents won't let us out of their sight.

'Hey! You! Rebecca Adlington!' Milo's voice cuts through my water-plugged ears. 'Are you trying to kill me or what?'

I turn my head, grinning as he splashes towards me – half doggy paddle, half front crawl. He rolls his eyes as he gets closer. 'Hellooo! We're not all Olympic swimmers, you know.'

'Wanna take a break?' We're about a quarter of the way round the island and a tiny cove has opened up in the midst of so much jungle.

'Definitely.' He sticks out his tongue and pants like a dog. 'I need a drink. My tongue's like sandpaper. We should have brought water.'

'There might be mangos over there.' I point towards a clump of trees on the edge of the cove.

Milo nods. 'That'll do.'

We flop onto the sand, too knackered to drag ourselves into the jungle to look for water or fruit, and stretch out our arms and legs. Neither of us says anything for several minutes, then Milo's stomach gurgles noisily, making me laugh.

He rolls onto his side to look at me. 'What's the first thing you're going to order back at the hotel?'

'Massive burger, fries, onion rings and a chocolate milk-shake.'

'You didn't even have to think about that!'

'I've been fantasizing about food for days.'

'Me too. I'm going to eat a bowl of Thai green curry the size of my head.'

We lapse into an easy silence again and I dig my fingers into the sand, raking them back and forth.

'Jessie?' Milo says.

'Yeah?'

'You do think they'll look for us, don't you?'

'Our parents?'

'Yeah.'

I turn to look at him. 'What makes you think they won't?'

'I'm pretty sure my mum and dad won't worry until we're at least a couple of hours late. They'll have to drive to the harbour and get a boat. What if they can't find us?'

'They'll find us.'

'You think?'

'Yeah, course.' I say the two words quickly before my voice can betray me. The truth is I'm scared too. I haven't even let myself think about how Mum and Dad will react when they realize that we haven't returned from our trip. They've been through so much already they'll fear the worst and... I stare out at the sea, focusing on the way the sunlight catches on the water, making it sparkle and glint. I can't do it. I can't let myself think about the anguish on my parents' faces, or the fear in their eyes when they're told I haven't come back.

'Good.' Milo lies back on the sand again and folds his hands under his head. I stare at his side profile for a couple of seconds then turn my face back up to the sun and close my eyes.

'I've been thinking about the phobia thing,' he says after a beat.

I tense. I still haven't told him about the snake. 'What about it?'

'Danny seems convinced that they're coming true but it's a coincidence, isn't it? We're on a jungle island, there are loads of spiders everywhere. We probably have dozens of them scuttling over us when we go to sleep.' I shudder but say nothing.

'And Jeffers falling off a cliff,' Milo continues. 'It was dark and he couldn't see where he was going because he'd lost his glasses.'

'There was rustling in the bushes,' I remind him.

'We were all hyped to hell last night and jumping at shadows. It was probably an animal.'

'That's what I thought,' I say.

Milo's brow creases as he tries to read my face.

'What is it?' he asks. 'There's something you're not telling me.'

I'm going to have to tell him. Danny's probably told Honor by now and she'll tell Meg, who'll probably ask Jeffers if he saw the snake and then everyone will know apart from Milo.

I sit up and brush the sand off my hands and legs. 'Another phobia came true.'

'What?' Milo sits up too.

'You weren't alone in the pit.'

'What do you mean *not alone*?'

'Danny saw a snake.'

His jaw drops and he stares at me with horrified eyes, unable to speak.

'It was a cobra. But it was OK,' I add hurriedly, 'because obviously it didn't bite you and—'

Milo scrabbles to his feet and heads back towards the water's edge, his face a fury. 'And Danny kept quiet about this?'

'He didn't want to scare you.' I put a hand on his arm but he snatches it away. 'Milo, if he'd said anything you would have freaked out. You wouldn't have been able to move, never mind get out of the pit.'

'Bullshit.'

'We saw you freak out before, remember? That time at the zoo. You wouldn't go into the reptile enclosure and—'

'Who else knows? About the snake?'

'I... just me. Danny said I was the first one he'd told.'

'Yeah, right.' He laughs dryly. 'Everyone knows, don't they? That's why no one has said anything because oh no, what if Milo freaks out again? What if he cries?'

'That's not true.'

'I just, I… argggh.' He presses his hands to his face and inhales noisily through his nose. His whole body is shaking.

'Milo.' I put a hand on his shoulder. 'It's OK. No one's going to judge you.'

He lowers his hands from his face and looks at me. 'Well, *you* wouldn't.'

'I'm scared too, Milo. What if the next phobia that comes true is mine? And I'm not talking about vomiting.'

'But my phobia is irrational. Yours is understandable…' He pauses, his gaze flickering towards my hands. 'You've got good reason to be afraid of fire.'

'Thanks for reminding me.'

'Jessie.' Milo clasps one of my hands between his as I try to turn away. 'I'm here for you if you want to talk about it.'

I shake my head mutely.

'I know it's not the same but we miss Tom too. I know he didn't come on holiday for a few years but… we knew him, we remember him. I can't… I can't believe he's really gone. I'm so, so sorry.'

I can't speak. My throat is thick with tears. Every word Milo speaks is like a knife in my guts. I don't want his sympathy. Not when what happened to Tom was my fault.

'Don't.' Milo grabs my hand as my fingers reach for the soft skin of my forearm. 'Jessie, please don't hurt yourself. Talk to me.'

'I can't, Milo.' I pull away and scrabble to my feet. 'I just can't!'

'Jessie, wait!' His voices follows me as I run towards the sea. It fades as I launch myself into the water, then disappears as I swim down, down, down and the sea washes the tears from my cheeks.

CHAPTER 24

DANNY

There's no sign of Milo and Jessie on the new beach when Danny swims back round the rocks empty-handed. As he walks out of the sea his mind whirs as he tries to process what he just saw. Did the Brothers Grimm steal Anuman's boots to frame Jeffers for the spiders? Have they been hiding the whole time? Creeping around in the dark and earwigging conversations? But why grab Jessie? Why not continue to hide and make more phobias come true?

But neither of the boys looked as though they'd been camped out anywhere and Jessie said all they had in their boat were a couple of day packs. It made more sense that they'd been hanging out by the hotel pool, getting more and more pissed off about what Jessie had done and decided to hire a boat to scare the hell out of her. So who *did* steal Anuman's boots? Either there's someone else on the island, or someone in the camp is responsible. But who? And why? The only people whose phobias haven't come true are him, Meg and Jessie.

So who's behind it all – Meg or Jessie?

He can't imagine Meg digging a pit, capturing a snake and luring her brother towards it. Jessie then? Two years ago he wouldn't have believed it of her but she's changed. There's a weird fearlessness she never used to have. Old Jessie would never have driven her chair leg into someone's hand. But why would she decide to torture her own friends by making all their phobias come true?

Does she think they don't care about her? Is that why she's lashing out? He's pretty sure no one's asked her about her brother. He was talking to Milo, Meg, Jeffers and Honor about Tom the night before they left for the island, when they were all sitting poolside. They all felt they should say something but no one knew what to say.

I'm sorry. That's what adults said when someone died, wasn't it?

I'm sorry.

How the hell would that help? He said sorry half a dozen times a day at school – when he forgot his homework, brushed past someone in the corridor or accidentally stood on someone's toe. How could those same two words be applied to someone dying? It wasn't enough. But what was the alternative? *I heard you watched your brother die. Holy shit, that's awful. How do you go on with life after something like that happens to you?* But he couldn't say that either because it was too raw, too brutal, so instead he'd chosen to say nothing at all.

As Danny draws closer to the small patch of shade where Meg and Honor are sitting, fanning themselves with palm leaves, he wrestles with himself. Should he tell them what he suspects about Jessie or should he keep it to himself? Honor senses that she's being watched and looks up. Her smile fades as she glances at his empty hands.

'Sorry,' Danny says. 'Your sunglasses were broken.'

She shrugs as though to say *never mind*, then leans over to Meg and whispers something in her ear. Danny turns away, paranoia running hot through his veins. Is she complaining to Meg about him? Telling her what a terrible boyfriend he is and how she's going to dump him the moment they get back to the hotel?

Danny's head pounds as he heads for the shore. It's this island, it's messing with his head. Honor probably wasn't even talking about him just then. There are a hundred things she could have whispered in Meg's ear. Why did he have to assume the worst?

He stops walking and rubs his hands over his face then stares up at the cloudless sky. He's tired and he's hungry. No wonder he can't think straight. He'll go back to the girls, grab whatever fruit he can cram in his mouth and find somewhere to have a nap. A good nap and he'll be thinking straighter again.

Yes, that's what he'll do. He blinks, the bright sun burning his retinas, and lowers his gaze to the beach. He blinks again.

There's a message, written in the sand less than a foot away from him, on the very edge of the sea.

One of you will die.

CHAPTER 25

JESSIE

I resurface, my chin clearing the water, then glance back at the beach. Milo's walking along the sand holding an armful of huge banana leaves. I tread water as he places two leaves on the sand, one vertically, the other crossing it horizontally.

T

He selects three more leaves and puts them next to the first two.

A

I wait for Milo to look out to sea but he doesn't. He continues to walk across the sand laying leaves down, one after another.

TALK

Arms empty he walks back into the jungle then returns after a few minutes, arms loaded up with banana leaves again. He spells out another word.

TO

He takes a step to his left and lays down more leaves. Only when he's finished placing the last leaf does he look out to sea.

TALK TO ME.

I stare back at him, my heart twisting in my chest. I don't know if I *can* talk to him. I haven't talked to anyone about what happened last year. Not to Mum and Dad, not to my teachers, not to my friends at school, no one. My parents tried to get me to go and see a counsellor. I made it as far as the chair in her office but, as soon as she tipped her head to one side and asked me how I was feeling, in a voice like warm honey, I was out of the door.

Mum drove me home and I locked myself away in my room. I knew my parents were worried about me but I couldn't drag myself out of the dark pit in my head. I didn't want to talk to them. I didn't want to talk to anyone. I just wanted the world to stop so I could get off.

Love wasn't a good thing, it was the worst thing in the world. If I hadn't loved Tom as much as I had then I wouldn't feel as though my heart had been ripped from my body. The answer was to stop caring. To shut myself down emotionally. For ever. I even googled 'how do you turn off your feelings?' but I didn't like the answers. I didn't want to go on medication or learn to meditate. I didn't want to dial my feelings down or learn to deal with them. I wanted to stop feeling. Full stop.

I knew psychopaths and sociopaths were in control of their feelings so I googled 'films about psychopaths and sociopaths' and watched every film on the list. Not one taught me how to turn off my emotions… until the last one. It was *Dangerous Liaisons* starring John Malkovich and Glenn Close. It was a period drama about a man and a woman battling each other for control and playing games with other people's lives. I was going to turn it off because… how could it be relevant to my life? But then Glenn Close's character had this scene where she talked about how she might appear calm on the surface but inside she was battling her emotions. She said that when she was fifteen and coming out into society she'd appear cheerful during dinner but, under the table, she'd stick a fork in the back of her hand. I don't know why that image lodged itself so firmly in my mind but it did. That's when I started twisting the skin on my forearm. It wasn't a fork in the back of my hand but it was near enough.

I look back at Milo, standing on the beach behind a row of banana leaves.

He just wants to talk.

Milo's eyes don't leave mine as I walk up the sand towards him, rubbing my hands over my biceps, even though it's not cold.

'That's um…' I incline my head towards the sentence made out of leaves, 'interesting.'

He half smiles. 'Nothing's ever easy with you, is it, Jess?'

'Ha! Says you.'

'So…' There's a shift in his expression. The sparkle disappears from his eyes and it's replaced with a strained seriousness I've rarely seen. He's nervous too. I can tell from the way he's repeatedly clenching and unclenching his hands.

He's torn. He feels like he should talk to me about what happen to Tom but he's scared to.

I don't know what I'll do if I open up. I could cry, I could rock, I could scream, I could pinch myself, I could run away. Or maybe all of them, one after another. I've been holding myself together for so long I'm scared that if I lift the lid on my emotions all the pain and the fear and the guilt I've been suppressing will bubble over and scald us both.

'Milo,' I say. 'I'll talk to you, but not about Tom.'

I can see the relief in his eyes. 'OK, that's fine. Whatever you want, Jessie.'

'Shall we sit down then?'

'Sure, 'course.'

We pretty much sit where we're standing – a good foot or so separating us. I run my hands over my hair and squeeze out the seawater. Then, not sure what to do next, I inspect my fingernails. Now we've agreed to talk we've both been struck dumb.

Out of the corner of my eye I see Milo rub a hand over the back of his neck. 'There's um… there's something we need to clear up.'

'What's that then?'

'I'm not in love with my ex.'

He raises his gaze from the sand and looks at me, as though challenging me to disagree with him.

'OK.' I cross my arms over my chest and hang on to my shoulders, suddenly, weirdly aware that, other than a bra and knickers and khaki shorts, we're pretty much naked. 'Your sister seems to think you are.'

'Meg thinks I'm in still love with Bella?' His brow furrows. 'But I was the one who split up with her. It wasn't working. We were arguing all the time and it was stressing me out.'

'She told Danny that you're infatuated with her. I think she told Jeffers, too.'

'Oh God.' He blows out his cheeks in frustration. 'Bella was – is – Meg's best friend. And she's pissed off with me for dumping her. I guess when we came here, she saw that I was...' He drifts off, suddenly unable to maintain eye contact with me.

'That you were what?'

My heart's thudding against my rib cage and I'm breathing so shallowly I feel faint.

'That I was...' He swallows uncomfortably and looks back at me. 'That I was spending a lot of time with you. And... I guess she... she...'

My stomach lurches uncontrollably. I feel like I want to cry or run or cover my ears and shout *LA LA LAH!* at the top of my voice but I'm rooted to the spot and I can't tear my eyes away from him.

'I guess she...' He swallows again. 'I guess she realized that I was... I am...' He takes a shaky breath. 'When my mum told me what had happened to Tom, I wanted to get on the Tube and come and see you. I wanted... I just wanted to hold you. I couldn't bear to think of you going through all that pain on your own.'

I wasn't alone, I want to tell him. *Mum and Dad were with me*. But pain isn't something you can share. You can't scoop out a handful and let someone else carry it for you. Other people around you may be in pain too and you can cry with them, talk to them and hug them, but your pain is your own.

Milo continues to look at me, his eyes swimming with emotion. If I reached out my right hand I could touch him. That's all I'd need to do to close the space between us. Reach out a hand. There's only a foot or so of sand between us but it so easily could be a mile.

Milo seems to sense my hesitancy because his head drops, his shoulders droop and his arms hang limply at his sides. It's as though something within him has crumpled, pulling his body down along with it.

'I'm sorry, Jessie. I shouldn't have put that on you. I know you just see me as a friend and—'

I twist towards him and reach for his hands. As our fingers touch he gasps, his breath juddering in his throat. His eyes search my face, bewildered and uncomprehending.

'I don't see you as a friend, Milo.'

It takes a second or two for my words to sink in then his face softens, his lips part, he tips his head down towards mine and he kisses me.

'You OK?' Milo asks as we near the island and the small strip of beach appears before us. We've swum around the whole island and we're both exhausted and dehydrated. After the kiss at the cove, and then some more kisses, we waded back into the sea. We set off at a pace, keen to return to the others before the sun set. It didn't take us long to discover that there was no beach on the other side of the island. It was pretty much one long line of rocks. Milo punched the air. I whooped with relief. No more running. No more creeping around. No more fear. We continued our swim, but at a more leisurely pace. No sign of Jack, Josh or their boat. They'd definitely gone.

'Jess?' Milo asks again. 'You OK?'

OK? I don't think I've stopped smiling once since he kissed me. We lay on the sand in the cove for what felt like for ever, just staring at each other, smiling and chatting, laughing softly. There were moments of silence too when he'd touch a hand to my cheek and shake his head softly as though he couldn't believe what had happened between us. I couldn't believe it either. We'd known each other since we were babies and there we were, lying on a soft white Thai beach, arms and legs entwined, looking into each other's eyes feeling like our lives had just begun. All the fears, all the worries, all the terror I'd felt about letting myself love him had evaporated the moment our lips touched and we kissed.

After an age we dragged ourselves up and ran, screaming and laughing, into the sea where we played like children, splashing each other and diving under the water to grab each other's legs. It was only as the sun began to sink in the sky that we realized why we were there in the first place.

'I'm good,' I say to Milo now. 'But I'm *starving*. I hope Jefferson's managed to catch something to eat.'

'That wasn't what I meant.'

I twist round in the water to look at him. 'What did you mean?'

'Are you OK with the others knowing about us?'

The *us* makes me smile. Among all the laughing and the playing and the kissing we haven't exactly had 'the chat'. Neither of us has mentioned the future or what will happen when we get home, but *us* makes me think that this isn't a one-off for Milo. It's not for me either.

'Yeah.' I smile. 'Of course.'

We don't hold hands as we walk out of the sea on tired legs but we do 'accidentally' bump against each other's shoulders, glancing and grinning and trying not to laugh. Only a fool would fail to notice that something's going on, but, instead of getting the third degree as we walk up to the others, no one gives us more than a nod in acknowledgement. Meg and Honor are sitting together, leaning against a thick-trunked palm, chatting conspiratorially, Jeffers is over near the rocks, wading in the water with a spear in his hand, and Danny is sitting alone by a fire that wasn't there when we left. His knees are gathered up to his chest and he's staring into the flames.

'All right, Dan,' Milo says, settling down beside him. 'We swam round the island. No sign of Jack and Josh, you'll be pleased to hear.'

He waits for a reaction but none comes. Instead Danny raises his chin to look at me as I pull a T-shirt over my wet bra. The strangest expression crosses his face. I force a smile despite the strange mood that's radiating from him like a black cloud. 'You all right?'

He smiles tightly. 'Are you?'

I look from him to Milo, but he looks as confused as I feel. What the hell happened while we were gone?

I drift away, towards Meg and Honor. They stop talking as I approach but, unlike Danny, they smile warmly. Well, Honor does. There's suspicion in Meg's dark eyes. I ignore it and crouch down. I'm shattered from all the swimming and all I want to do is stretch out on the sand and sleep but I need to find out what's going on with Danny. Is it something to do with Bella? Does he still think that Milo's leading me on? But why look so angry with me and not Milo? It doesn't make sense.

'You all right?' Honor asks. 'You were gone *ages*. Did you see them? Are they still here?'

I shake my head. 'Nah, they've gone.'

'Oh thank God.' She exhales heavily. 'That's one less thing to worry about.'

'Talking of worried...' I glance back at Danny, who's still staring into the fire, either listening to Milo talk, or completely ignoring him, I can't be completely sure. 'Is he OK?'

'Yeah, I think so, why?'

'You sure? Has something happened since we left?'

'Nothing exciting. Danny swam to the old camp to look for my sunglasses and Jeffers asked him to look for some fishing hooks but he came back empty-handed.'

'Nothing happened while he was gone?'

'Not that he mentioned. Why?'

'He just... He seems a bit off with me, that's all.'

'Why would he be off with you?'

'I don't know.'

'He's...' She pauses. 'He's not been himself for a few days. He's really jumpy.'

I look at Danny. His face looks drawn, despite the healthy tan. 'We've only got two more nights here and then we can all go back to normal.'

Go back to normal? I don't even know what that means. I don't know about the others but this island has changed me and not just physically – I don't think twice about stripping down to my bikini anymore. It's not down to Milo and what happened in the cove either; something shifted in my head before that. Maybe it's the way we've all had to pull together since Jack and Josh appeared. I don't feel like an outsider anymore. We're all in this together.

'Guys!' Jefferson traipses up the beach with a medium-sized fish hanging from the tip of one finger. As he approaches the fire Danny says something to Milo then scrabbles to his feet and heads off in the other direction.

'See,' Honor hisses. 'He's not just being weird with you. He's off with everyone.'

'I think we should pack up,' Jefferson announces. 'Get back to our old camp for the night. It won't take me five minutes to start another fire.'

Milo shakes his head. 'We can't. Danny said it's been trashed. Those two knobheads couldn't just leave, could they?'

'They trashed my camp too,' Jeffers says miserably.

'Have you been back there?' I ask.

'Yeah. I managed to salvage a few bits and bobs, mostly stuff I'd hung in the trees.' He nods towards his rucksack. 'It's all in there, everything I've got left. Everything else was burnt.'

'I'm sorry.'

'It's just stuff.' He shrugs then looks back at Milo. 'Did they burn all the wood in the old camp?'

'I don't think so. Dan said there wasn't a fire, just a big mess.'

'No point us chopping down a load of trees here when we can reuse the timber. I think we head back to our old camp through the jungle and get it sorted. It'll be dark soon so we really need to get going if we want to be set up for the night.'

'I'm in.' Meg gets to her feet and holds out a hand to Honor.

'Yeah.' She nods. 'Me too.'

As Milo gets to his feet he glances at me. 'Coming?'

I nod and take the hand he offers me, but as I try and get to my feet my legs wobble beneath me and I plop back down again.

Milo smiles. 'Is our Olympic swimmer tired by any chance?'

'Shattered. But I can't leave you guys to do all the hard work.'

'Tell you what,' Jeffers says. 'Why don't you stay here with the rucksacks? That way we'll all make it through the jungle a bit quicker. We'll pop back and grab them when we're done. Have a nap,' he adds. 'You look shattered.'

'Danny!' Honor shouts. 'We're going to the old camp. Are you coming?'

Danny doesn't reply. He's standing at the water's edge at the far end of the beach staring down at his feet.

'Leave him.' Jeffers touches her on the shoulder. 'He's in a weird mood. Coming, Milo?'

He nods. 'You guys go on ahead. I'll catch up.'

We both watch as Jeffers and Honor disappear into the jungle. Meg, trailing behind, turns to look back at us. Her eyes dart from Milo to me and she frowns, then swiftly turns and runs to rejoin the others.

'She knows,' I say.

'Of course she does.'

'She doesn't look happy about it.'

'She'll get used to it.' He bends down to kiss me. 'I wish I could stay here, with you.'

'Why don't you?'

'Because some of us aren't slackers!' We both laugh then he kisses me again and stands up. 'Seriously, though. Do you want me to stay?'

'No.' I smile up at him. 'I'll be fine. I just need a half-hour nap.'

He reaches round, pulls a thin blanket from his rucksack and hands it to me.

'Just don't sleep too close to the fire.' A split second after he says the word 'fire' he widens his eyes in horror as the implications of what he just said sink in.

'It's fine.' I reach up and squeeze his fingers. 'I know what you meant.'

CHAPTER 26

DANNY

Danny stares down at his feet, his stomach hollowing and twisting like a shell. It's gone, the message in the sand.

One of you will die.

Of course it has. It's been washed away by the sea. Or was it even there in the first place? It was, he knows it was. He wouldn't have rushed over to Honor and Meg, his heart in his throat and his forehead beaded with sweat, if there wasn't anything to panic about. But when he'd reached them and they'd both looked up with alarm written all over their faces he'd found that he couldn't speak. He had a choice – tell them the truth and terrify them or keep it to himself and deal with it. But he hadn't dealt with it, had he? He'd plonked himself down by the fire and stared into the flames hoping an answer would magically come to him. He could tell Jeffers, of course. That was the first thought that leapt into his brain. But Jeffers would immediately take charge, making decisions and telling Danny what to do like he was a little school kid who couldn't do anything for himself. No, he wouldn't tell Jeffers. He wouldn't tell anyone until he knew who he could trust. He'd keep it to himself and work out who was behind it.

Only the message had unnerved him so much he couldn't think straight.

One of you will die.

Die. Not fall in a pit with a snake, not wake in the night covered in spiders, not fall off a cliff before dawn. Die.

It wasn't a vague threat; it was a message meant for him. Your greatest fear is coming true next, Danny. Honor's going to die.

Two nights, that's how long they had left before help would arrive. Just two nights, forty-eight hours. It was nothing; a weekend would pass in a heartbeat back at home. One minute he'd be traipsing out of the school gates then he'd blink (or at least it would feel that way), and he'd be traipsing back in again. Forty-eight hours on the island was a different matter. So much could happen in such a small passage of time, so much had *already* happened.

How would they try and kill her? he wonders. Drown her? He won't let her go into the sea alone. Burn her? He turns instinctively to look at Jessie, curled up near the fire. He can't even begin to imagine what she went through. And he doesn't want to. Besides, she's one of the suspects.

Might they stab her? Hack her to death? The thought of anything, *anything*, happening to his girlfriend makes him want to vomit with fear.

The answer is not to sleep. He'll sit by the fire and stay

awake for forty-eight hours, keeping watch until someone comes to rescue them.

As he stares down at the sand he suddenly becomes aware of how rapidly his heart is beating in his chest and of the blood thumping in his ears. He looks at his hands. They're trembling uncontrollably.

Breathe, he tells himself. *Breathe, it's just a panic attack.*

But then his vision starts to blur and he's hot, so hot and sweaty he feels as though his skin is wrapped in clingfilm and it's tightening around his chest and his heart is beating faster and faster and faster. He drops to his knees and splashes seawater onto his face, but as he closes his eyes all he can see is Anuman's face, his skin leathery and grey, pulled tight over his bones and his jaw, slack and open, his tongue lolling out of his mouth.

Death is the one thing you can't control.

The tremors in Danny's hands grow stronger as he presses them against his own face and his fingertips tap, tap, tap on his cheekbones and temples. His arms begin to vibrate, his shoulders shake and his whole body quivers and quakes as his vision blurs and his heart throws itself against his rib cage, beating faster and faster and faster.

It's a panic attack. It's just a panic attack.

But his body has stopped listening to his mind and his breathing is sharp and shallow and the sea's growing darker and narrower and his world's turning black.

This is what death feels like, says a voice in his head.

He tries to shout for help but there's no air in his lungs.

It takes every ounce of energy to crawl out of the sea and back onto the sand.

Danny lies on the sand for what feels like for ever, waiting for the final lurch of his heart. But his heart doesn't stop beating and he doesn't black out. Instead, very, very gradually his pulse begins to slow, his breathing deepens and his vision returns to normal. He reaches his fingers into the sand and rakes it over and over, relishing the sensation of the soft grains under his fingertips. Every muscle in his body feels weak and exhausted and his brain feels numb. It was a panic attack, just a panic attack. Honor's not going to die.

As he continues to dig his fingers into the sand he hears a soft whimpering sound from further up the beach. He freezes, listening intently. The sound gets louder. It's not whimpering anymore. It's a screech of pain. He looks towards Jessie, the only other person on the beach apart from him. She's lying with a blanket wrapped around her but one corner is in the fire and flames are leaping at her feet.

CHAPTER 27

JESSIE

Eighteen months earlier

Tom hasn't been himself for weeks. He's never really been keen on spending time with the family, not since he hit his teens anyway, but we hardly see him anymore. It's not as if he's at work, he quit his job as a service station chef a couple of months ago. He just hangs round the house all day, playing PlayStation and watching films in his room or else sneaking down to the shed at the bottom of the garden to drink and smoke. Mum and Dad don't know what to do. They've tried sitting him down and having a word with him. Dad went for the tough love approach, Mum was more understanding, but it didn't change anything. It's as though my brother's built a huge, invisible wall around him that none of us can smash through. Mum got in touch with a couple of his friends to ask if they knew what was wrong but they said they hadn't seen him for ages. They'd invited him out for drinks, they told her, but he'd either turn up for one and then leave or not turn up at all.

Dad thinks Tom's struggling because most of his mates have left London. Unlike my brother, who went to catering college, his friends went to university in different parts of the UK, then got jobs elsewhere and haven't come back. I've seen some of their Instagram accounts, showing off about their fancy cars, their action-packed holidays and their fit girlfriends. Tom still lives at home and he split up with his girlfriend six months ago. When I asked him why, he just shrugged and said, 'Shit happens.'

I think that's when Tom *really* started getting depressed. Because that's what's wrong with him. Depression. I might be young but I'm not stupid. I know that's why he stopped going to work and lay in bed all day after they sacked him. There's a part of me that feels sorry for him but I'm angry with him too. He's all Mum and Dad can talk about – *Tom this, Tom that. What are we going to do about Tom?* I know they've tried to get him to go and see the GP but he didn't turn up. When Mum confronted him about it he said there was nothing wrong with him and he just wanted to be left alone.

Earlier tonight he came down to the kitchen while I was doing my homework, a bottle of vodka and a pack of fags in one hand, and he stood at the counter, staring at me. I looked up at him and said, 'All right?' and he shook his head and said, 'No, not really.'

'Why?'

'Life.'

'What's wrong with it?'

'Everything.'

'So change it then.'

He laughed then. 'I wish it was that easy.'

'Just get a job,' I said. 'That'll help.'

He gave me a long look then said, 'Will it?'

'I dunno. At least then you'd have some money to do stuff.'

'Like what? Buy stuff I don't really need? Go out drinking? Go on holiday? All that stuff is meaningless.'

'No, it's not.'

'No, I guess it's not when you're fifteen.'

I rolled my eyes.

'Jessie,' he said softly. 'Do you ever think about death?'

I sat back in my seat and stared at him. 'No.'

I glanced towards the kitchen door, hoping Mum and Dad would walk through it. But the door was shut and Mum and Dad weren't in. They hadn't been out in for ever, not even to the cinema, and when they were offered a weekend on the Isle of Wight to celebrate one of their oldest friend's fiftieth birthday they agonized over it for days. I heard them, chatting in the living room about whether it was a good idea to leave me and Tom alone. Mum was worried that Tom would get too drunk to look after me. Dad said that I was sensible enough to knock for the neighbours if anything happened. It took him a while to convince her but he got there in the end. I was pleased. With any luck they'd have a brilliant time and wouldn't be so stressed out when they came back.

'I do.' Tom leant back against the counter and folded his arms over his chest. 'I think about death a lot.'

'Well, you shouldn't,' I said. 'That's morbid.'

'I'm not scared. I used to be, when I was kid, but I'm not anymore.'

He might not have been scared of death but I was scared of him, listening to him talk like that. I felt completely out of my depth. Was he thinking about killing himself? Was that what he was hinting at? Well, he needed to get that thought out of his head straight away. I had to change the subject.

'You know the NCT group are thinking about Greece next summer, don't you?' I said. 'For the group holiday.'

'Why are you telling me?' He laughs dryly. 'I haven't been for years. I'm too old for that crap, Jess. What twenty-three-year-old goes on holiday with their parents and a bunch of randoms they met bouncing on birthing balls?'

I'd thought mentioning a holiday would give him something to look forward to but he wasn't interested. There had to be something I could say to stop him thinking dark thoughts and give him something to get excited about.

'Will you teach me how to bake?'

He laughed softly. 'You? Bake? Since when?'

'Since *Bake-Off*. I want to learn how to make cakes and… and bread.'

'I'm not exactly Paul Hollywood.'

'I don't care. Will you teach me?'

The strangest expression passed over his face and he rounded the counter and wrapped me in his arms.

'You're such a kind-hearted girl, Jessie. Stay that way. Don't ever let go of that bit of you.' He hugged me tightly and kissed me on the top of my head. 'I love you, you know that, don't you?'

I stiffened. We weren't a very huggy family and physical affection made me feel awkward. So instead of saying, 'I love you too,' I said, 'Yeah, yeah' and wriggled out of his arms.

I wake with a start. The alarm clock on my bedside table glows 1.43 a.m. Something's wrong, I can feel it in the pit of my belly, but it isn't until I sniff the air that I realize why I've woken up.

Smoke. Instinctively I turn to look out of the window, shoving the curtain out of the way to peer outside. Directly below my bedroom the garden is shrouded in darkness but light is dancing in the window of the shed at the end of the path. Light... or... I squint my eyes. Flames!

I slam open the door to Tom's room but there's no one inside. I pound down the stairs and, without stopping to pull on my shoes, I yank open the kitchen door and run down the path in my bare feet, heart pounding.

'Tom!' I thump my fists against the shed window then jump back as the searing heat of the glass burns into my flesh. 'Tom!'

I run to the door. I can feel the heat radiating off the wood like a furnace so I rip off my T-shirt and wrap it around my hands. But when I shove on the door it doesn't budge an inch.

'Tom! Tom! Someone help me! Help me!'

I go back to the window and look inside. Where the piles of hay for my guinea pig used to be now there's a column of flames, licking the back wall of the shed from the floor to the wooden shelves holding Dad's tools. My heart races as I search the flames and the thick black smoke for my brother. Maybe he's not in here. Maybe he went to the pub with his friends? But then I see him, a dark, slumped shape on the floor, pressed up against the door.

'Tom! Tom, wake up!' I stare in desperation at my neighbour's house. A bedroom window light comes on and a figure appears at the window. 'Help!' I wave my arms. 'Help!'

I run back to the shed door and throw myself at it, not registering the heat that radiates down the right side of body. I throw myself at the door again and again, screaming my brother's name. I need to get him out of there. I need to… I need to…

I stare desperately around the garden, looking for something, anything I can use to break open the door, and then I see it, the ugly ornamental water fountain Dad bought for Mum one Christmas. It's plastic and it runs on batteries but it's heavy. I pick it up and approach the shed, still screaming my brother's name.

There's a curtain of flames behind the window now. As I hurl the fountain against the glass they blow out towards me, licking at my hands, my arms and my neck. It's so hot I feel as though I've been dropped into the heart of a volcano.

And everything goes black.

CHAPTER 28

DANNY

Danny sprints across the sand as Jessie twists and turns on the sand, sobbing and flailing. He picks up a flip-flop, lying abandoned beside a rucksack, and brings it down hard on the blanket, slapping out the flames that were licking at Jessie's feet then he rolls her across the sand, moving her a safe distance from the fire.

'Stop! Stop!' she screams.

He stops rolling her and crouches beside her. 'You're OK. It's all right. It's over.'

She stares up at him, her face and hair crusted with sand and her eyes wide and fearful, then she wriggles out of the cocoon-like blanket and shuffles away from him. 'Danny, what the hell were you doing?'

'You were on fire!' His heart is still thumping like a boxer, his whole body buzzing with adrenaline. 'You were shouting for help.'

'I was dreaming!' There are tears in her eyes now and

he watches, horrified, as they spill down her cheeks. 'I was dreaming about my brother.'

He looks from her distraught face to the blanket, lying in a heap at her feet, and then to the fire. He can still see the indentation in the sand where she lay. There's no way she could have kicked the blanket into the fire with it wrapped so tightly around her. Someone must have put the corner in the flames. He glances back, towards the jungle, half expecting to see evil eyes glinting out at them from between the trees.

'What did you say your phobia was?' he asks Jessie.

She looks at him and frowns, her face wet with tears and her eyes red and shining. 'What?'

'On the first night, when we were sitting around the fire. What did you say your phobia was?'

'I… I…' She runs her hands over her face, brushing the sand from her cheeks. 'Vomiting. I said my fear was vomiting. Why?'

A cold chill pricks at Danny's spine as he glances back towards the forest. 'You lied, didn't you? Like I did.'

'I don't… I don't understand what that's got to do with anything. Danny, I just woke up. I don't know what's going on.'

His gaze drifts towards the sea and the small patch of sand where he'd had his panic attack. *One of you is going to die.* He'd narrowed down his list of suspects to Jessie and Meg, and he'd been so sure it was Jessie he could barely bring himself to look at her when she and Milo came back from swimming round the island. But Jessie's worst phobia just came true and there's no way she faked it. He saw the flames!

'What is it, Danny?' Jessie asks. 'What are you looking at? What's going on? You're scaring me.'

He doesn't reply. Instead he reaches down, selects Jefferson's rucksack from the pile near the fire and hauls it onto his back.

'Danny!' Jessie calls as he runs into the jungle. 'Danny, where are you going? What's going on?'

Danny runs at a steady pace, or as steady as he can in a pair of Milo's flip-flops that slip and slide under the soles of his damp feet. He grips the rucksack straps with both hands and keeps his gaze fixed on the jungle floor. It's as though the motion of his body has cleared his mind, and the fog of dark thoughts that have been plaguing him for days are gone.

When he arrives at the small cave, hollowed into the cliff by millions of years' worth of weather, he shrugs off the rucksack and drags it inside. He discovered the cave when he was looking for Honor on the first day and ended up jumping off the cliff to get back to her. He'd peered inside it, half expecting to see a snake or some other kind of creature slithering within, but it was unoccupied. Now, he drops to his hands and knees and crawls inside. There's just enough space for him to sit down, legs crossed, with the rucksack in his lap. He eases Jefferson's neatly packed belongings onto the ground and sorts through them. There's some food – dried meat strips, a couple of cans of corned beef, some beans and several bottles of isotonic water. There's also a first-aid kit, some paracetamol and ibuprofen, a waterproof sheet and a length of cord. He unravels the cord and wraps it around each of his hands and pulls, hard. Strong, good. He places it on the floor then flips open the first-aid kit. There are bandages inside, wound tightly and unopened, some wads of dressing and some tape. He sets them down by the cord, along with both bottles of water and some of the food, then he crawls back out of the cave and straightens up. Taking a deep breath he screams at the top of his lungs.

CHAPTER 29

JESSIE

'Jessie! Are you OK?' Milo comes rushing towards me as I stumble out of the sea and make my way across the sand. 'What's happened? You look like you've seen a ghost.'

I shake my head but it doesn't clear my thoughts. 'I've just been for a swim to the cove we found. Something really horrible happened and I thought some time alone would help, but I'm still a bit freaked out.'

'Is it them?' He gently guides me down onto the sand then wraps an arm around my shoulders. 'Have Jack and Josh come back?'

'No, no. Nothing like that. I had a nap, like I said I would, by the fire. And I had a really upsetting dream. About...' I search Milo's eyes, 'about Tom. I was outside the shed, trying to get in to save him and—'

'It's OK.' He pulls me closer. 'It's OK, Jessie. You don't have to talk about it if you don't want to.'

'No, no. I do. I really do.'

It is as though the dream has unlocked something in my brain and there's so much… stuff… swirling in my head that I have to talk to let it all out.

Milo listens intently, his eyes not leaving my face as I tell him everything – about my brother's depression and the conversation we had in the kitchen.

'I freaked out when he started talking about death,' I say. 'It scared me so much. I felt completely out of my depth and I didn't know what to say, so I changed the subject…' Hot tears roll down my cheeks. I try to rub them away but new tears immediately take their place.

Milo pulls me into a hug, pressing my cheek into his chest. I can hear his heart pounding – strong and steady – and I close my eyes. Talking about Tom makes it real. As words leave my mouth images flash up in my head: my brother's face, his tired eyes, the long, loose shape his body made pressed up against the kitchen counter, the pack of cigarettes in his hand and the bottle of vodka by the sink. I don't want to relive what happened. I want to slam the door shut in my brain, lock it and run away. Every muscle, every tendon, every ligament in my body is tensed and primed to pull away from Milo and scrabble to my feet. But I can't keep doing that. I can't keep running for the rest of my life.

'It wasn't your fault.' Milo strokes my wet hair back from my face. His eyes are shining with compassion, his brow is knitted into a frown and his mouth is a thin, worried line. 'You know that, don't you?'

'But it was. Don't you understand? It *was* my fault. I shouldn't have gone to bed. I should have stayed up all night talking to him. I should have hidden the lighter or poured the vodka down the sink. If he'd never set foot in that shed he might still be alive.'

'But...' He pauses uncertainly.

'Go on.'

'Your brother's death was an accident, Jessie. That's what the coroner ruled. Tom got drunk, passed out and dropped his cigarette. That's what started the fire. He didn't commit suicide. He didn't mean to die.'

'And that's what makes it so much worse.'

'It was an accident, Jessie; a terrible, tragic accident. You couldn't have known what was going to happen. No one could.'

Milo holds me as I burst into tears. I haven't talked about Tom's death to anyone other than the police and Mum and Dad, and even then I didn't go into detail because I didn't want my parents to have the same awful images in their heads as I do. Telling Milo about my brother is like reopening a scar; the pain's as fresh as the day Tom died.

'You have to let it go,' Milo says softly. 'This weight that you're carrying around inside you; you can't torture yourself with *could have been* for the rest of your life. Tom wouldn't want you to do that. I didn't know him as well as you did but I'm pretty sure of that.'

'But I don't know how to let it go. I keep rerunning what happened that day in my head. What if Mum and Dad hadn't gone to the Isle of Wight? What if I hadn't gone to bed when I did? What if I'd taken Tom's lighter? What if I'd stayed up all night talking to him? I was the only person who could

have stopped what'd happened and I didn't, Milo, I didn't…'
My voice cracks. I feel as though someone has stuck a knife
between my ribs and they're gutting my heart.

'Sssh… sssh… sssh…' He sways me from side to side, his
cheek against the top of my head, his voice a whisper that
mingles with the soft lapping of the sea.

'It's OK,' I hear him say as Jeffers calls out to ask if I'm
all right. 'She'll be OK.'

Will I? I want to believe him but I can't.

We work side by side, making a new roof for the shelter:
a tired, companionable silence sealing us off from the rest of
the world. Milo glances at me as he weaves banana leaves
together. *How are you?* he asks wordlessly. I nod in reply and
shoot him a small smile. My brain feels thick and woolly, my
eyes swollen like two split boiled eggs and emotionally I'm
spent. Making a roof for the shelter is about all I can deal
with right now. It's like basket weaving, desert island style.
Meg and Jefferson are a good hundred metres or so away,
fishing on the rocks, and there's no sign of Danny or Honor.

'Milo,' I say. 'There's something I haven't told you.'

He takes a leaf from the pile then cries out in pain as it
cuts him, and he sucks his finger. 'Sorry. What was that?'

'Earlier, when I woke up from my nightmare, Danny did
something really weird.'

'What do you mean?' He looks at me in surprise.

'He was slapping the bottom of my blanket with a flip-
flop, then he rolled me around in the sand, screaming that
I was on fire.'

'Holy crap! Are you OK? You're not—'

'Burnt? No. No more than I was already. There was something else. He said he knew I'd lied about my phobia, then he grabbed Jefferson's rucksack and ran off into the jungle.'

'So he just left you there? On the beach? After he saw you catch fire?'

'That's just it. I'm fine.'

'Are you sure?' He runs his hand down the length of my shin, his touch featherlight. He does the same on my other leg then changes position to look at the soles of my feet. 'Does your skin feel OK? It's not tender or anything?'

'No. It's fine. No fresh burns.'

'No pain when you woke up?'

I shake my head. 'No, nothing.'

'So maybe it was just the blanket that was on fire?'

'I guess so. I… I didn't really look at it.'

He bites down on his thumbnail and stares out to sea. 'You know this means everyone's phobia has come true apart from Danny and Meg's?' He pauses then looks back at me. 'She freaks out at the sight of blood but I can't remember what he's afraid of.'

I frown, trying to remember. 'Something about a bucket.'

'Claustrophobia! He's scared of enclosed spaces… Oh God.'

'What?' I ask.

'Jack and Josh had already left when your blanket went up in flames.' He grimaces. 'So whoever's behind all this is still on the island.'

I rest my head in my hands and exhale noisily. I thought

217

we could relax now, sit it out until our parents rescue us. 'You think we're still in danger?'

'Yeah.' He looks over towards the rocks where Meg is sitting cross-legged with a homemade fishing pole in her hands and Jeffers crouched beside her. 'You don't think someone we know could be behind it?'

'You think Danny set me on fire! Milo, there's no way. Absolutely no way. He was *terrified*.'

'So that just leaves my sister.'

'No.' I shake my head. 'No way. Besides, she wasn't even on the new beach. She was over here with you guys.'

An expression I can't read crosses his face. 'No she wasn't.'

I look at him in alarm. 'Where was she?'

'In the jungle. She said she needed a wee. She said she'd meet us here.'

'No.' I shake my head. 'No way. Meg's been a bit off with me this holiday but she's not a psychopath. She wouldn't deliberately set light to me.'

'You're right.' He rubs his hands over his face and groans. 'Of course you are. I can't believe I'd even say that. Seriously, this place is getting to me. Big style.'

'Well, whoever's behind it knows what we're really scared of.'

'What do you mean?'

'Well, I lied, didn't I?' I say. 'Like Danny said. That first night when I said my fear was vomiting. Whoever did this knows I'm terrified of fire, not sick. And… oh my God…' I touch a hand to my lips as a memory comes flooding back.

'I know why Danny ran off. He didn't say "you lied about your phobia". He said "you lied about your phobia *too*".'

'So he's not really claustrophobic?'

'No, but I don't know what he's really—' I break off as the bushes rustle behind us and Danny emerges from the jungle. He looks a state – absolutely dripping with sweat, his dirty hair slicked back and his T-shirt and shorts clinging to his body.

'You guys all right?' He shuffles towards us with Jefferson's rucksack in one hand. He drops it onto the sand. Before I can ask him about his phobia he says, 'Where's Honor?'

I twist round, searching the beach, the sea and the edge of the forest for a small blonde figure. I can't remember the last time I saw her. All my attention was on Milo as I dragged myself out of the sea.

'She's collecting empty bottles...' Milo turns to point towards the remains of the shelter. There's no one there. 'Oh. She must have gone off to the waterfall.'

'When?' Danny asks.

Milo shrugs. 'I'm... not sure. I didn't actually see her leave.'

'Jessic?' Danny asks.

'I haven't seen her. Not since I swam over from the new beach.'

'And when was that?'

'I'm not... I can't be sure.'

'Think! How long?'

'I don't know... an hour... maybe two?'

219

All the colour seems to drain from Danny's face. 'For God's sake! Honor's been gone for up to two hours and none of you thought to look for her?' He glares down at me. 'And you call her your friend? If anything's happened to her, I'll never forgive you.'

'Danny, wait!' I shout as he turns and sprints back into the jungle. 'I'm sure she's fine. She'll just be—'

Milo ducks down to grab a bottle of water. 'He's right,' he says. 'She's been gone too long. We need to look for her. *Now.*'

We head for the waterfall, running at first, then walking as the undergrowth grows thicker and our throats dry from repeatedly shouting Honor's name. Danny leads the way, followed by me, then Milo.

'Where did you go?' I ask as he holds a vine up for me to duck under. 'When you took Jefferson's rucksack.'

He waits for Milo to pass under the vine too then swipes a hand over his forehead, slicking away the sweat that covers his brow.

'I wanted to see what he had in there,' he says as he falls in step with me.

'And?'

'Food, mostly dried and canned meat. A first-aid kit. Some other prepper bits and bobs. But mostly food. No wonder he was happy setting up camp on his own.'

My stomach rumbles at the thought of meat and I'm tempted to ask Danny if he's got any of Jefferson's food that he could share with me. Instead I say, 'Do you still think Jeffers is the one behind the phobias coming true?'

Danny gives me a sideways glance. 'Not unless he deliberately threw himself off the cliff.'

'He didn't. I was there.'

'Did you see who was in the bushes?'

'No. I—'

'Could you see all the others?'

'Well, no, not really. It was dark and we were all curled up around a pile of rucksacks. I couldn't see anyone until Jeffers started stumbling through the clearing.'

'So it could have been Meg, in the bushes?'

'What could have been Meg?' Milo says from behind us. Danny turns sharply. 'Nothing.'

'He knows,' I say. 'About the snake. I told him.'

'Yeah.' Milo raises his eyebrows. 'Cheers for that, mate.'

Danny looks affronted. 'For what? Keeping quiet so you wouldn't freak out?'

'You could have told me. I'm not eleven anymore.'

'Yeah, I know. But you wouldn't have been able to sleep, would you? Knowing there were bloody great cobras slithering all over the place. You wouldn't have come into the jungle to get water or look for food.'

'I'm here now, aren't I?'

'Guys.' I touch their arms. 'Can we not do this now? Please? We're supposed to be looking for Honor.'

The expression in Danny's eyes switches from pissed off to concerned in a heartbeat and he nods sharply. 'You're right. We can talk about this later.'

221

'And he thinks Jeffers is a control freak,' Milo mutters under his breath as Danny breaks into a slow jog.

'Don't,' I say. 'The last thing we need is more arguments—'

'Wait!' Milo grabs my arm as I move to follow Danny. 'What's that?'

He points at a shrub, further down the route, just to our left. At first all I can see are flat, shiny leaves, but then I spot it, a flash of pink among the green. I crouch down and pull it out. It's a flip-flop – pink with white polka dots and a sparkly, silver toe strap.

Milo reaches to touch it. 'Is that—'

'Honor's. Yeah. She's been wearing them all holiday.' I look at him. 'She never takes them off.'

As Milo searches the undergrowth for Honor's other flip-flop I shout for Danny, screaming his name. He comes running, fear etched into every line of his face.

'That's Honor's,' he says, immediately spotting the flip-flop in my hands. He spins on the spot, staring wildly around the jungle as though he's expecting his girlfriend to walk out from the trees at any second. 'Where did you find it?'

We show him the spot and, like Milo, he crouches down and rummages among the scrub. He searches the next bush and the next one, muttering under his breath. When he stands up again his whole body is beaded with sweat.

'Have they gone?' he asks, looking from me to Milo. 'The brothers? Have they definitely gone?'

Milo and I share a panicked look. Danny's thinking what we're thinking, that Honor wouldn't just lose a shoe and carry on without it. I have a flashback to Josh and Jack shunting me through the jungle and my blood runs cold.

'Yes,' Milo says. 'They've definitely gone. We told you, remember. You were sitting by the fire when we came back from our swim.'

'You're sure? You're positive there's no way they're still on the island?'

'We swam all the way round,' I say. 'There was no sign of them, or their boat.'

Danny stares at me. His pupils are huge, blocking out the pale blue of his irises, making his eyes look black. He looks horrified, transfixed, as though he's watching the end of the world play out in front of him. The expression on his face makes all of the hairs on my arms go up.

'What?' I ask. 'Danny, what is it? Why are you looking at me like that?'

He shakes his head mutely.

'Dan?' I can hear the panic in Milo's voice but I can't tear my eyes away from Danny.

'Danny!' A cold chill passed through me as though someone just walked on my grave. 'Danny, talk to us! Do you know what's happened to Honor?'

He shakes his head mutely and a single tear weaves its way through the dirt and grime on his cheek. An image flashes up in my mind of Honor lying dead in the jungle, her blonde hair splayed out, blood clouding her eyes and dribbling from her mouth.

'TELL US!' I scream as I grab him by the shoulders and shake him. 'TELL US WHAT'S GOING ON!'

Danny doesn't shrug my hands from his shoulders. He doesn't move. He doesn't blink. But he does say something. He stares straight at me and says: 'I found a message in the sand. It said, *One of you will die*.'

I pick at the fish in the metal tray. I'm starving, but there's a knot of worry in my stomach that's stopping me from eating. We searched for Honor. We headed to the waterfall first, but she wasn't there. Nor was she up in the clearing. Unsure where to go next, we ploughed back into the jungle and started walking in a straight line, or as straight a line as we could. We shouted Honor's name until our throats were raw and dehydration began to set in, Milo's water bottle long since drained. As the sun began to set we had no choice but to head back to camp. Danny cried the whole way and I held Milo's hand, squeezing it whenever a wave of panic surged through me. Was Honor dead? Was that why we couldn't find her?

One of you will die, the message said. Just thinking about it made me want to burst into tears.

'We can't just pile into the jungle in the dark,' Jefferson says now, putting down his tin and standing up. He's remarkably energetic considering he and Milo just lugged all our rucksacks back to camp from the new beach. 'People will get lost or hurt. We need a cohesive plan.'

Danny, standing by the fire with a flaming torch in his hand, shakes his head. 'Sod a plan. I'm going back in. I'll search all night if I have to.'

I get to my feet. 'I'm coming too. We should go in pairs, that way no one else gets lost.'

Meg raises an arched eyebrow. 'There's five of us.'

'So a three and a two then. Does it matter?'

'That depends if you get to go with Milo or not.'

I shoot her a look. 'What's that supposed to mean?'

'Meg—' There's a warning tone to Milo's voice.

'What?' She looks from him to Jefferson. 'If we're going to look for Honor we need to do it properly, not wander around holding hands and mewing at each other.'

I laugh. 'Seriously?'

Milo rolls his eyes. 'We didn't swim round the island with our eyes closed, you know.'

'Are you sure? It took you long enough.'

I stare Meg out, irritation burning in my chest. She's not the only one who's worried about Honor, but she's taking it out on the wrong people.

'What do you think we were doing?'

'You tell me,' she narrows her eyes. 'Maybe you were too distracted to look for Jack and Josh.'

'Or maybe you don't think I'm good enough for your brother,' I snap. 'Is that it? Is that why you're doing this? How about you just come out and say it to my face instead of trolling me behind my back, telling everyone who'll listen that he's still in love with his ex. I know for a fact that you deliberately told Danny so he'd warn me off.'

'Whoa, whoa!' Danny holds his hands up, palms out. 'Don't bring me into this.'

'You're not special, Dan,' I say. 'She told Jefferson the same thing too.'

'Actually,' Jeffers says, 'Meg told me that Milo was a complete arsehole to Bella and he'd cheated on her multiple times. That's the reason I tried to warn you off him, Jessie.'

Milo stares at his sister in disbelief. 'You told him I was a cheat? Seriously? That's absolute crap and you know it. I've never cheated on anyone in my life. Why would you say something like that?'

'Because you're an arsehole!' She glares at him but her eyes are shining with tears. 'You're completely self-obsessed. And it pisses me off to see girls throwing themselves at you.'

'Hang on,' I say. 'I haven't thrown myself at—'

'I didn't say you did, Jessie. And this isn't about you. It's not even about Milo. Not completely. It's about me.'

'Huh?' Jefferson says.

'We were friends.' Her voice cracks. 'Us six. Right from the beginning. I loved our holidays. I looked forward to them because you guys treated me differently than people at school. You looked at me differently. You liked me for a start—'

'Is this about the bullying at school?' Milo interrupts.

I look at him in surprise. Neither he, nor Meg, has ever mentioned her being bullied before.

'That's part of the problem, Milo, yes.' She swipes at her eyes with the back of her hands. I can't tell if she's crying because she's angry or because she's upset. 'That and the fact you always talk over me instead of letting me speak.'

'OK, OK.' He holds out his hands in surrender. 'I won't say a word.'

'I *liked* how I was with you guys.' She looks from me to Jeffers to Danny. 'I felt like part of something, like... I dunno, like... you were my tribe. I felt safe with you. I felt good about myself. And then...' She pushes her dark hair away from her face and stares into the fire. 'And then you all started coupling up and everything changed.'

Jeffers clears his throat.

'Well, clearly you didn't, Jeffers, and that's why I threw myself at you. Remember, that summer when were all fourteen? Everyone was flirting – Honor and Danny, Milo and Jess... and we were left on our own...'

He shakes his head, warning her not to go there. He knows what she's about to say, we all do, and he doesn't want her to embarrass herself.

'And I tried it on with you.' Meg closes her eyes at the memory. 'And you turned your cheek when I tried to kiss you.'

'Meg...' he says softly.

'No, it's fine. Honestly. It's fine. I kind of guessed you were gay. I mean, not that I would expect you to fancy me if you were straight but, for me, it was just... I felt humiliated. Not by the rejection. Because I'd thrown myself at you. But I was so bloody lonely...'

'Oh, Meg,' I say. 'I didn't know.'

'Don't.' She swipes at her eyes again. Her voice has softened and she looks like she's struggling to hold it together. 'Please don't feel sorry for me or I'll... Anyway, yeah, I was being bullied at school. Milo knew but I swore him to secrecy because I didn't want you guys to look at me differently like… like I was some kind of victim.'

I make a noise in protest at the same time Danny says, 'We wouldn't have done that.'

'Wouldn't you? Are you sure?' Meg says. And she's right. We would have treated her differently if she'd turned up one summer and told us about the bullying. We'd have seen a different side to her, a more vulnerable Meg. We'd have overcompensated to make her feel better.

'Anyway,' she continues, 'I haven't got much of a life outside of these holidays. Our parents are stricter with me than Milo. They'd deny it but they'll happily let him go out whenever he wants whereas, for me, I've got to text to say where I am and make sure I'm back by a certain time. Not that,' she adds quickly, 'I've got anyone to go out with. Apart from Bella. Well, I *had* Bella.'

Milo drops his head into his hands and sighs deeply.

'Yep,' Meg says. 'Bella. My only real friend back at home. And Milo decided to hook up with her. So then I had no one. Because all of a sudden my best friend wanted to hang out with my brother rather than me. I knew it wouldn't last. Milo's fickle.' She looks at me. 'He doesn't mean to hurt people but he does and—'

'Meg.' Milo looks up from his hands. 'You know I didn't mean to hurt Bella. It just… it just ran its course.'

'And then I had to pick up the pieces. At school, because obviously she wasn't going to come anywhere near our house again.'

'Yeah, but…'

'And now you've decided you want Jessie.' She tips a hand towards me. 'Jessie who's lost her brother and is just about as vulnerable as someone can get. What happens when that runs its course eh, Milo? Who's going to be there for her?'

'It's not the same,' Milo objects, 'I don't think—'

'No,' she snaps. 'You don't think, do you? Not about anyone else? And that's the issue. There's one person – one – in our whole group who takes the time to talk to me, *properly* talk to me, and that's Honor. And she's probably dead.'

She turns away, hot angry tears spilling onto her cheeks.

'Meg.' I touch her on the shoulder but she shrugs me off, scrambles to her feet and runs off down the beach.

There's an awkward pause as the rest of us glance at each other, unsure what to do, then Milo sighs.

'I'll go after her. She's right, this is my fault.'

The air is thick with tension as we head into the jungle, flaming torches held aloft. Milo and Meg have paired up but they're not speaking, other than to bicker about which direction they should head in. I'm with Jeffers and Danny, who are also having a power struggle about where we search.

'I think we should go that way.' Jeffers points beyond the waterfall, to the other side of the island. 'The vegetation is thicker there so she's more likely to get lost.'

'She wouldn't go through that,' Danny says, 'and if someone took her, surely it would be a lot more battered. I think we should go that way.' He points to the right.

'But that leads up to the clearing and you've already checked there, haven't you?'

'Yes, but we didn't explore the jungle at the base. Look, Jeffers, you're the survival expert but Honor's my girlfriend. She wouldn't have gone deeper into the island Unless…' The muscles in his jaw pulse. 'Unless she was forced.'

'All right then.' Jefferson shrugs. 'Right it is.'

'For now,' he adds under his breath.

An hour or two later, when Jefferson suggests we give up for the night, I wearily agree. My throat is red raw from shouting Honor's name, my feet are aching and my skin is on fire from being bitten so many times. Even Danny, who's become more and more fraught and short-tempered the longer we've been searching, begrudgingly agrees.

'We did our best,' Jeffers says as we trudge back to our camp, a note of despair in his voice. 'It's so dark now that we could end up injuring ourselves or getting lost too if we keep looking. With any luck Milo and Meg have found her or she's back at the camp, wondering where the hell we all are.'

As we step through the trees I look hopefully towards the roaring fire, but there's no one sitting beside it. There's no one in the shelter either, or on the beach. Honor hasn't come back.

Danny hugs himself as he shifts his weight from foot to foot. I've never seen him so agitated. 'I can't. I can't just sit and do nothing.' He moves to step back into the jungle but Jefferson grabs his arm.

'At least wait until Meg and Milo get back. They might have found her.'

Danny shrugs but he doesn't join us as we settle down by the fire, swigging at our water bottles. Instead he paces up and down the beach, his eyes never leaving the jungle.

'Do you think she'll be OK?' I ask Jefferson.

I wait for his reassurance, for the swift *Yes, of course* that will lift the weight from my chest but, instead of nodding reassuringly, he sighs.

'If she's got water and a safe spot, raised off the ground, she should be fine.'

'And if she didn't wander off…'

'I'm not convinced someone's taken her. There are other reasons why she might not have responded when we shouted her name.'

'You think she could be hurt?'

He sighs again. 'I don't know. I just hope she's OK.'

We lapse into silence but Jefferson's comments have unsettled me and now all I can think about is Honor, lying unconscious somewhere.

One of you will die.

I can't – won't – imagine her dead.

After an age the sound of footsteps, snapping twigs and low voices drifts towards us. I turn, hopefully, but only two people step from between the trees and onto the beach. One look at Milo and my heart sinks deeper in my chest.

'We looked everywhere.' He digs his torch into the sand and runs his hands over his face. He looks as tired and as broken as I feel.

'We shouted and we shouted,' Meg says, looking at her

brother. There's a softness to her gaze that suggests that they've sorted out their issues. 'We couldn't find her.'

Danny comes running over, sweaty and pale in the light of the fire. 'What is it? What's happened?'

'Nothing.' Milo gives him a look. 'I'm sorry, Dan. We didn't find her.'

Danny crumples into himself, sinking to his knees, his hands in his hair, his arms covering his face. In an instant Meg is at his side, her arm hooked over his shoulders. Danny flinches as she touches him and pulls away.

'It's OK,' she says soothingly. 'We'll find her. As soon as the sun comes up we'll set out again and this time we'll find her.'

'It'll be OK, Dan. We'll find her,' the rest of us chorus. 'Don't worry. I'm sure she's fine.'

But there's a hollow ring to our voices that wasn't there when we set out to search.

CHAPTER 30

DANNY

Day six on the island

Danny lies very still on the sand, his cheek hot and clammy against the palm of his hand. Over in the shelter, where the other four are sleeping, someone just moaned softly and shifted position. The sun has finally risen, peering above the horizon, streaking the sky with warm oranges and deep reds. Danny shifts onto one elbow and listens for sounds of wakefulness in the shelter, then silently gets to his feet. If anyone wakes up it's game over. They won't let him go back into the jungle on his own. They'll insist on coming with him.

A noise, a strangled cry, makes him freeze and he listens intently, barely daring to breathe. Is it an animal, a bird or... something else?

Adrenaline surges through him as he steps away from the shelter. He moves lightly, a bottle of water in one hand and a knife in the other, stepping slowly and carefully until he's deep enough in the jungle that the others won't hear the snapping branches and breaking twigs. Then he starts to run. He hasn't slept and his mind is a dark whirl of fear and anxiety, one phrase going round and round his head:

One of you will die.

He'd never seen anyone go as white as Jessie did when he told her about it. It was a good job she was holding on to him at the time because she looked like she was about to collapse. Milo wasn't any steadier on his feet, but the shock wore off faster and the questions came thick and fast. Where exactly had he seen the message? At what time? Was it before or after they set off for their swim?

Danny told them everything (although he kept his real phobia to himself). He even crouched down and scratched the earth with a stick to show them the shape of the letters. He'd assumed it was down to Jack and Josh, he told them, a final warning message before they left, to freak everyone out.

Who else could have written the message? Meg? One of the others? Or someone else? Someone hiding in the depths of the jungle, watching every move they make.

Danny had never felt as scared and as panicked as he did combing the jungle with Milo and Jessie, searching for any trace of Honor. Nor when he'd headed back in the dark with Jeffers and Meg joining the search party.

One of you will die.

Only two people's phobias hadn't come true. Meg's fear of blood and his phobia, his real one – of someone he loves dying.

He speeds up, jumping over tree roots and leaping over tangled foliage, his heart thundering in his chest and sweat dripping off his face. What if Honor's become so dehydrated she's passed out? What if something, or someone, attacked her and she couldn't fight back? What if she's dead? No… no… he pushes the thought out of his head. He loves her and that love will keep her safe. It will wrap her like a blanket and protect her. He won't let Meg kill her. Because he's certain now. Meg's the only one who hasn't had to face her phobia yet. She has to be the one behind all this.

When Danny returns to the camp the others greet him like a long-lost son.

'You're back! Oh my God!' Meg throws herself at him, wrapping her arms around his neck. 'We thought you'd disappeared too.'

Danny's skin crawls as she buries her face into his chest and he fights the urge to shake her off. He thought Honor was a good actress but Meg is next level. He can't believe none of the others can see through the act. All that stuff earlier about her being bullied at school, feeling left out in their group and her crocodile tears about Honor. She may as well have jumped up and down waving a sign saying, *I'm making your phobias come true because I hate you all.*

'We thought something had happened to you!' Meg says as she pulls away and her eyes search his face. 'Where've you been? What happened?'

Danny shakes his head as Milo and Jessie congregate by him, their faces tight with worry. There's no sign of Jefferson.

'Any sign of Honor?' Milo asks.

'No, I um…' Danny clears his throat. 'I thought I heard something. Someone… crying but it… it must have been an animal. I went into the jungle, I looked everywhere but there's no sign of her. She's just…' He looks Meg straight in the eye. 'She's vanished.'

'We'll search again,' Milo says. 'Now you're back. We've made a plan. We split into two groups again and we comb every inch of the island. We'll take Jefferson's food supplies and as much water as we can carry and we *will* find her.'

'We'll go in two groups again, but me, Jefferson and Danny in one group and Jessie and Meg are the other. Everyone OK with that?'

Jessie nods towards Meg and smiles. ''Course.'

Danny stares at her in disbelief. What the hell is she doing? Yesterday he pretty much told her that Meg was behind the phobias coming true and yet here she is, smiling and nodding as though nothing has happened and all is good with the world.

Meg tried to burn you alive, Jessie! he wants to shout. *She's not your friend!*

Maybe he should confront Meg now before they go and look for Honor again. But what if no one backs him up? After her little sob story earlier, Jessie's treating her like they're besties and Milo's stupidly contrite. And besides, Meg's clever, she'd find a way of blaming Jack and Josh or pretend there's someone else hiding out in the jungle.

He feels frozen by indecision. Should he say something or not?

'There you are!' Jefferson strolls out from between the

trees with what looks like a large lizard slung over one shoulder. 'Where've you been?'

As Danny repeats his story about hearing a noise in the jungle Jefferson slings the lizard over the roof of the shelter then rummages in his bag, looking for something.

'Only one trap worked,' he says. 'The second one was triggered but there wasn't anything in it. Must have escaped.' He looks up. 'Meg, have you got my knife?'

'No.' She shakes her head lightly. 'I washed it and gave it back to you, after I gutted the fish last night.'

Jefferson frowns. 'Are you sure? It's not in your day pack?'

'A hundred per cent,' Meg says.

'Milo?' Jeffers asks. 'You haven't got it, have you?'

'As if! You never let that thing out of your sight.'

'And I haven't got it,' Jessie says before Jefferson can ask her. She pulls the blanket tighter around her shoulders. 'You must have lost it.'

'I never lose anything.' Jefferson gives her a pointed look. 'One of the rules of survival is...' he tails off. 'Anyway, Dan? Have you seen it?'

Danny runs his hands over the deep pockets of his cargo shorts. 'Nope!'

'Meg, are you *sure* you didn't put it in your bag?' Jefferson asks.

'You can check it if you want.'

'I'd rather you did that. It's your stuff. I just want to get this monitor lizard gutted before it goes on the turn.'

'OK. No worries.'

Danny watches, his arms folded over his chest as Meg

reaches for her day pack. Unlike everyone else who packed waterproof bags in shades of grey, black or navy, Meg's got a canvas bag she bought on a Bangkok market stall, embroidered with flowers and birds. As she pulls it towards her Jefferson sighs audibly. He'll make them turn the camp upside down to find that knife, Danny thinks with a stab of irritation. He won't let it lie if he thinks one of his prized possessions is lost.

As Meg opens her bag Danny's pulse pounds in his ears. Meg seems to freeze, so do the others. Even the sea seems to pause its gentle lapping of the shore. But Danny's heart hasn't stopped. It's thumping in his chest, every beat a weighty punch that makes him feel sick. Lying just inside Meg's bag, with its eyes closed and mouth stretched wide in a silent scream, is a monkey head. And it's swimming in blood.

Meg doesn't scream. She's doesn't tremble or cry. As she stares down into the bag her eyes don't betray the fact that her phobia has just come true, but Danny spots something else – a grin – the smallest of smiles that plucks at her lips.

And that makes him run.

CHAPTER 31

HONOR

It's damp, dark and cold inside the cave but it's far less scary than what lies beyond the jagged, rocky mouth. As darkness fell Honor shuffled as far inside as she could, frantically checking the moss-lined walls and leaf-strewn ground for spiders as she inched her way backwards. She kept on moving until her back hit a cold, rocky wall, then she gathered her knees to her chest and burst into tears. She didn't cry for long. She couldn't risk her nose becoming so stuffy she couldn't breathe. Instead she channelled her fear and her frustration into anger and, using all the strength she had, she tried to pull her bound wrists apart. The tape held firm. And it didn't budge from her ankles when she frantically wiggled her feet back and forth in an effort to loosen it.

She hadn't planned on spending the night in the cave. After her kidnapper left her there, she tried to escape. She shuffled out of the cave on her bum, the fabric of her shorts catching on rough bits of stone, her breath coming in short, sharp, terrified bursts.

When she finally made it to the entrance of the cave she stared out at the small clearing and the wall of trees behind it, trying to get her bearings. If she could just find her way to her friends – even if she had to bum-shuffle or hop the whole way in her bare feet – her nightmare would be over. They'd pull the tape from her lips and the gauze from her mouth. She'd tell them what had happened and they'd help her, they'd protect her. They'd make sure she was safe until her mum turned up to rescue her. The thought of her mum, sipping cocktails by the pool with the other parents, totally oblivious to what her daughter was going through, brought fresh tears to Honor's eyes. It had just been the two of them – Thea and Honor against the world – for so long. They had a brilliant relationship, the best, and her mum was happy, finally, for the first time in years. It was almost a relief when Adrian, Honor's dad, moved out five years earlier and the rows finally stopped. Her dad's bellowing voice and her mum's desperate, screechy retorts had had a big impact on twelve-year-old Honor. She swore she'd never have a relationship like her parents'. She wouldn't put a child, or herself, through that kind of hell. She crept into herself, hiding bubbly, exuberant Honor away, only bringing her out when she stepped out on stage. Danny was there for her when she went on her first group holiday without her dad and she was so grateful. She stopped seeing him as a loud, annoying boy. Instead she viewed him as a kindred spirit. Someone who understood how lost she felt. They grew closer on the next holiday, and the one after that, and when he asked her to be his girlfriend on his fifteenth birthday she felt like the happiest girl in the world. That was two years ago and she's been playing the part of the perfect girlfriend ever since.

Exhausted and trembling, she sat in the mouth of the cave and tried to work out which way to go. Was the beach to her left or to her right? She couldn't hear the sea or feel a breeze on her cheeks. The air she drew into her nostrils was thick, cloying, hot. Where was she? It was as though she'd fallen asleep on the beach and had woken up in the heart of the jungle. Even if she hadn't been utterly terrified when she'd been led through the jungle, there was no way she could have memorized the route. Other than the beach, the waterfall and the clearing at the top of the cliffs, there were no other distinctive features on the island, no way of orientating herself. As she looked from left to right, searching for footprints, for trampled vegetation, for something, anything to tell her which way to go, movement at the base of a palm tree made her turn sharply. She watched, heart pounding, as a grey-black monitor lizard slowly emerged from between the fronds of a shrub. It moved slowly on short stubby legs and scaly clawed feet. It was huge, maybe a metre and a half long. Honor held herself very, very still as its head swung slowly from left to right and its snake-like tongue flickered in and out of its mouth. It was tasting the air, she realized with horror, and picked up on her scent. Were monitor lizards dangerous to humans? Was it venomous? Jeffers would know. Why hadn't she listened to him? Why had she laughed along with the others when he'd tried to share what he knew?

The lizard stopped moving its head from side to side. Its head wasn't pointed towards her but Honor could tell that it was watching her with its unblinking black eye. She wanted to scream. She wanted to stand up and jump up and down as she shouted at it to 'Go! Go! Get away!' But she couldn't do either of those things. All she could do was inch herself back into the cave, praying that the lizard wouldn't follow.

She wouldn't leave the cave that night, she decided as she slowly shuffled backwards. The jungle was too dangerous, her hands and feet were bound and if she got lost in the dark she might never find her way out. Better to remain in the cave and escape when dawn broke.

Now, as the darkness of the world outside the cave begins to lift, it is as though someone has turned up the volume of the jungle too. The incessant chirping of crickets that kept her company as night fell is joined by the hollow whoop of macaques and the caws, shrieks, hoots and cries of birds. The world beyond the confines of the cave is waking up but Honor hasn't slept. She's remained awake, staring into the darkness, listening for animals and insects, praying that her kidnapper won't return until she's made her escape.

The tape around her wrist is weakening. She's been rubbing it against the sharp spots on the wall behind her for hours and now there's mere millimetres between her and freedom.

She grits her teeth against the pain that's burning through her forearms, biceps and shoulders and speeds up, sawing the last few threads against the jag of rock then stops, dropping her hands to the floor. She inhales deeply through her nose then wrenches her wrists apart. She feels the tape tighten against her skin and then – SNAP – it breaks. She slumps forward and slowly, tentatively rolls her shoulders forward. Her anguished scream is smothered by the mesh in her mouth and the tape still binding it closed. She rips it away, not caring as it lifts a layer of skin from her lips, and pulls the gauze from her mouth. She grabs at the bottle of water by her feet, unscrews the lid with trembling hands and gulps desperately, barely swallowing as she tips the water into her parched mouth and down her throat. She drains every last drop then tosses the bottle away and reaches for her ankles, running her fingernails over the tape, looking for the edge. She finds it, but as she picks at it a noise makes her look up. It's coming from outside the cave. Someone, or something, is crashing through the undergrowth.

Heart pounding, Honor tips forwards onto her knees and drags herself to the mouth of the cave. What if it's her kidnapper returning to check up on her and force her to drink water again? She freezes as someone steps through the trees. Someone she loved. Someone she trusted. Someone who now absolutely terrifies her.

'Hello, babe,' Danny says.

CHAPTER 32

DANNY

Fourteen hours earlier

Danny watches from between the trees as the others mill around the camp, fixing it up. Milo and Meg are erecting pieces of wood by knocking them into the soft, sandy soil with the flat of the axe, under Jefferson's careful guidance, while Honor is weaving banana leaves together to make a roof. Interesting, Danny thinks. He could have been murdered back at the cave and none of them, not a single one, would have heard him scream.

He waits patiently, watching as Honor gathers more leaves then sits cross-legged on the sand to continue weaving. Danny turns his head, alerted by movement beyond the rocks. Jessie's in the sea, face down, arms and legs powering through the water. She's heading away from the new beach, to the right, as though she's circling the island again.

Danny creeps closer to the beach. He keeps low and shoves Jefferson's rucksack into a bush, then, as Milo smashes the axe against a tree trunk, he hisses Honor's name. When she doesn't react he picks up a small stone and skims it across the sand so it lands beside her. She twists around and gasps, just as Milo uses the axe again.

Danny presses a finger to his lips and, with his other hand, beckons her. She grins and gets to her feet. Her smile makes his heart ache. She's always loved surprises. He'll never forget the look of delight on her face when she got home from school one day to see him sitting on the wall of her house with the biggest bunch of roses that he could afford. He had to skive the last hour of school to get there on time but it was worth the week of detentions he was handed the next day. He'd do anything to make her smile.

'Dan!' she says as she draws closer. 'Where've you been? Do you fancy a swim? I'm boiling.'

'Actually, there's something I need to show you.'

'Show me?' She raises her eyebrows. 'Like what?'

'Something I've found in the jungle. It's beautiful. You'll love it.'

She doesn't look convinced. 'Is it some kind of creature?'

'No, no, nothing like that.' He takes her hand. 'You trust me, don't you?'

'Of course.' She smiles up at him, but it doesn't reach her eyes.

There's a nervousness about her gaze, a wariness that's been growing over the last few days. Doesn't she trust him? The thought hurts his heart. If she's scared of anyone it should be Meg.

'Come on then.' He gives her hand a reassuring squeeze. 'Let's go.'

'Where are we going?' Honor asks. 'Dan, we've been walking for ages. I feel bad about leaving the others to do all the work and it's getting dark. Are you sure we're going the right way?'

Danny sighs. He thought it would be easier than this. Honor's always been up for adventure and trying out new things and this whining is completely out of character. He squeezes her hand again, partly to reassure her, partly to stop her from turning back.

'Nearly there.' He's just spotted a tree that looks like an old man with a walking cane. The cave isn't very far away. He needs to talk to Honor now, before she sees it and gets spooked.

'Babe,' he says as they continue to walk, him striding purposely onwards, her checking the ground, hanging back. 'Have you told anyone what my real phobia is?'

'What?' She looks at him in surprise.

'Have you told anyone that I'm not really claustrophobic and that I'm actually scared of...' he tails off, not wanting to say his real phobia aloud.

'No.' She shakes her head. 'Why would I do that?'

He stops walking and turns to face her, taking both of her hands in his. 'Are you absolutely one hundred per cent sure?'

'Yes!'

'You didn't accidentally let it slip to Meg while you've been having one of your little chats?'

'No!'

'Are you positive? What about when you were drunk? Can you swear you didn't say anything then?'

'No! I didn't! Ow, Danny!' She tries to twist her hands out of his. 'You're hurting me. Stop it!'

'Do you swear on your mum's life?'

'What?'

'Swear on your mum's life that you didn't tell Meg what my real phobia is.'

'I swear. Danny, you're scaring me. Please, please, let's go back to the camp. We can talk there.'

To his horror her eyes fill with tears. This isn't what he wanted. It isn't what he wanted at all.

'We can't go back to the camp.' His voice is little more than a croak. 'It's dangerous.' He tugs on his girlfriend's hands, pulling her through the trees towards the cave.

'No.' She digs her heels into the ground and leans back, trying, and failing, to stop him dragging her with him. 'Tell me what's going on.'

'Meg's dangerous.'

'What?'

'She's been making all our phobias come true. She's the one who tipped the spiders on you.'

Honor's jaw drops. She doesn't say anything for several seconds, she just stares at him.

'No.' She shakes her head decisively. 'Meg wouldn't do that.'

'Why not?'

'Because she's my friend.'

'She's not. She's not anyone's friend. It's all an act.'

'Danny, that's mad.'

'It's not mad, it's…' he tails off. His head feels thick, as though part of his brain has been replaced with cotton wool, but he knows in his heart that he's doing the right thing. This conversation – Honor defending Meg – is the reason why he couldn't suggest that she just hide for the next few days. She wouldn't go along with it. She'd head back to camp, tell Meg Danny's 'crazy' theory and unknowingly place herself right in the lion's den.

'Danny…'

He looks at his girlfriend now, pale, sweating and shaking as she tries to twist her hands free from his, and his heart aches in his chest. There's a part of him that wants to tell her about the *One of you will die* message, and another part that knows that would be a huge mistake. She'd completely freak out and there'd be no talking her down. She'd probably try and swim to the mainland and end up drowning herself. This is the only way he can keep her safe.

'Come on, babe.' He pulls her towards the cave. 'Not far now.'

'Danny, no! Stop it! Please, Danny, don't do this!'

He works quickly, binding Honor's wrists and ankles with the cord he stole from Jefferson's rucksack. He tries to block out the sound of her screams, her sobs and her pleading voice, telling him to stop. He's just trying to keep her safe, to keep them both safe. If she was telling the truth and she didn't tell Meg what his real phobia is then all he's got to worry about is being tricked into entering a small, confined space. But if she did tell Meg? Well, that's why he's keeping her safe.

He glances at the remains of the first-aid kit – the wadding and the tape – lying against the cold cave wall. Earlier, when he stood outside the cave and screamed, no one on the beach heard a thing. He picks up the tape and gauze. The others will send out a search party once they realize that Honor is missing. He can't risk Meg hearing Honor shouting for help.

'You need to drink some water,' he says placing the plastic bottles next to his sobbing girlfriend. 'And have a bit of food.'

Honor stares at the tape and gauze in his hand and whimpers in fear, twisting her bound hands behind her back. 'No, Danny, please. Don't do this. Dan, please.'

He unscrews the water and holds it to her lips. Honor shakes her head violently and pulls away from him. 'No?' he says and rips the top off the dried beef. 'Do you want food first? Babe, it's really important that you drink and eat something. I'm not sure when I'll be able to come back again.'

'Danny, please,' Honor begs as he pulls a piece of biltong out of the packet. 'Whatever it is you think I've done I swear I didn't do it. I love you.'

'Done?' He looks at her in shock. 'You haven't done anything! I'm doing this to keep you safe.'

'How does tying me up keep me safe? Danny, this is

insane. Untie me and take me back to the others! The boys from the hotel have gone. We're safe now. We're all safe.'

'Oh, Honor.' He shakes his head sadly. 'You have no idea how much danger you're in.'

'Untie me!' she begs. 'Danny, please. Why are you doing this? Is it because I've been off with you? Because I have, I know I have. I haven't been happy for a while I just… I just… I didn't know how to tell you. I was scared of how you'd react.'

'Scared?' he looks at her in confusion. 'Why would you be scared of me?'

'I know you love me, Danny, but you can be really controlling and I just… I didn't know how to talk to you, to tell you how unhappy I've been. I didn't want to upset you.'

Danny's confusion morphs into surprise. 'Controlling? I've never stopped you from doing anything.'

'Not physically no, but… you always want to know where I am and who I'm with. You text me all the time and if I don't reply, you ring and ring and leave voicemail after voicemail and…' Tears well in her eyes. 'It's too much, Danny. I can't take it anymore.'

'But… but that's not controlling. That's me making sure you're OK. I worry when I don't hear from you. I think something bad's happened. I can't sleep if you haven't sent me a photo of you in your room at night. I just need to know that you're safe.'

'I get that, I do. But it's not just the texts and the calls. It's the paranoia too, the way you look at me when I talk to other boys. I can't even joke around with Milo these days without worrying that you're going to give me a dirty look or freeze me out. It's not right and it's not healthy for us to be joined at the hip the whole time. I think you should talk to someone when we get back to the UK. You know you've been talking about your mum in your sleep again and—'

'No.' Danny holds up a hand. 'You don't talk about her. Do you understand? You DO NOT talk about her.'

'OK, OK. I'm sorry. But we can talk about us, can't we? We can talk about what's been going wrong and put it right.' She shrieks as he tears a piece of tape off the roll with his teeth. 'You can't do this. I'll suffocate. It's going to get dark soon and there are creatures in the jungle. There's spid—'

'You'll be fine.' He gives her what he hopes is a reassuring look. She's trying to talk her way out of the cave, manipulating him into letting her go but it's not going to happen. She didn't see the message on the beach. She has no idea how much danger she's in. She'll thank him for saving her life one day. He just needs to keep her safe until help arrives and then it'll all be over.

'I'll be back as soon as I can,' he says. 'I'll check on you a couple of times a day to give you food and water.'

She tries to scream as he sits astride her and pushes her down so she's lying flat on the cave floor. Before the sound can leave her mouth he smothers it with his hand.

'You'll be fine,' he says as he gently pushes the gauze into her mouth then secures the tape over the top.

She'll be fine, he reassures himself as he scrabbles back out of the cave, leaving Honor lying on her back, frantically kicking and twisting as she tries to sit up. *We're both going to get off this island alive.*

CHAPTER 33

JESSIE

Now

We head in the opposite direction to Milo and Jefferson, whose cries of 'Danny! Honor!' creep through the gaps between the trees. We walk in single file, Meg first, carrying a flaming torch, then me. Before we left camp, as Meg hunted around for her water bottle, Milo reached for my hand. He didn't get the chance to do more than squeeze it before his sister returned but it was enough; the smallest of gestures to check I was OK.

'I've never, ever seen Danny react like that.' Meg's voice, barely more than a whisper, drifts towards me on the hot, humid air. 'When I opened my bag he took off like a rocket.'

'I know. I've never seen anyone look as terrified. His scream!'

'It's this place. This island... we shouldn't have come here. It was a stupid idea. And it was a mistake to sit it out and wait for help. Honor was right, we should have made oars and tried to row back to the mainland.'

'We'll find her, and Danny.' Even to my ears my voice sounds strained. 'And even if we don't, this place will be crawling with adults when our parents get here. We'll all be back on a boat to the mainland in no time.'

We're seventeen years old, months away from being adults ourselves, but I've never felt more like a child. We don't know what we're doing, playing at survival, making fires, spearing fish. We've been biding our time until we're rescued, knowing that we won't really starve and, sooner or later, we'll be tucked up in fresh, crisp sheets with running water on tap and cool showers to wash the grimy memories from our skin. But not Anuman. No one's going to rescue him and return him to his family. He's never going to see them again. Even with everything that's been going on I haven't forgotten about him. I think about him every time I see the boat gently bobbing on the shore with Anuman's boots poking out from beneath the tarpaulin. I try to block out the fact that he's dead. I can't think about death – that final black hole of a full stop that we fall into at the end of our lives – without feeling as though I'm spinning, untethered, a hundred miles above the Earth.

Meg swears under her breath and slaps at one of her arms. 'If I never see another sand fly again it'll be too soon.'

'I don't think I've got a single inch of skin that isn't covered in bites,' I say.

We fall silent as we continue to walk. Meg's day pack bounces on her back as she neatly hops over a fallen tree. I jump over it too, narrowly avoiding a gecko.

'Meg,' I say, as she pauses to scratch at her arm, 'I'm sorry you felt left out. I… it never occurred to me that you were feeling that way. I assumed you didn't like me.'

She glances back at me. 'Of course I like you, Jessie.' She smiles. 'How were you, how was anyone supposed to know how I felt? You're not mind readers.'

'No, but…' I shrug.

'I should have said something before, years ago, but I didn't want you guys to feel sorry for me.'

'I know that feeling.'

'Of course you do.' She touches a hand to my forearm. 'And I'm sorry I didn't ask you about Tom. I was scared. I didn't know how you'd react. How do you… how does anyone talk to someone about something like that?'

'I don't know.'

I look at her, at her grubby cheeks, her bright brown eyes and the dark tendrils of hair that surround her face. 'Are we OK now?'

'Of course we are.'

'And Milo?'

She smiles. 'He's my brother. He'll always be a twat.'

'Hug?'

She opens her arms, being careful not to set light to overhanging branches with the torch, and we share a brief, sticky hug.

'Everything's going to be OK,' she says. 'Come on, let's find Danny and Honor.'

She lifts a vine for me to stoop under and I have the strongest sense of déjà vu. Meg continues to walk, then, sensing that I'm not directly behind her, turns sharply.

'Jess?' Meg says again, making me jump. 'You're not ill, are you?' She hands me her water bottle. 'Here, drink this.'

I shake the bottle. 'There's not much left.'

'You have it.'

I take the smallest sip then screw the lid back on. 'Honor might need it,' I say, as Meg gives me a questioning look.

We trudge, rather than walk. I don't know how long we've been in the jungle but it feels like hours. We finished the last few drops of water ages ago, my feet are aching and I'm dripping with sweat. Neither of us has said a word for ages, other than to shout Honor and Danny's names, and our voices are starting to go. Neither of us would admit it but we're starting to give up hope. How can two people just disappear? The island's big but surely they can hear us. Unless they don't want to be heard…

'Jess.' Meg stops abruptly. 'I'm going to have to stop for a bit. I feel a bit faint.'

'Here, let me take that.' I reach for the torch, then tap her day pack. 'I'll take that too.'

She shrugs it off and sinks down. Her legs give way before I can warn her to check the ground for snakes and spiders. She rests her back against a tree then slumps forward, her head in her hands. Even by the faint light of the torch I can see how pale she's become in the last few hours. There are dark circles beneath her eyes that weren't there before.

She looks up at me. 'I'm not sure how much longer I can keep walking.'

'It's fine, have a rest. Once you're feeling up to it we should head to the waterfall, get some fresh water.' I pause, listening for the sound of rushing water, but all I can hear are birds, cicadas and my own laboured breath. I don't want to say this to Meg but I'm not entirely sure where we are. We started at the waterfall, moved on to to the cliff top and the plan was to do a complete circle, but I've got a horrible feeling that we're lost.

I'm not sure Meg could make it back the way we came, not without food or water. I could kick myself. *Why* didn't I grab a bottle of water too? Jefferson has been drumming it into us the whole time we've been here – *don't go anywhere without water* – but Danny's sudden sprint into the jungle completely freaked me out.

Maybe we should just sit it out. Or try and climb a tree like Danny and Jeffers did when they were hiding. An idea hits me and I look up into the trees, scanning the gloom for any sign of fruit. If we could just find a mango or a coconut the moisture would keep us going, for a few more hours at least.

'Jessie,' Meg says. 'Why don't you sit down? You look exhausted.'

'I'm all right,' I lie. 'I'm just trying to—'

An ear-splitting scream fills the jungle, then it stops as suddenly as it started. It lasts for a second, maybe two, and then it stops as suddenly as it started.

Meg jumps to her feet and stares at me. She's thinking the same thing as me.

'That was Honor,' I breathe.

It's not easy to work out where the scream came from but we head in the general direction, adrenaline powering our exhausted legs and fear making us forget our parched mouths. We reach a knot of undergrowth so tightly woven there's no way through it.

'Which way now?' Meg asks.

I shake my head. 'I don't know.'

Without any sound to guide us it's impossible to know where to run next. I turn in a circle, tipping the torch low to see which direction looks the least overgrown, and then I see it, a pink and white flip-flop embedded under a log.

'This way!' I beckon Meg. 'She went this way!'

We run and we leap, scratching our arms as we shove thorny branches out of our way, our lungs burning, our legs aching, and then finally, just when I think I can't run anymore I see a gap in the trees, a small patch of rough ground beyond, and Danny, lit by a flaming torch, crouched in the mouth of a cave. As he adjusts his position I catch a glimpse of blonde hair and a pale flash of skin.

'Honor!' I clutch Meg's arm. 'He's found her. Oh thank God.'

Danny's got his back to us so I can't see his face but he looks as though he's just fought a war. His hair's in ratty tendrils that cling to his scalp, his green T-shirt has a dark stripe of sweat between his shoulder blades and the soles of his grubby feet are striped with blood.

'Dan!' Meg shouts, nudging me as she pushes past. 'How is she? What happened?'

Danny's expression as he turns to look at Meg is like

nothing I've ever seen in my life. But it's not the terror in his eyes that makes all the hairs goes up on my arms, it's his howl of anguish. It's the noise an animal makes when a predator's stalking its young. Danny's not helping Honor to escape the cave, he's sitting astride her, pinning her arms to her side.

'I won't let you take her away from me, Meg. You'll have to kill me first.'

I grip Meg's shoulder, stopping her from taking another step. She doesn't resist. Danny's guttural yell is so powerful it's as though a gust of wind has blown her back towards me.

As he shouts at her, gesturing wildly, telling her to stay away, Honor tries to squirms out from beneath him. She's caked in dirt, her fingernails are black and there are red sores around her wrists and mouth.

'Help!' she screams as she tries to shuffle out of the cave, her bloodshot eyes wide with terror. 'Help me!'

Danny lunges after her, grabbing her by the ankle. She lets out a terrified scream, her fingernails scraping through the dirt as he yanks her backwards.

'What the hell!' Meg pulls away from me, crossing the small clearing in a dozen strides. She crouches beside Honor and gathers her into her arms. She strokes her hair away from her face and makes soft, sympathetic noises, telling her everything's going to be OK.

'Get off her!' Danny grabs the back of Meg's T-shirt and hauls her away. 'Don't you dare touch her.'

'Danny!' I shout, but it's as though he's forgotten I even

exist. All his attention is focused on Meg. His cheeks are flushed, his eyes are dark and he's muttering something I can't hear.

'Get off me!' Meg twists sharply and thumps at his arm with a clenched fist. 'Get your filthy hands off me!'

As Danny slackens his grip on Meg's T-shirt I let out a sigh of relief. The next second he grabs a handful of her hair and yanks her to her feet.

As she screams in pain I leap forward. 'Danny!' I shout. 'What the—'

I stop in my tracks as he pulls a knife – the one Jefferson lost – out of the pocket of his shorts and holds it to Meg's throat. Honor, curled up in a ball on the ground, whimpers with fear.

'Danny...' A cold chill runs through me, paralysing my limbs and freezing my brain. I can't make sense of what I'm seeing. Meg's clawing at the arm around her throat and Honor's feet are bound with tape.

'It's OK, Honor,' Danny coos. 'It's OK, babe. You're safe. She can't hurt you now.'

'Danny... you need to let Meg go.'

He jolts at the sound of my voice, but when he looks in my direction it's as though he's staring straight through me.

'Danny,' I say again. 'You're hurting Meg. Let her go.'

He shakes his head, pulling her closer. She squeals in pain and grabs at his arm, digging her fingernails into his tanned skin. Danny doesn't react.

I look from his impassive expression to Honor's

tear-streaked face to Meg's bewildered, terrified eyes. I feel like I'm in a nightmare but no amount of telling myself to wake up is going to make it stop.

'It was Meg,' Danny says. 'It was always Meg.'

'What was?' she screams. 'What was me?'

'Sssh. Sssh. Sssh. Sssh.' He angles the knife so the sharp tip dents the soft skin of her neck. She whimpers but says nothing. She stares at me imploringly, silently begging me to help her.

'Meg made all the phobias come true,' Danny says. 'I couldn't work out why but then she explained it. She wanted to punish us for leaving her out of the group and—'

'I didn't,' Meg gasps. 'I didn't punish anyone. I haven't done any—'

'Sssh.' A shallow pool of blood appears around the knife edge and she moans in fear.

My heart's beating so quickly I feel sick. 'Danny, put the knife down. Please, you're hurting her.'

'Good. She was going to kill Honor.'

The blank look in his eyes has been replaced by a new, manic intensity. I don't know if he's eaten something poisonous by accident or if he's ill but something's very, very wrong with him. Whatever he thinks Meg has done he utterly believes it. My only hope of talking him out of hurting her is to go along with it. If he thinks I'm on his side, that I believe him, he might listen to me.

'Is this about the phobias?' I ask. 'Remember we talked about them… the spiders and the snake in the pit?'

Danny's expression shifts the tiniest bit, from anger to

relief. He wants – needs – an ally. Whatever it is he believes he needs someone else to back him up.

'I got it wrong,' he says, 'when I blamed Jeffers. It was Meg all along.'

'Meg hasn't done anything wrong,' Honor says from the ground. Without either of us noticing she's shifted away so she's out of Danny's reach.

The light in his eyes goes out instantly. 'She tricked you,' he says. 'She tricked all of us. She put that monkey's head in her bag and thought that would make her look innocent.'

Honor and I share a look. The horror I feel is reflected in her eyes.

'She had it all planned,' Danny continues. 'From the moment we set foot on the island she—'

'WHAT THE HELL?'

Milo explodes out of the jungle, his eyes dark and furious. Jeffers follows, a split second behind.

'Milo, no!' I run towards him, blocking his route to Danny. If he attacks him Meg will get hurt. Or worse. God only knows what Danny's capable of right now. 'Jeffers, stop him! Stop him!'

The panic in my scream has an immediate effect on Jeffers. He launches himself at Milo like a rugby player, whipping his legs out from beneath him, sending him sprawling to the ground.

'He's not well!' I shout as Milo kicks out at Jefferson. 'Danny's not well. Don't... please... don't...'

Milo glances at me and, for one horrible second, I feel the full force of his rage – I'm defending the boy who's got a knife to his sister's throat – but then he looks away sharply and gets to his feet.

'Let her go.' His whole body shakes as he stares at Danny. It's taking every ounce of willpower he's got not to launch himself at him, fists flying.

'Tell them, Danny,' I shout. 'Tell them what Meg's done.'

Milo snaps round to look at me and it's back, the anger and recrimination behind his eyes. *Trust me*, I will him, *please, just trust me*. Jefferson, standing beside him, nursing his elbow shoots me a confused look.

'Go on,' I say. 'Tell them about the phobias.'

Danny's gaze doesn't shift from Milo. The air is charged with tension. There's so much hostility and anger it feels like a nuclear bomb, waiting to go off. If it does it will devastate us all.

'He's not going to do anything,' I say. 'Are you, Milo?'

A tendon pulses in his jaw. 'I'll listen if he lowers the knife.' As he speaks a bead of blood dribbles down Meg's neck towards the top of her T-shirt.

'Danny,' I say. 'Can you do that? Move the knife away from Meg's neck? She's not going to go anywhere or try anything. Are you, Meg?'

Her skin is pale and clammy and her knuckles are white from clinging on to Danny's arm, but the terror in her eyes has been replaced by cold defiance. Now the shock of being grabbed has died away she's ready to fight back.

'Meg?' I say again.

She gives me a long look. 'I hope you know what you're doing, Jess.'

'Is that a yes?'

She presses her lips together, struggling with the decision. 'I won't run.'

For a couple of seconds Danny does nothing, but then he slowly relaxes his grip on Meg's throat and the tip of the knife lifts from her skin.

'The phobias,' I remind him. 'Tell the others what you know.'

'Meg's been trying to punish us,' he says, 'by making our phobias come true.'

Milo's lips part in protest but he swallows the words back.

'It began with you,' Danny says, looking at him. 'I don't know how she dug the pit, or even if she did, but she made sure there was a snake in there before she lured you towards it.'

'Snake?' Jeffers says. 'I didn't see a snake.'

I hold up a hand. 'Just let him continue.'

For once he shrugs and lets it drop.

'The spiders were next,' Danny says. 'Meg covered Honor with them and took off Anuman's boots to make prints in the sand. She wanted us to believe that Jefferson was responsible.'

Meg catches my eye and lightly shakes her head. I don't want Danny to think we're colluding against him so instead of shooting her a sympathetic look I glance away.

'I don't know why she lured Jefferson off the cliff next, instead of leaving him until last, but she did. Then she set light to Jessie's blanket and tried to burn her alive.'

'Bullshit!' Milo says, disguising it as a cough. If Danny

264

notices he doesn't let on. He's caught up in his tale, his eyes darting manically from left to right, as though he's expecting someone else to come leaping out from the jungle.

'Then she left me a message in the sand.'

'What message?' Honor asks. She's backed herself all the way to Jefferson's feet, frantically picking at the tape that binds her ankles whenever Danny's eyes are averted.

'*One of you will die.* She meant you, babe.'

Jefferson leans closer to me. 'What's wrong with him?' he hisses in my ear.

'Meg left her own phobia for last,' Danny continues, 'which was stupid but she thought she'd got away with it by then. The way she smiled when she opened her bag… who does that? A psychopath, that's who.'

Milo stiffens. 'What the hell are you talking about?'

'Show him, Jessie,' Danny says. 'You've got the bag.'

'This bag?' I unhook Meg's day pack from my arm and hold it out towards him.

'Yeah. Tip it out.'

I invert the bag and shake the contents onto the dusty jungle floor. An empty bottle of water falls out along with some suntan lotion, a half pack of chewing gum, some fishing twine and half a dozen pretty shells.

'Where is it?' he asks. 'Where's the monkey head?'

Meg's jaw drops. 'The what?'

Danny points at the day pack. 'How'd you get the blood out?'

There are water stains along the base, the embroidery is unravelling and there's a dirty footprint near one of the handles but there isn't a drop of blood on the bag. There's never been any. I thought I knew where this conversation was going but Danny's completely thrown me. I don't know what this means. I feel completely out of my depth. I want to help him but I don't know how.

'Danny, I'm not sure what you're talking ab—'

'You swapped it!' He tightens his grip around Meg's throat, making her squeal in shock. 'She must have two,' he says to us.

'Danny, stop!' I say. 'You're cutting off her air supply. Danny! You promised me you wouldn't hurt her.'

'But she's tricked me. She's tricked all of us.'

'It's Meg's bag. I promise! Look, there's the rip from when she caught it on a thorn, there's the stain at the bottom from where her pen leaked while we were on the boat. This is her bag, Danny. There isn't another one.'

'But you were all there. You saw her open it.' There's so much anguish on his face I can barely bring myself to look at him.

A memory flashes up in my brain, of Danny screaming as he sped into the jungle after Meg opened her bag. And just like that the final piece of the jigsaw slots into place.

'Meg's phobia,' I say. 'It's blood.'

'Yes.' He nods wildly. 'But she set it up. She killed the monkey. She put its head in her bag. We all saw it.' He's breathing quickly now, his chest rising and falling.

'You saw it,' I say carefully. 'Just like you saw the other phobias come true.'

'Yes,' he says again. 'Yes, yes.'

266

'Only…' I try to swallow but my mouth is so dry I can't.

'Only what?' Jefferson asks. 'What is it, Jessie?'

'Danny… you were the only one who saw the phobias come true.'

'That's not true.'

I unwrap the blanket from around my neck and hold it out to him, running it through my fingers to show him the edges. 'Look, it's not burnt.' I take a step towards him. 'Look at the blanket, Danny. It's not singed or blackened. It wasn't on fire. Neither was I.'

His eyes, clouded with confusion, flick from the blanket to my legs and feet. 'I saw the flames, Jessie. I swear. I definitely saw them. You must have… you must have put something on your skin, something to heal it and the blanket… you must have… you must have…' The words fall away and he shakes his head. 'I know what I saw.'

'You saw a snake too, didn't you? In the pit with Milo. But Milo didn't see it. Neither did Jeffers. And the spiders, the ones that crawled all over Honor…' I glance down at her. 'Danny said they were crawling all over you. Did you see them? Feel them?'

She shakes her head, not daring to look at him. 'I… I was having a nightmare and then… then all of a sudden I was awake and Danny was slapping me and shouting and I heard the word *spiders* and I freaked out.'

'Did you see them?' I ask again. 'Any of them? Did you see a single spider?'

She shakes her head. 'I… no… I didn't. I thought he was telling the truth.'

'I *was* telling the truth,' Danny shouts, making her jump. 'I was, babe. They're lying. They're all lying. Meg's got to them. She's turned them against me. But I didn't imagine anything. Jefferson fell off the cliff. I wasn't the only person who saw him fall, Jessie did too.'

'Yes, Danny,' I say. 'I did. But no one pushed him. It was dark. He didn't have his glasses on, he couldn't see where he was going. It was an accident.'

'There was someone in the bushes.'

'No one was in the bushes.'

'It was Meg.'

'It wasn't,' Honor says. She pushes her hands through her hair but they only travel a few inches until they catch in the tangled, dirty mess at the roots. 'She was lying right next to me the whole time. She was still there when Jessie screamed.'

'But... but...' Danny says desperately. 'What about Anuman? Someone took of his boots.'

'Anuman's boots are still on his feet,' I say. 'I saw them earlier. They're poking out from the tarpaulin, just like they have been every day since he died.'

'Jessie's right,' Milo says and Jeffers and Honor both nod.

'But... but...' Danny presses a hand to the side of his head. He screws up his eyes and roars as though something is slicing through his brain.

My eyes fill with tears and I press my fingers over my mouth, stifling a sob. This is tearing him apart.

'Our phobias haven't come true, Danny,' I say softly.

'Jefferson fell off a cliff but the other stuff – the snake, the spiders, the fire, the message, the blood. None of it happened. Meg's not making our phobias come true. You're not well, Danny. The things you saw are all in your head.'

CHAPTER 34

DANNY

It all began on the second night on the island. He was drunk, stumbling away from camp, feeling the warmth of the sea breeze on his skin as he neared the boat. The others were asleep, knocked out by the vodka and rum; most of them in the shelter and Jessie curled up on the sand, a safe distance from the fire. Even Anuman was flat out on his back, mouth open and snoring softly. But Danny couldn't sleep. Honor's voice was on a loop in his head.

'I'm going back tomorrow. I don't want to be here.'

He didn't want her to go back to the hotel where she'd shut herself off from him with a book or avoid him completely. There was no way they'd sort out the issues in their relationship if she did that. They needed to do it on the island, where there were no distractions and where they could fall asleep in each other's arms at night and wake up to the sunrise each morning. They could walk hand in hand down to the beach or swim in the waterfall pool. The island was Danny's best chance of getting Honor to fall back in love with him again. If she left he'd never get the opportunity to put things right.

The idea to cut the engine starter cord had come to him in a flash – quite literally – as he sat alone at the fire and drained the last of the vodka. But it wasn't the tiny sparkling flames that lit up the darkness that had caught his attention, it was the glint of the knife lying on top of Jefferson's rucksack. Danny couldn't see the boat in the distance but he knew it was there, bobbing around on the sea, taunting him, reminding him that tomorrow it would carry Honor away from him. Anger bubbled in his belly. It wasn't fair, not when he was fighting so hard to save their relationship. He reached for the knife and stood up, swaying slightly as he fought to keep his balance. He hadn't been able to stop his mum from leaving him but he could stop Honor.

Less than five minutes later the starter cord was severed, the pull handle lobbed far out to sea. He woke up the next day, foggy and confused. His head hurt and everyone was moaning about being hungover. It wasn't until he saw the empty vodka bottle in the sand that he remembered what he'd done. By cutting the starter cord on the boat not only had he forced Honor, and everyone else, to remain on the island, but he'd pretty much single-handedly destroyed Anuman's livelihood. He'd pay for the starter cord to be fixed, he told himself. He'd borrow some money from Honor's mum and pay her back when they returned to the UK.

Only Anuman never discovered what he'd done to his boat. He died and Meg discovered that the starter cord had gone. Danny couldn't admit what he'd done, not then as they panicked about getting Anuman help and not later when the reality of their situation sunk in. He could never, ever, tell any of them what he'd done. They'll never forgive him. And he doesn't blame them. He doesn't forgive himself.

Honor. He glances at his girlfriend, crouched at Jefferson's feet like a frightened child. She looks at him, only for a split second, but it's long enough for him to register the fear in her eyes.

How has his life gone so horribly wrong? He was happy once, wasn't he? He had a girlfriend who loved him and friends who laughed at his jokes. When he clambered into Anuman's boat six days ago did they sail into a nightmare? Is the island a dark force that will destroy them all? Or is he dreaming? Is that what this island is – a dark, twisted fragment of his imagination where all his worst fears come true? But if it's a nightmare why can't he wake up? He's already jumped off a cliff. Nothing happened. Is it hell? Did the boat sink when it left the harbour and his bloated rotting body is floating out to sea? Because it feels like hell, with his pounding heart and his bleeding feet and the grotesque twisted faces swimming in and out of his mind.

He clutches his head, stumbling forward now, not running, as a lightning bolt of pain tears through his head. His eyeballs burn behind his screwed shut lids and he feels as though he is flying and twisting, turning and landing and there's the pain again. And the voice, the voice he's spent so long trying to push out of his head.

Danny! Danny! Oh God! No! No! Danny! Danny! Hold on!

He sinks to his knees, his hands over his ears but he can still hear it, his mum's ear-splitting scream.

CHAPTER 35

JESSIE

As Danny drops to the ground Milo rushes forward and gathers Meg into his arms. He half carries, half pulls her back to the safety of the edge of the jungle. At the same time Jefferson scoops Honor up and, lifting her over his shoulder, carries her back to the trees.

'Jessie!' he shouts. 'Come on!'

But I don't follow.

'Jess!' Milo's yell follows Jefferson's. 'It's not safe.'

He continues to shout after me as I walk slowly across the clearing towards Danny, still crouched low beside the cave, one hand pressed to the side of his head, the other clutching the flaming torch. His eyes follow me as I duck down to pick up the knife and throw it behind me, but no emotion registers on his face. He stares at me blankly – not afraid, not curious, not relieved, nothing. It's as though he's looking straight through me.

'Danny?'

He flinches at the mention of his name but he doesn't speak. He just keeps on staring.

'Danny, I want to help you.'

I glance over my shoulder, to check on the others. Jefferson's set Honor back on the ground and she and Meg are clinging to each other and sobbing. Jefferson and Milo are watching me, their hands clenched at their sides.

'Danny,' I say again. 'Talk to me. Tell me what's going on. Let me help you.'

His shakes his head. It's the tiniest of movements but it's enough for me to know that he's listening.

'You don't want help?' I ask. 'Or you don't believe me?'

'I don't believe you.' His voice is a low guttural moan.

'Why not?'

'You're all in it together.' He stands up suddenly, making me jump, and waves the torch in front of him. The flames dance and spark in front of his face.

'What is it we've done, Danny?'

'YOU'RE ALL LIARS!'

The force of his scream makes my heart gallop and I tense, prepared to turn and run if he attacks. But I don't turn and I don't run. I stay rooted to the spot, my hands hanging loosely at my side.

'It's OK to be scared, Danny.'

'I'm not scared of you.'

'What are you scared of?'

'Whoever's behind all this.' He waves the lit torch from side to side. 'Whoever wants to punish me, to make my phobia come true.' I pause. He's never told me what he's

275

scared of but I'm starting to guess. 'Why did you tie Honor up?'

'To protect her. I had to keep her safe.'

'You thought someone wanted to hurt her?'

'Not hurt her! Kill her! And if she dies I may as well die too! But I get to decide that. Not you! Not them!' The flames jump and leap as he waves the torch from side to side. It hasn't rained in Thailand for weeks and the jungle is tinder dry. If he sets fire to one plant the whole island will go up in flames.

'OK, OK!' I hold up my hands. 'Please be careful, Danny. Just watch the torch.'

'What about it?' He waves it from side to side, making the flames dance in the air. 'It's not real.'

'What isn't?'

'The torch, the jungle, the island, us. None of it's real.' He presses the flat of his hand against a palm tree and rubs it up and down. 'Look.' He holds his palm out, showing me the red raw skin. 'It doesn't hurt. You can't feel pain in dreams.'

'So that's what this is, a dream?'

'No, it's a nightmare!'

I fight to control my breathing. To slow it down. I need to keep him calm until help arrives.

'OK,' I say. 'Let's say it is a nightmare. Now you know that you can control how it ends.'

Danny frowns. 'What do you mean?'

'It's called lucid dreaming. You can take control of what happens. You get to decide.'

'So...' He shrugs. 'If I decide to cut my own throat I'll still wake up?'

I feel sick. This was a terrible idea.

'No, no. What I mean is, if the dream is making you feel scared or stressed, you can choose to be happy or peaceful instead.'

'I want to be happy,' he says flatly.

'OK. Good.'

'It's not working.' His expression shifts. 'You know why, Jessie? Because everything I touch turns to shit, everything I do ends in failure and everyone I love leaves me.'

'That's not true.'

'Isn't it?' he shouts, spreading his arms so wide that the flames from the torch lick at the trunk of the nearest palm tree. 'Honor wants to leave me! My mum left me. Eight years! She hasn't been to see me once in eight years! What kind of woman walks out on her son and never sees him again?'

A terrible wave of fear crashes over me. It's the same fear I felt when Tom talked to me about death – that I'm completely out of my depth. I just want to ignore it or run away but I can't do that. If I leave now he's going to hurt himself or set the whole island alight.

'Dan,' I say hesitantly. 'Why haven't you seen your mum?'

'Because she's with him. John. The arsehole she left my dad for.'

I take a steadying breath but my heart is ricocheting off my ribs. 'That's not true, is it?'

'Yes it is!' His eyes rage. 'She lied to me and said she and dad were splitting up because they'd grown apart when all the time she was sleeping with John from work! Dad said she'd been having an affair for ages before he found out. I tried to make her stay. I begged her. I screamed at her that I was her son and if she moved out that meant she loved John more than she loved me. I was nine years old. NINE YEARS OLD and my mum left me behind.'

Instinctively I reach for the soft skin of my forearm. But I don't twist it to numb the pain I'm feeling for Danny. Instead I stroke my fingers over my rough burnt skin. *You can still help him, Jessie,* Tom's voice says in my head. *You can do this.*

'Where's your mum, Danny?' I ask softly.

'I don't know.'

'Yes, you do!'

'No.' He presses a hand to the side of his head and winces, screwing his eyes tightly shut. 'Don't. Please. Don't.'

'What happened to her, Danny, after she left to move in with John?'

He shakes his head and loosens his grip on the torch. It dips down to the ground and the flames lick at the parched earth. 'Stop it! Stop asking me about her! I'll burn the whole island down. I will! I swear!'

'What happened to your mum, Danny?'

'None of this is real.'

'You're real. I'm real. And what happened to your mum is real. Tell me what happened to her, Danny!'

He starts to cry, silently at first, then loud, broken sobs that make him jerk and twist.

'What happened to your mum?'

'No... no... I can't...' He crumples and sinks to his knees, one hand gripping the torch, the other slapping himself on the side of the head.

'Say it, Danny.'

There's a pause, a terrible weighty pause that seems to go on for ever and then Danny throws the torch away from him and doubles over, hugging his head in his hands.

'She's dead!' he sobs. 'She's dead, she's dead, she's dead.'

I hold Danny as he cries, his head on my shoulder, rocking and shushing him as though he were a tiny baby, the torch – extinguished – lying blackened and burnt on the ground beside us. I cry too, silent tears for Danny, for his mum, for Tom, for my family, for me. I didn't think Danny and I had anything in common but we are more similar than I ever could have known. We are both broken, shattered by grief, carrying the shards of what could have been in our hearts.

I close my eyes and listen to the sounds of the jungle, the caws and calls, the whoops and wails carried on thick, humid air that wraps us like a blanket. We are lost in death but surrounded by life. I have never felt so small or so insignificant as I do right now, a tiny speck on an enormous planet, but I have also never felt more grateful to be alive.

The gentle squeeze on my shoulder doesn't startle me. I heard the footsteps growing closer, the snapping of branches and the swish of leaves.

'Jessie,' Milo says softly. 'Our parents are here. They've come to rescue us. Someone overheard Josh and Jack talking and they realized we were in trouble. Jefferson's dad hired a boat. We're going home.'

CHAPTER 36

DANNY

Three weeks later

'She's dead. She said she'd never leave me but she did. She said she'd never love anyone as much as she loved me. She said I was her everything. She said a lot of things and none of them were true. She's dead. And she's a liar.'

The psychiatrist leans forward in her chair, her gaze not wavering from Danny's face. 'That's how you felt, after your mum died?'

'Yeah.' He stares down at his hands, twisting almost of their own accord in his lap.

'You felt betrayed? Angry?'

He shrugs. 'I don't know how I felt. I was nine.'

'Yes,' she says softly. 'You were very young.'

'I saw her die.'

The psychiatrist's brows knit together in sympathy. 'I can't begin to imagine how awful that must have been.'

'She was screaming my name, when she lost control of the

car. We were hurtling towards a truck. It was like everything was suddenly in slow motion, kind of jerky like someone was pushing play then pause, you know?' The psychiatrist nods minutely. 'And I was shouting to her to turn the wheel but...' He pauses. 'Maybe that was just in my head. The car flipped over. I don't know how many times it turned in the air but I can remember the seatbelt cutting into the side of my neck and how much it hurt.' He presses a hand to his collarbone, nursing the scar with his fingers. 'When the car finally landed on the motorway Mum screamed and it was...' He shakes his head. 'It was...'

The psychiatrist hands him a box of tissues but he shakes his head and swipes roughly at the tears on his cheeks.

'It was the worst sound I've ever heard in my life, but... but what scared me more was when...' He stares at the ceiling, tears clouding his eyes, and takes a deep, juddering breath. 'What scared me more was when she stopped.'

The psychiatrist says nothing but Danny can feel her eyes on him from across the room and the wave of sympathy that wraps itself around him.

'She was... she was taking me back to Dad's house and I spent the whole journey going on at her, trying to make her feel guilty for leaving me, telling her that John didn't love her the way I loved her and that she'd broken my heart. The last... the last thing she heard me say was that... was that... I hated her.' He crumples forward, tears streaming down his cheeks, and cradles his head in his hands. The pain of the memory rips through him, tearing at his heart.

'She knew you loved her,' the psychiatrist says softly,

which makes him cry harder. 'I didn't know her and I didn't know you then, but I am certain of that.'

'How?' He looks up at her. 'How can you know that?'

'Because all children say they hate their parents at some point in their lives. As children we throw all kinds of emotions at our parents because we feel safe doing so. We know that, no matter what we say to them, they'll still love us. I'd be more worried if you hadn't been able to tell her how frustrated and angry you were.'

'So you're worried about me?' He swipes at his tears again then laughs dryly. 'I didn't know you cared.'

The psychiatrist smiles warmly. 'Tell me what happened after the accident, Danny. You mentioned earlier that you saw things as a child, dangerous things.'

'Yeah.' He nods, feeling he's on more emotionally stable ground now that he's not talking about his mum anymore. 'After... after the accident... I... I started seeing danger everywhere I went.'

'What kind of danger?'

'I'd um... I'd imagine terrible things happening to my friends, my dad and my nan. Friends would be climbing trees and I'd get really scared because I could imagine them falling out and lying sprawled on the ground with a broken neck or something. And if we were playing football in the park I'd freak out if a dog got too close to us in case it savaged one of my friends. I'd go into my dad's room at night and get scared that he was dead. I'd have to hold a hand over his face to make sure I could feel his breath on my palm.'

'You saw danger everywhere you went. In everyday life.'

'Yeah.' He nods.

'It sounds as though you were suffering from post-traumatic stress disorder. Did you tell anyone about the disturbing things you were seeing? Your dad or a teacher?'

He shakes his head. 'No. I didn't want them thinking I was mad.'

'Did you feel like you were going mad?'

'Yeah, a bit. No, a lot. I couldn't sleep at night because every time I closed my eyes I'd hear Mum screaming and I'd see... I'd see...'

'It's OK, you don't have to go there again.'

'Good.' He sighs with relief. 'It was so bad, the not sleeping and the seeing stuff and then, one day, when I was in the supermarket with Dad I thought I saw Mum. She was pushing a trolley with a little baby in it and I nearly ran up to her and hugged her and then I realized that it wasn't her. But thinking that she was alive, that she'd had a baby with John was... it was easier to imagine that than accept she was dead so I... I made myself believe it was real. If a kid at school asked why my mum didn't drop me off or pick me up anymore I told them it was because she had a new family.'

'But your friends, and Honor, they knew the truth.'

''Course.' He nods. 'Their parents told them that Mum was dead but I forbade any of them from ever mentioning it. When Jefferson brought it up I beat him up.'

'So you tried to control the way you felt by controlling the way other people viewed you?'

'I guess so.'

'And did that impact on your relationships, do you think?'

He sighs heavily. 'You mean Honor?'

'How would you describe your relationship with her?'

'Was I controlling, is that what you mean?'

'That wasn't what I asked.'

'Well, you should have, because I was. I wouldn't have admitted that three weeks ago, but I can now. I was possessive and jealous and I was really, really scared of her leaving me.'

'How are things between you and Honor now?'

'We've split up.'

'Were there repercussions because of what happened on the island?'

'Well, yeah, obviously. Honor's mum wanted to report me to the police. She said I should be locked up for what I did, but the others talked her out it.'

'Your friends?'

'Some of the other parents. They said I wasn't well, that none of it would have happened if Anuman hadn't died. They said I should get help, though. That's why Dad sent me to see you.'

'That's not quite what I mean. How has Honor been since you were all rescued?'

'She won't talk to me. She won't see me, neither will Meg and I don't blame either of them.' He shrugs. 'I did something so awful I don't know if I can ever forgive myself.'

'And your other friends? Have they supported you at all?'

'Jessie has. She rings me a lot. And Jefferson... he messages sometimes... he's trying to understand. So's Milo, I think, but,' Danny rubs away a tear, 'he's still angry. I'm not surprised after what I did to Meg.'

'You were ill, Danny. You had a breakdown.'

'Yeah, but why? That's what I don't understand.'

'I think it's possible that, when your guide had a stroke and died, it brought back memories of your mum's death that you'd been repressing for years. It shattered the safe, controlled world you'd created for yourself. All the mental defences you'd erected were pulled down and it was as though you'd become a terrified nine-year-old boy again, seeing danger everywhere.'

'Why didn't that happen to Jessie? She saw her brother die.'

'Maybe because she was older when it happened to her. Maybe she has different coping mechanisms. We're all so different from each other, Danny. We don't know why one person develops PTSD and another doesn't. The important thing is that you shouldn't feel ashamed of yourself for what happened. You were mentally ill.'

Danny considers what she just said and shrugs. 'So... Anuman dying... that's why I saw the phobias coming true and the others didn't?'

'Yes. And you had no way of protecting yourself. You couldn't concoct a story that would allow you to hide from the threat so you faced your fears straight on.'

'I kidnapped my own girlfriend.'

'Because you thought someone was going to take her away from you for ever. In your own way you were trying to do what you couldn't do when you were nine. You were trying to protect yourself from pain. Does that make sense?'

'Yes. No. I don't know.'

She smiles sympathetically. 'We've still got a lot to cover and plenty of sessions in which to do that.'

Danny twists his hands together in his lap. There's a question he's been wanting to ask his psychiatrist all session but he's afraid of her answer.

'What is it?' she asks softly, as though sensing his dilemma. 'What's troubling you?'

'Am I...' He forces himself to look up at her. 'Am I a monster? Am I a psychopath?'

She shakes her head gently. 'No, Danny. You're not.'

And that makes him cry.

CHAPTER 37

JESSIE

Six weeks after the escape from the island

I crouch down beside the grave and trace a finger over my brother's grave.

THOMAS ARTHUR HARPER
BELOVED SON AND BROTHER

It's the first time I've seen his grave since he died. I haven't been able to face it before but it feels right today, in the spring sunshine with the sun gently warming my cheeks and new leaves budding on the trees.

'I know you don't particularly like flowers.' I crouch down and lay the small posy of daffodils and tulips on the cropped green grass. 'But I wanted to bring you something.'

I thought, when I got up this morning, suddenly certain that today was the day I wanted to visit my brother, that I'd have so much to say to him, but now that I'm here all the

287

words and phrases that were spinning in my head on the bus have grown still and faded away. Instead my heart is beating out its own message to my brother, each pulse steady and weighted with love.

Danny isn't the only one who's been to see a counsellor. I've been seeing one too. I spent a lot of time talking, and even more crying. For the first few sessions I was angry. Angry with Tom, angry with myself, and angry with the counsellor for not giving me a salve that I could use to heal my grief. But there is no salve or sticking plaster that can take away the pain of loss, and time doesn't heal. But I am learning how to reconnect with my feelings without feeling crushed by the weight of them. I am relearning how to trust and to love, not just others but myself too.

As I stand up I sense someone watching me and turn to see Milo walking down the path towards me, his hands in his pockets and an uncertain smile on his face. He looks relieved when I smile back. It's still new, our relationship, and we're treading lightly, getting to know each other slowly rather than rushing in, giving each other the space we both need. I look back at my brother's grave. Today is my eighteenth birthday. As a child he'd always be the first one to rush into my room and jump on my bed and shout 'Happy birthday!' in my ear. I had to come and see him today. He had to be the first person I shared my birthday with.

I close my eyes and I picture my brother. I see the gentle wave of his hair, the rough stubble on his jaw and the bright blue of his eyes. And then I see him smile.

ACKNOWLEDGEMENTS

Huge thanks to my amazing editor Emily Kitchin, who understood the story I was trying to tell in *The Island* and whose editorial notes really helped me up the tension, conflict and the mystery in the book. Thank you for being such a pleasure to work with and for being such a champion of Young Adult novels, and of *The Island* in particular. Thanks also to the team at HQ HarperCollins for all their support and hard work particularly Katrina Smedley, Isabel Smith and Melanie Hayes. I'd also like to thank Jon Appleton for doing such good work on the copyedit. Huge thanks to Kate Oakley for creating such a vivid and eye-catching cover. I fell in love with it the moment I saw it.

Thanks as always to my incredible agent Madeleine Milburn and everyone at the agency, particularly Hayley Steed, Liane-Louise Smith and Alice Sutherland-Hawes, for your belief in me and my books, and all your hard work.

I'd like to thank all the book bloggers, librarians, booksellers and reviewers who adore young adult fiction as much as I do and who help spread the word. And thank you to the readers who took the time to contact me to let me know how much they enjoyed my previous book *The Treatment*.

It's been a bit of a wait between books but I hope you think it's worth it.

Finally, all my love to my amazing family – Jenny and Reg Taylor for reading everything I write, to my brother and sister David and Rebecca Taylor for pimping my books on social media, to their partners Sami Eaton and Lou Foley for putting up with them, to my nieces and nephews Sophie Taylor, Rose Taylor, Frazer Eaton, Oliver Eaton and Mia Taylor (Sophie and Frazer, I expect you to read this book!), to my amazing in-laws Ana Hall, James Loach, Angela Hall and Steve and Guinevere Hall. And last but by no means least, my own amazing family, Chris and Seth. Thank you for letting me witter on about my plot lines over the dinner table and for chiming in with ideas and thoughts. I mostly ignore your suggestions but it's good to talk! I love you more than you can ever know.

For anyone who'd like to keep up to date with my books do please join my mailing list: https://cltaylorauthor.com/newsletter/ or get in touch on social media.

Thank you for reading *The Island*. I hope you enjoyed it.

Cally

www.cltaylorauthor.com

FB: www.facebook.com/callytaylorauthor
Twitter: www.twitter.com/callytaylor
Instagram: www.instagram.com/cltaylorauthor
YouTube: www.youtube.com/cltaylorauthor

Keep on reading for an extract from the gripping and twisty YA debut from C.L. Taylor, *The Treatment...*

Chapter One

They're still following me. I can hear their footsteps. They think I can't hear them because I put my headphones on the second I walked through the school gates. But they're not plugged in. I heard every word they said as I walked down Somerset Road.

'Why are you walking so fast, Drew? Don't you want to talk to us?'

'She can't hear us.'

'Yes she can.'

'Oi, Drew. Andrew!'

Lacey and her gang of sheep think it winds me up, calling me Andrew, they think it's funny. I don't. My dad gave me my name because my hazel eyes and chubby cheeks reminded him of the child actress in the film *E.T.* He thought it was a pretty name, unusual too. Drew Finch. My name is all I've got to remember him by other than a folder of digital photographs on my computer.

Mum doesn't talk about Dad any more – she hasn't since she married Tony. Mason, my fifteen-year-old brother, refuses to talk about Dad too. Not that Mason's here to chat to. He's been sent to a school hundreds of miles away, hopefully to learn how to stop being so irritating. It's weird, my brother not being at home. He was never much of a conversationalist but God was he noisy. He'd bang and crash his way into the house, kick his shoes off, stomp up the stairs and then slam his door. Then his music would start up. It's eerie how quiet it is now. I can hear myself breathe. I think the silence unsettles Mum too. She's always tapping on my door, asking if I'm OK. Or maybe she feels guilty about sending Mason away.

I speed up as I reach Jackson Road. It's the quietest street on my walk home and if Lacey and the others have followed me this far it can only be because today's the day they go through with her threat. Lacey's been saying for weeks that they're going to pin me down and pull up my shirt and skirt and take photos of me with their mobile phones. I've tried talking to her. I've tried ignoring her. I've spoken to my Head of Year and we've been to mediation, but she won't leave me alone. She's clever. She never says anything in front of any of the teachers. She hasn't posted anything on social media. She hasn't touched me. But the threat's still there, hanging over me like a noose. Whenever I go into school I wonder if today's the day she'll go through with it. It's not about hurting me, or even about humiliating me (although there is a bit of that). It's about fear and control. We were best friends in primary school and I was the one she opened up to when her parents were getting divorced. She's the big 'I am' at school but I know where her vulnerabilities lie. And she hates that.

I slow down as I reach the High Street and my heart stops double thumping in my chest. I'm safe now. The street's full of shoppers, drifting around aimlessly or else speed walking madly like they *must* get an avocado from the grocer's before it closes or the world will end. Someone brushes past me and

I tense, but it's just some random man with a beanie and a swallow tattooed on his neck. I glance behind me, to check that Lacey and the sheep aren't following me any more, then I reach into my pocket for my phone, select my favourite song and plug in my headphones. Just two terms of school left and I'm free. No more Lacey, no more lessons, no more –

My breath catches in my throat as my arms are pinned to my side and I'm half carried, half shoved into the side alley between Costa and WHSmith. A hand closes over my mouth as I'm bundled past a skip and forced to sit on a pile of bin bags. They've got me. They've finally made their move. But it's not Lacey or one of her cronies who forces me to the ground as I thrash and squirm and try to escape.

'It's OK. Don't be afraid.'

The woman keeps her hand tightly pressed to my mouth but her grip on my shoulder loosens, ever so slightly. Her pale blue eyes are wide and frantic and her long brown hair, pulled into a tight ponytail, is damp with sweat at the roots. There's a deep crease between her eyebrows and fine lines on either side of her mouth. She's probably as old as my mum but I'm too shocked to hit out at her. All I can do is stare.

'Drew? It is Drew, isn't it?' She glances at her hand, still covering my mouth. 'Promise me you won't scream if I take it away.'

I nod tightly, but the second she lifts her palm a scream catches in the back of my throat.

'Drew!' She smothers the sound with her hand. 'You mustn't do that. I'm trying to help you. I'm trying to help Mason.'

I tense at the mention of my brother's name. How the hell

does she know who he is? He's over two hundred miles away and we haven't heard from him in over a month.

'My name is Rebecca Cobey. Doctor Cobey,' the woman says, shuffling closer on her knees. We're completely hidden from view behind the skip but she keeps glancing nervously back towards the street as though she's scared that someone will discover us. 'I worked at the Residential Reform Academy. I was Mason's psychologist. He gave me something to give to you.'

She lets go of me and reaches into the pocket of her jeans. There's a loud bang from the street, like a car backfiring, and all the blood seems to drain from her face. I've never seen anyone look so scared. For several seconds she does nothing, she just listens, then she pulls her hand out of her pocket.

'Here,' she says in a low voice, as she thrusts a folded piece of paper at me. 'I've got to go. I can't talk. It was a risk just trying to find you.' She scrabbles to her feet and pushes a stray strand of hair behind her ear. She glances towards the street then back at me. 'I would have got him out if I could. I would have got them all out.' The word catches in her throat and she presses a hand to her mouth. 'I've said too much. I'm sorry.'

She darts out from behind the skip, sprints down the alley towards the street and turns right, disappearing from view.

I sit in stunned silence for one second, maybe two, surrounded by split bin bags and the smell of roasted coffee beans and then I launch myself up and onto my feet.

'Wait!' I shove the piece of paper into my pocket. 'Doctor Cobey, wait!'

* * *

4

I can see her long, dark ponytail bobbing above her khaki jacket as she speeds down the street ahead of me, weaving her way through shoppers, briefly stepping into the road when there are too many people to overtake on the pavement.

'Doctor Cobey!' I shout as the distance between us decreases and a stitch gnaws at my side. 'Wait!'

I am vaguely aware of people staring at me, of toddlers in buggies gesturing, of car drivers slowing to gawp, of cold air rushing against my face and my heart thudding in my ears. I don't know why I'm chasing the woman who just grabbed me, smothered me and terrified me. I was lucky she didn't hurt me, but I can't shake the feeling that if I let her get away I'll never see her again. She knows something about Mason. Something she was too afraid to tell me.

I see the car before she does. I hear the engine rev and the black flash of the bonnet as the lights change from green to amber at the crossing and Dr Cobey steps into the road. One second the car is a hundred metres away, the next it's at the crossing. The engine roars and there is a sickening thump as Dr Cobey's body flies into the air.

Chapter Two

'He didn't stop. I can't believe he didn't stop.'

'Did anyone get the registration number?'

'Don't move her! She might have broken her back.'

Within seconds a crowd gathers around Dr Cobey's body and I am shoved and pushed further and further away. I don't push back. I don't shout, cry or explain. Instead I stare at the back of the man standing in front of me. But it's not his black woolly jumper I see. Imprinted on the back of my eyelids is Dr Cobey's broken body; half on the pavement, half on the road, her legs twisted beneath her, her neck lolling to one side, her blue eyes wide and staring, a single line of blood reaching from the corner of her mouth to her jaw.

'She's not breathing.'

'I can't find a pulse.'

'Can anyone do CPR?'

The driver of the car aimed straight for her. He revved the engine. He wanted to hit her.

'She was scared. She thought someone was after her.'

'What was that, love?' A heavy-set woman in her fifties with wiry bleach-blonde hair and bright pink lipstick nudges me.

I glance at her in surprise. Did I just say that out loud?

The woman continues to stare at me but my lips feel as though they have been glued shut. She loses interest when the man on the other side of her starts shouting into his mobile phone.

'The High Street. Near M&S. Road traffic accident. It was bad. I don't know if she's breathing or not. Someone's doing CPR. He said he was a doctor.'

The crowd presses against me on all sides, gawping, commenting and speculating.

'There's still no pulse!' shouts someone near the road. 'Where's that ambulance?'

As I take a step to the side to try to force my way through the crowd someone grabs hold of my left hand. An elderly woman gazes up at me as I twist round. She's so short I can see the pink scalp beneath her fine white hair.

'My boy,' she says, squeezing my hand tightly, 'my boy was killed the same way. She will be OK, won't she?'

I'm torn. I want to check on Dr Cobey but people have started to shout the word 'dead' and the old lady holding my hand is quivering like a leaf. She looks like she's about to faint.

'Are you OK?' I ask.

She doesn't shake her head. She doesn't answer. She just keeps staring hopefully up at me, tears filling her milky eyes.

'Is there someone I could call for you? A relative, or a friend?'

She continues to look at me blankly.

I don't know how to deal with this. I glance to my right,

to where the woman with the bleach-blonde hair and pink lipstick was standing but she's disappeared, replaced by a couple of scary-looking builder types. What do adults do in this situation?

'Would you . . . would you like to sit down somewhere and have a cup of tea?'

The old woman nods. Tea, the magic word.

***

I hear the wail of the ambulance sirens as the owner leads us to a table at the back of the café. The old lady is resting her weight on my elbow, telling me that I'm 'kind, so kind'. I want to tell her that I'm not kind. That I'm selfish and ungrateful and lazy and all the other things Tony and Mum accuse me of being. I want to tell her that someone deliberately ran over Dr Cobey but I can't, not when there's a bit of colour in her cheeks and she's stopped staring at me with that weird freaked-out expression.

I wait for her to drink half a cup of tea, my feet tap-tap-tapping on the wooden flooring, as she sips, rests, sips, rests and then, when she reaches for the slice of carrot cake the café owner brought her and takes the tiniest of nibbles, I excuse myself, saying I need to use the ladies'.

I slip into the single stall toilet at the back of the café. I hold it together long enough to close the door and lock it and then I rest my arms on the wall and burst into tears. I'm still crying when I sit down on the closed toilet lid and reach into my pocket. Tears roll down my cheeks as I pull out the note that Dr Cobey thrust into my hands. They plop onto the paper as

I carefully unfold it. I read the words Mason has scribbled in blue biro. I read them once, twice, three times and the tears dry in my eyes.

I'm not sad and confused any more. I'm terrified.

Chapter Three

Help me, Drew! We're not being reformed, we're being brainwashed. Tell Mum and Tony to get me out of here. It's my turn for the treatment soon and I'm scared. Please. Please help.

My hands shake as I reread the words my brother has written. Two weeks ago he was sent to the Residential Reform Academy in Northumberland after he was excluded from his third school in as many years. My brother is a gobby loudmouth, always out with his mates causing trouble, while I like being on my own with my books and music. He speaks up, I keep my head down. We couldn't be more different. Tony, our stepdad, said the RRA was the best place for him. He said that, as well as lessons and a variety of activities, Mason would be given a course of therapeutic treatments to help him deal with his issues. He didn't mention anything about brainwashing.

As soon as I read the note I rang Mum but the call went straight to voicemail. By the time I'd got myself together enough to leave the toilet cubicle the old lady's friend had turned up at the café to take her home. She tried to offer me a tenner, to thank me for my help, but I said no and hurried out of the café, pressing my nails into my palms to try to stop myself from crying. I ran all the way home, only to find that the house was empty when I let myself in. It always is when I get back from school.

I put the note on my desk and run my hands back and forth over my face to try to wake myself up. I feel fuzzy-headed and tired after everything that's happened but there's no way I can sleep. I need to talk to someone about Mason, but who? There are a couple of girls at school that I sit with at lunch but I wouldn't call them friends. Friends trust each other and share everything. Lacey taught me what a bad idea that is.

I pull my chair closer to my desk and open my laptop. I'll talk to someone on the Internet.

But which 'me' should I be? I've got four different names that I use. There's LoneVoice, the name I chose when I was fourteen. It's a crap name, totally emo, but there was a song in the charts with a similar name and it was going round and round my head. LoneVoice is sociable me. He/she chats on music forums about singers, songs in the charts, that sort of thing. XMsZaraFoxX is feistier. She's the kick-ass main character in my favourite PS4 game *Legend of Zara* and she wades in if someone's being out of order on the gaming site. RichardBrain is serious and academic. I log on as him if I want to talk about psychology. Then there's Jake Stone. I invented him to mess with Lacey's head. She thinks he's nineteen and a model and she's a little bit in love with him.

I never set out to be a catfish. I just wanted to be anonymous, you know? I wanted to be able to chat to people without them making assumptions about me based on how

I look, how old I am, where I live and what my gender and sexuality are. The first time I joined a forum I didn't say anything. I didn't ask any questions or join in with the chat. I lurked and worked out who the funny one was, who was controversial and who was a bit of a knob. I watched how they interacted with each other, just like I watched the kids in the canteen at lunchtime.

It was my dad who got me into people watching. If I got bored in a restaurant or train station he'd gesture towards people on a different table, or standing in a huddle on the platform, and he'd ask me to guess who liked who, who had a secret crush and who felt left out. He taught me about body language, micro expressions and verbal tics. He showed me how much people give away about themselves without realizing it. I didn't realize at the time that was he teaching me psychology. That's what he did for a living. He was . . . is . . . an educational psychologist. He'd probably have a field day if he knew about my different internet 'personalities'.

I log onto the psychology site where I hang out as RichardBrain. If anyone can help me make sense of what just happened with Doctor Cobey it'll be them.

Actually, no. They'll ask me what I know about her which is precisely nothing.

Dr Rebecca Cobey

I type her name into Google and click enter. The first link is to a LinkedIn profile so I click on it and scan the page. She's a psychologist . . . blah, blah, blah . . . she worked at the University of London as a Senior Lecturer . . . responsibilities blah, blah, blah and . . . I frown. It says she left three months ago but there's no mention of where she went. No entry that says she worked at the RRA.

Were you lying to me, Dr Cobey? You had a note from Mason. How could you have got that if you weren't at Norton House too?

I stare at her profile photo. She's smiling into the camera, her brown hair long and glossy, her blue eyes sparkling. She looks so happy. So alive. And then she's not. She's lying crumpled and broken at the side of the road, staring unseeingly at the sky as blood dribbles from her mouth to her chin. I shut down the browser but the image of her lifeless face is burned into my brain. I have to find out if she's still alive.

**

I ring the hospitals first, asking if they've admitted anyone by the name of Dr Rebecca Cobey. The first receptionist I speak to tells me she can only release patient information to next of kin. I wait a couple of minutes then I ring back, using a different voice, and say I'm Dr Cobey's daughter. This time the receptionist tells me there's no Rebecca Cobey listed. I try the other hospital in town but they claim they don't have her either. Finally, I ring the police who confirm that there was a motor vehicle accident on the high street but they can't tell me what happened to the victim.

'I was there,' I tell the female police officer. 'The car sped up. It deliberately knocked her over.'

'Can I ask how old you are?'

'Sixteen.'

'OK,' she says and then pauses. This is the bit where she

laughs at me or puts the phone down. But she doesn't. Instead, she says, 'What's your name and address? I'll need a contact number for your parents so I can arrange for someone to come to your home to interview you.'

'Of course. My name is Drew Finch and I live at—'

'Drew,' Mum says from the doorway, making me jump. 'Is everything OK?'

Chapter Four

Mum frowns as she reads Mason's note. Tony, sitting beside her on the sofa, reads over her shoulder.

'Who did you say gave this to you?' Mum says, looking up.

'I told you, a stranger.'

'Did she tell you her name?'

'Well, she . . .' I tail off. I don't like the weird way Tony's looking at me. It's like he's *too* interested in what I'm saying.

Mum glances at Tony. I hate how she does that – deferring to him as though she's incapable of making a decision without his opinion. She was never like that with Dad. She made all the decisions in our house back then. Dad used to joke that, ever since the motorbike accident where he lost his right leg from the knee down, Mum wore the trousers because they didn't look right on him any more.

Tony runs his hands up and down his thighs as though he's trying to iron out invisible creases in his suit trousers. 'Have you spoken to the police about what you saw?'

'I rang them earlier. They said they'd send someone round to take a statement from me.'

'I see.' He glances back at Mum but she's looking at Mason's note again. It quivers in her fingers like a pinned butterfly. She's rereading the bit where Mason says how scared he is. I can just tell.

'Jane.' Tony places his hand over the note, blocking her view. 'We talked about this. Remember? About Mason trying to avoid facing up to his responsibilities. We both know how manipulative he can be.'

'He's not manipulative!' Mum shifts away from him so sharply his hand flops onto the sofa. 'My son might be a lot of things but he's not that.'

'He's a liar, Jane. And a thief. Or have you already forgotten that he stole from you.'

'Tony!' Mum glares at him. 'Not in front of Drew. Please.'

It's not like I don't know all this already. They sent me upstairs when we got home from school but I didn't go into my room. I sat cross-legged on the landing instead and listened to Mum lay into Mason about nicking twenty quid from her bag. She told him how disappointed she was. How Tony was at the end of his tether. How they knew Mason had been smoking weed out of his bedroom window. 'And now you're stealing!' she cried. 'From your own mother. What did I do to deserve that, Mason? What did I do wrong?' She started crying then. I heard Mason try to comfort her but she wasn't having any of it. She told him that he'd pushed her to the edge and she had no choice but to agree with Tony and send him to the Residential Reform Academy.

Mason wasn't the only one who gasped. I did too. When Tony had first mentioned sending Mason away (another conversation I'd eavesdropped) Mum was really against the idea. I wasn't. Mason might be my brother but he can also be a prize dick. He wasn't always a dick. He was pretty cool when we were kids but he changed after Dad disappeared. He stopped watching TV in the living room with me and Mum and holed himself away in his room instead. And if he wasn't in his room he was out with his mates on their bikes or skateboarding in the park. He started finding fault in everything – in me, in Mum, at school. He talked back to his teachers, he started fights and he smashed stuff up if he lost his temper. After he was excluded, I barely saw him. When I did he'd make snidey comments about me being the favourite and accuse me of sucking up to Tony.

'You've got no personality,' he'd shout at me. 'That's why Tony likes you.'

He really bloody hated Tony. He made no secret of that.

'Drew,' Tony says now. 'If this woman told you her name you need to tell us what it is.'

'I know but . . .' I pause. Tony's the National Head of Academies which means he knows the people who run the RRA. If he contacts them, Mason will get into trouble. He's not supposed to have any contact with the outside world while he's away. He wasn't even allowed to take his phone or iPad with him. I shouldn't have said anything about this in front of Tony but I was so freaked out by what had happened it all came spilling out before I knew what I was doing.

'But what?' He sits forward so he's perched on the edge of the sofa. 'Just tell us her name, Drew.'

'I'm going to ring Norton House,' Mum says, before I can reply. She reaches into her handbag for her phone and swipes at the screen.

'Jane.' Tony touches her arm. 'Let me deal with this. If you get in touch, Mason will be getting exactly the reaction he was hoping for when he smuggled the note out. He –'

'Yes, hello.' Mum twists away from Tony. 'I'm calling to enquire about my son, Mason Finch.'

'Mum!' I jump out of my seat. 'Mum, please! Don't tell them about –'

She waves me away.

'Yes, that's right. I just wanted to check that he's OK.' She covers the mouthpiece with her hand and gestures for me to sit back down. 'They're just going to find out how he's doing.'

'Honestly, Jane . . .' Tony gets up from the sofa. He walks over to the window and stares out into the street with his arms crossed over his chest. A bead of sweat trickles out of his hairline and runs down the side of his face. He swipes it away sharply, as though brushing away an annoying fly. The toe of his right shoe tap, tap, taps on the carpet as Mum continues to hold. I've never seen him look this unsettled before.

'OK,' Mum says into the phone. 'Right, OK. I understand. No, there's nothing else. Thank you for your time.' She removes the phone from her ear and ends the call. 'He's in pre-treatment and can't be disturbed, but they're going to WhatsApp me some video footage so I can see that he's OK.'

Tony doesn't react. He continues to stare out into the street. A new bead of sweat runs down the side of his face. He doesn't swipe it away.

'Mum,' I say, but I'm interrupted by the sound of her phone pinging.

'Here we go. They've sent the video.' She taps the empty seat next to her, gesturing for me to join her on the sofa. Tony doesn't move a muscle as I cross the living room.

Mum touches the screen as I sit down next to her. An image of Mason, sitting in a beanbag chair with a PS4 controller in his hands, jumps to life. There are two boys sitting either side of my brother, both on beanbags, both holding controllers. All three boys are laughing their heads off. They look like mates, kicking back in one of their bedrooms rather than three kids who've been sent away to overcome their 'behavioural problems'.

'Can I look at that for a second?'

Mum doesn't resist as I take the phone from her hand and click on the video details.

'What are you doing?' she asks.

'Checking the date the video was taken. They might have sent you footage of when he first arrived.'

'And?'

I stare at it in disbelief. 'It was taken today.'

'There you go, then.' Tony swivels around so he's facing us. 'And you still claim your son wasn't trying to manipulate you, Jane?'

Mum sighs heavily and looks at me. 'What do you think, Drew? He looks fine, in the video, doesn't he?'

There's desperation in her eyes. She wants me to tell her there's nothing to worry about.

'No one's being brainwashed,' Tony says. He's not sweating any more and his foot has stopped pounding the carpet. If anything he looks ever so slightly smug. 'All the kids get a couple of weeks to settle in followed by an intensive course of therapeutic treatment to help them overcome their behavioural issues. If Mason passed a note to someone – and I'm of the belief it was written before he left – it was done because he's still resistant to the idea that he needs to make some positive changes in his life.'

Waffle, waffle, waffle. Tony might be convincing Mum with his pseudo psycho-babble but I'm not so sure.

'What kind of therapeutic treatment?' I ask.

'Um.' Tony runs a hand over his thinning hair. 'It's . . . er . . . cognitive behavioural therapy, modelled especially for adolescence.'

He's right. Cognitive behavioural therapy isn't brainwashing. It helps you change the way you think and behave. But if it's all so innocent why has he started sweating again?

ONE PLACE. MANY STORIES

Bold, innovative and
empowering publishing.

FOLLOW US ON:

@HQStories